SETHU

The Cuckoo's Nest

olive turtle

NIYOGI BOOKS

Published by
NIYOGI BOOKS
Block D, Building No. 77,
Okhla Industrial Area, Phase-I,
New Delhi-110 020, INDIA
Tel: 91-11-26816301, 26818960
Email: niyogibooks@gmail.com
Website: www.niyogibooksindia.com

Editor: Vibha Chakravarty Kumar
Design: Nabanita Das

ISBN: 978-93-89136-21-0
Publication: 2019

Printed at: Niyogi Offset Pvt. Ltd., New Delhi, India

Dedicated to my mother,
who made me dream…

Foreword

Renowned writer Sethu's (Sethumadhavan's) latest contributions to the arena of fiction is a new a novel titled *The Cuckoo's Nest.* It is about a nun who, after quitting the nunnery out of frustration with the loss of the real spirituality and mysticism inside the four walls of the convent, decides to establish a 'Nest' for forlorn young girls. It is a daring attempt by Madam Agatha, the ex-nun, to step into the realm of charity, the monopoly of the church and other corporatised religious institutions she had grown up in. The challenge is to give a safe haven to girls in their youth who have, owing to harsh circumstances, eloped from their blood relationships without consent. The risk is their youthful age and the 21st century religious, social, political, racial, and financial scenarios. Although she has formed a Trust comprising a retired chief justice, a professor, and other eminent personalities in town, the decision-making in complex cases rests upon her alone. Here, we meet with an empowered woman who has matured out of her paradoxical experiences inside a nunnery for a considerable period.

Sethu has imbibed the nuances of a woman's mind who has left the convent life, and is to be commended for creating a character like Madam Agatha. She has transformed herself from a religious entity into a secular personality. Religious or racial differences will not bother her in welcoming girls or women into the peaceful, nurturing, and liberating haven she has created. She is the paragon of compassion, care, and understanding but never devoid of discipline and strong will. No special religious prayer is allowed to be recited in public. Well aware of her past, she is reluctant to dwell on the closed chapter of her life as she has begun it all afresh. Her sole desire is to enable the little birds who had sought her help in dark times of their lives, to strengthen their wings, and assist them in taking flight. Her dream is materialised in many cases but met with negative forces regarding some rare species.

Colonel Annie Fernandez, Secretary Sarala, Security Guard Karuppayyan, Nest residents Kadambari, Lisie, Gouri, Sabeena, Ranjini, Kamakshi-Kamalakshi (twins from the slum), Didi, Apoorva and Parveen Singh, et al, are the multi-raced sparrows in this abode of love. Haryanvi girl Parveen Singh, who has fallen in love with Salim, a Muslim boy, persuades her father Risal Singh—along with 'holyman' Swamiji and the likes—to join the Nest, which unveils the real visage and certain unlawful activities carried out by some members of certain Khap Panchayats. The novelist seems to be concerned about such events occurring in the northern part of India.

Feminism captured in strengthening women in adverse situations is handled with aplomb in the narrative. The omniscient author-centred narration is applied well. The narration swings from past to present poles as smoothly as a clock's pendulum. There are ample examples of analepses and prolepses in the narrative, with philosophical revelations seeded in abundance. The narrative is more akin to an omnibus of short stories. The author assuredly deserves credit for a heart-touching narrative, empowering readers from different walks of life.

Dr Sister Jesme

(Author, ex-nun, retired principal)

A Rainy Evening

It rained. And it rained continuously. There were pools of water at many places in the campus, where sparrows were enjoying a rare summer bath.

Unexpected rains after a few weeks, or possibly a couple of months. Unseasonal rains, Kadambari thought. Normally, it did not rain in this part of the country during the months of *Ani* and *Adi* (June-July). But it was not so in her Devagiri area, a temple town in the valley east of the Western Ghats. Normally, the monsoons kept their appointed dates, and when it defaulted for some reason and the village ponds and wells went dry, the panicky elders congregated in the temple compound and debated on the possible reasons. After lengthy arguments and counter-arguments based on astrological signs, it would be the privilege of the senior-most astrologer—considered to be the custodian of the wandering planets closest to the heavens—to pronounce the ultimate verdict.

'It's unusual!' The old man would announce, as if it was something new. 'Sometimes, even the heavens do miss the calculations. After all, they don't have computers!'

As a practising astrologer he might have reasons to attribute, reasons ordinary mortals could not question. But the youngsters were not patient enough to listen to their boring lectures full of incoherent sentences, archaic terms, and astrological jargon. Pointing to the lashing rains, they retorted aloud: 'Why blame the heaven? When the people on earth tend to deviate from righteous path, it is time for those above to teach them a lesson or two. Natural disasters like draughts, heavy rains, and floods follow. What's surprising is that we haven't learnt enough from a couple of successive draughts in the past.'

No arguments on that. Elders nodded unanimously and the youngsters were happy. At last, they were being heard. So this year, the monsoon was going to be bountiful, and they waited for it.

But it was in Devagiri, the forgotten temple town far away, Kadambari sighed. So long since she had left the place…when was it?

It was still raining twenty minutes later. Kadambari looked at the unusually dark and gloomy skies that were indicating how unseasonal rains could be really nasty—much like a cloud burst. She looked at the tiny watch on her wrist—the first automatic watch she had ever seen—that Appa had presented to her when she had stood first in her matriculation class. Although Amma, too, was very happy about it, she did not like the way Appa was pampering the daughter with such an expensive present. She was a young girl yet to start a real life, and she must not be allowed such luxuries at this age.

A round watch with a golden dial, glittering numbers, and a gold-plated strap was a big hit among her friends in the class too. Her bosom friend, Pavizham, could not conceal her envy.

'Something poor people like us couldn't afford,' she sighed.

'We are not that rich. But Appa likes me so much!' she retorted quickly.

Pavizham frowned, as if not impressed. She was still looking at the golden strap, which looked almost like a bangle.

'Do you want to wear it for some time?' asked Kadambari.

'Could I take it home and show Amma?' she asked hesitantly.

'Appa would be angry,' she replied quickly.

The cuckoo clock on the inner wall chirped—a strange noise that Kadambari hated. But Madam Agatha was visibly excited when a gracious patron, a wealthy NRI businessman settled in Malaysia, presented it during his recent visit.

Kadambari remembered that this businessman had also run away from home at a very young age when an unfortunate incident had turned his life topsy-turvy. During his high school days, he was accused of stealing a precious gold ornament from the neighbour's house where a wedding was being celebrated. Despite pleading innocent, nobody believed him—including his father, who was a lazy drifter and never bothered about his family. The boy was apprehended and sentenced to serve a three-year term in a juvenile prison. While in prison, his outlook about the outside world changed completely. And after his release, he did not go back home but got on a train to nowhere, which ultimately took him to Bombay... His true story began after that.

After becoming a successful businessman in Malaysia, a choice meeting with Sister Agatha—who was then a senior sister at a convent—turned him into charity activities, particularly those relating to youngsters. His acquaintance with Agatha continued even after this chance meeting—during his occasional visits, he made it a point to meet her and exchange pleasantries. Incidentally, he was one of earliest patrons of The Nest.

An old story. And a memorable one, too. Agatha had been careful not to talk about her past. And understanding her reluctance, Kadambari had not touched upon that topic, waiting for the Madam to open up on her own.

'As you know, we had twin births, Kadambari,' she used to say. 'Some swamijis called the earlier one *poorvashram*. You may call it so if you want. Although one would have plenty to say about that *avatar*, it would be better to keep that rusty can of the past unopened.'

Kadambari could understand that swamijis, reverend fathers, and sisters often avoided talking about *poorvashram*. It was a prohibited area for others, and there was no point in prying...

The bell in the central hall rang. It was time for the morning meditation.

Most of the girls had assembled in the hall. Madam Agatha had requested that there should be no loud prayers or chanting of bhajans of any community in the open hall. If one wanted, they could do so privately in their room, without disturbing the peace of others. This would be an absolutely secular space, and only those who believed in secularism and tolerance could join—as she had insisted right in the beginning. Such free thinking would be liberating, thought Kadambari, who did not know her religion. But she was apprehensive as to whether it would be pragmatic in the highly polarised world of today. But her roommate Gouri was confident that Madam Agatha was capable of performing the impossible.

'I'm no longer a Christian but I believe in the Almighty. I believe in the teachings of Jesus and the messages of Sri Krishna, Siddhartha Gautama, and Prophet Muhammad,' she had once said, adding, 'Wasn't it George Bernard Shaw who once said that there is only one religion, though there are a hundred versions of it?'

Having been a nun for long, she was unhappy about the way religion was being practised these days. The divide and tension in the name of religion was on the increase globally; even in a secular country like ours, politicians and religious groups promote these divides against the much-touted syncretism. But she was all for meditation and yoga, which would promote a healthy mind and body. She meditated regularly and practised yoga in the morning.

Again, there was no compulsion in Kilikoodu, or The Nest—the shelter for girls, that one should pray or meditate. 'This is not an orphanage run by the mothers or a *madhom* run by the *swamins*,' Agatha used to say. 'I had never asked you about your religion or caste. Neither did I listen to your private prayers to find out your religion. Your prayers were nothing but your attempt for a private communication with the Almighty. If you believe in it, do it, that's all. I hated these stereotyped choirs and bhajans. And those measured sermons? A bunch of lifeless words in a hoarse voice. One has to remember that this is the age of computers and digital printing,' she would mutter, adding, 'Boring, so boring. Those lengthy, hackneyed speeches to the dumb audience, who have their own views on matters concerning human existence.'

But Agatha had no qualms about admitting that she was once Sister Agatha of the convent; that too, for a fairly long period. She had quit on her own—before they could throw out the defiant nun who had inappropriate questions to ask on many issues. She would have asked the same questions had she been a *sanyasin*, too. No religious heads like questions, particularly in open congregations in the presence of others. They expect the followers to obey them blindly. But Sister Agatha had too many questions to ask… and that, too, on uncomfortable issues. 'How dare a senior sister of a convent raise questions? We respected your age, else we had our own replies to such naughty questions,' another sister had whispered in her ears.

Of course, she had some crazy thoughts on motherhood too. Motherhood was a precious gift from God, and mothering a child, an invaluable blessing. It was not a title which could be conferred upon a person, since it had clear-cut genetic connotations and the onus of social acceptance. And the term 'orphanage'? She detested it. Nobody was an orphan in this world. Every single human being was sent to this world with a definite mission, good or bad, and only circumstances had led them into such situations.

'Then why didn't you marry a man of your choice and deliver a sweet baby?' Kadambari once asked. Frankly, Agatha did not like that kind of liberty taken by a young girl as her, but she controlled herself. It was a private moment and they were alone.

'Good question, young girl,' Agatha, the eternal spinster, had a broad smile on her face. 'I simply could not tolerate a man. I couldn't live with one. If the Almighty had blessed me with a divine conception like that of Mother Mary, I would have been happy to bear that child.'

This hatred towards men…was there another story behind it? Kadambari suspected it but did not want to probe further, because she was sure that one day it would come out on its own.

She was someone who believed earnestly that nothing could be kept secret beyond a reasonable period in this modern world.

On that day, Kadambari was not in the mood to do anything. She suddenly remembered the letter she had scribbled hurriedly to Appa without much detail about her present whereabouts. She had only hinted vaguely that she was in a place almost like her home in faraway Devagiri, where five handicapped girls used to assemble in the attic of flower man Shankararaman's house for working on the garlands for the Karumariamman temple.

She had no regrets that she had given incomplete information in her first letter to Appa. Appa and Amma would have been very anxious to know more about her well-being. But when she was indicating that she was in a flower man's home, she was only trying to console the worrying parents. To some extent, I was not far from the truth, she told herself. As the name itself would have suggested to some extent, Kilikoodu (a nest) was another shelter for girls who were in similar situations, but not necessarily handicapped.

Yes, Appa, I had not lied to you—I'll never do that… I did not want to disturb you further. A flower merchant like yourself would understand only the beautiful world of flowers, and I wanted to assure you that I was not far away from it. After all, a cuckoo's nest was no different. We're all close to nature, she told herself.

A home, not far away from home, Kadambari murmured to herself. After all, what difference did it make? Both were not my homes. Did I ever have a nest of my own? Am I not like a migratory Siberian bird?

Kadambari at Kilikoodu

Kadambari vividly remembers the morning when her lean teenager self was at the gate of Kilikoodu, the famous nest of Madam Agatha.

It was an unusually cloudy and sultry morning, and Kadambari was tired, hungry, and thirsty after a hectic bus journey from the temple town of a border village. She had to jostle through a crowd of shabbily-dressed villagers even to find a place for setting her foot. It was one of those market days when the nearby villagers rushed to the town to do their weekly purchases. The pungent smell of tobacco, rotten fish in a basket, and last evening's arrack was nauseating, and Kadambari was trying her best to keep some distance from it all. She somehow managed to grab the rod above, and stood with her eyes closed as if in penance—not knowing precisely what she was doing, where she was going and what the purpose of the travel was.

A new town in a new state, a neighbouring one though, with a similar culture and habits.

Her feeble attempt to ring the bell of The Nest had woken up the snoring gatekeeper, Karuppayyan. Furious at being disturbed during his early morning nap after last night's vigil that had kept him up—not to mention the heavy dose of arrack—he stared at the girl with bloodshot eyes. He was a tall, fat man with a bulging belly and a thick moustache. His attitude was rude and non-compromising, true to what his duty demanded. His night duty was to end within an hour, after which he could go home.

'*Po, po* (go, go). Not today. This is not the day for you. Come on Saturdays!' he screamed. Saturdays were for beggars, when the gate would be kept open for a couple of hours at noon. It was common knowledge in town that free food would be served to the sick and old ladies at that time.

Kadambari was startled for a moment. She, the daughter of flower man Shankaraman and darling of the temple town, had been taken for a beggarwoman. Do I look like one, she asked herself. What did this hefty fellow think of himself? Did he think he was the owner of The Nest?

'*Ayya, ayya*, (a salutation) listen, I'm not a beggar. I have come to meet Madam Agatha.'

'Meeting the Madam? No way! Go away. She doesn't see anybody without appointment.'

'Just five minutes, *ayya*. Have mercy on me. I have travelled a long distance in a crowded bus.'

'I don't care how you travelled. Get lost fast, otherwise I would fold and throw you in that dustbin of the municipality,' he growled, pointing to a dustbin near the compound wall while trying to pick up some choice expletives.

Kadambari eyed the half-filled dustbin. She was relieved that though big, it couldn't possibly accommodate a tall girl like her.

'*Ayya*, please,' as a last-ditch attempt, she was trying to hold the tall iron gate firmly and push it open.

It was then that he hurled expletives at her in a loud voice. This commotion at the gate caught Madam Agatha's notice, as she was out on her morning stroll in the garden. She shouted at Karupayyan to stop yelling and wait for her.

Madam Agatha went to the gate herself, and looked at the girl outside with an unusual curiosity, devoid of any compassion.

'Who are you? What brought you here?' she shouted in her coarse voice.

Madam Agatha was a short, stout woman who looked like a stubborn stickler to rules. She had the face of a tough matron and the gruff voice of a jail warder.

Somewhat relieved at the unexpected response, Kadambari tried to put on a tearful face and pleaded.

'Allow me inside ma'am. I need only five minutes. Just five minutes.'

Strangely, Madam Agatha seemed to be awfully confused about the face she ought to put on in front of unwelcome visitors—that, too, simple-looking girls—a face of a condescending matron of a destitute home or a friendly matron of a college girls' hostel.

Anyway, Kadambari was happy that at last she could get a thin rope to latch on to.

'I'd heard a lot about your Kilikoodu and your benevolence. You are known the world over for your kindness and empathy.'

Although immensely pleased, Agatha avoided showing it on her tough countenance.

'OK, OK. But I was on my morning stroll. After this, I have my routine—yoga, bath, meditation, browsing the newspapers, etc. The whole schedule might take a couple of hours. No compromise on that. I follow this relentlessly unless I fall ill for some reason.'

'No problem, ma'am. I shall wait here at the gate. But please tell the gatekeeper not to abuse me. I have not heard such dirty language directed towards a young college girl like myself ever in my life.'

'Oh, you're a college girl! I'm sorry about that. I'll tell him to mend his ways. Anyway, come inside. I would give you 10 minutes first, and then get on with my routine.'

And so, they were in the lobby at last, ignoring the murmurs of the gatekeeper. Madam was relaxing on her imposing couch, covering her sweaty body with a Turkish towel. Kadambari chose to stand obediently with a glum face.

Throwing a cursory look at the girl and listening casually, Madam mumbled:

'Yet another case of a run-away girl, isn't it? What's happening to this wretched world! As if they're all waiting for some flimsy reason to flee. Spat with one's own parents on trifles, casual punishment by teachers, dumped by a boyfriend and so on... Come on, tell me, in which group should I put you? What cock and bull story do you have to narrate? Don't you, the NexGen girl, have the guts to face the harsh realities of life?'

'None of these,' Kadambari said firmly. 'I have a real story of my own—one you would not have heard so far. No cocks and bulls in between. But I need time.'

'Okay. But this is not story time, young girl! Madam Agatha is a busy woman, especially so in the morning. Come on, what do you want from me now?'

'A little space in The Nest for this hapless sparrow.'

'Ha, ha. A little space for a hapless sparrow in The Nest,' Agatha chuckled aloud. 'Surprising, that even a born-tough Agatha can melt in front of this hapless sparrow. But I'm sorry, girl, The Nest is full. As you would have heard, we don't just take strangers without proper introduction. I'm used to all sorts of cooked-up tales and sob stories of girls on-the-run. No different from what you come across in the morning papers. Mind you, this is neither a reformatory nor a home for the destitute. Madam Agatha has a strict set of rules.'

'I will observe all the rules of The Nest.'

'Okay. Let me see. Let me complete my daily routine. By now, the other girls might be wondering who this wonderful girl could be, who has made their Madam bend her rules!'

'Heaven is great. I shall wait, Madam!' Kadambari bowed her head in an unusual show of reverence.

To Be or Not To Be

'Aren't you a Hindu?' Agatha's eyes were riveted on her face. Through her prying eyes, she was trying to find out whether Kadambari was trying to fool her.

Kadambari was puzzled for a moment and could not reply. Madam had to repeat the question.

'Come on, tell me. Aren't you a Hindu?'

'I don't know, ma'am.'

'A Christian?'

'Don't know, ma'am.'

'A Muslim. But your attire doesn't reflect so!'

'Frankly, I don't know who I am.'

Agatha stared at her in disbelief. In this highly polarised modern era, here is a girl from a temple town who claims she does not have a religion of her own.

'Then what about your parents, didn't they have a religion of their own?'

'They did. They were Brahmins.'

'My God! Then you are a Brahmin girl. What's wrong in admitting that? Did somebody warn you that Madam Agatha wouldn't accept Brahmin girls? Either you're bluffing or you are trying to cover up something cleverly, for your own purpose.'

'Not at all, ma'am.'

'Then are you an atheist or a die-hard communist?'

On reaching my goal after crossing too many hurdles, why this quiz—that, too, to one who didn't know how to lie, wondered Kadambari.

'Not really. I don't know how a four-year-old orphan picked up from a temple compound by a childless couple would have a religion of her own, or whether she knew she would be a communist when she grew up. What she did know was to cry aloud when hungry or when hurt.'

'Still, you were brought up like a Brahmin girl with all their rigid customs and practices, right?'

'Almost. I had undergone all those and never resisted even once, since I didn't know much about it. I obeyed them blindly because I loved them so much. I owed my entire life to them. Without probing about my background, they had treated me as a gift from goddess *Karumariyamman* for their long prayers and penances; they took care of me and made me one among them, amidst abuses and sarcastic comments by the community. For some devout elders, I was nothing but an illicit child deserted by a couple to cover up their guilt.'

'Then why now?'

'It's a long story, ma'am. Better that I narrate it later.'

'Fine. But a generous Brahmin couple who brought you up to this stage and then suddenly made your life miserable, so as to force you to run away...there appears to be a disconnect somewhere! Anyway, this is the first time I have ever asked any girl about her religion and caste. Perhaps the last time, too. I normally keep such things out of this campus. But I felt you were trying to reveal less and conceal more, which put me on the alert, since you are a stranger.'

Madam Agatha was waiting to hear the story, but Kadambari hesitated for a moment. This was not the time to narrate a long story in a few sentences. But to satisfy Madam, she tried to evade a direct reply to the question.

'Religion and caste were of no consequence until I had reached this age. When I completed my matriculation as a topper and was aiming for admission to the medical college, and my parents were beaming with joy and excitement over it, problems suddenly cropped up—usual jealousy, gossip, canards spread by people with motives. But Appa, who did not believe them in the beginning and even scoffed at his critics, later reached a stage of succumbing to wild stories...'

'Frankly I'm surprised. In this age, they could not stand up to such canards!'

'And there was the question of my looks.'

'What's wrong with your looks? You're very pretty. An adorable child for any parent!'

'That was precisely the problem. Orthodox elders like Sastrigal could not stand the thought of an ill-gotten child of a flower man surpassing his daughters in studies and looks.'

'A flower man?'

'My Appa had a flower stall in our temple town, near the Kurumari Amman temple. A reputed family handling the flower business for generations... Forgive me ma'am, some other time.' Kadambari was visibly tired. Her mind was in turmoil.

'Okay. Some other time, when you're a little more relaxed,' Madam agreed.

Time for Trust

After renouncing the order of the church and discarding the holy robe she had worn for decades—and planning to start a charitable institution, it was the senior journalist, social worker and activist Mu. Ka. Raja, who was first consulted by Agatha.

Strangely, her acquaintance with him had started on a sour note a few years back, when she was the warden of the college girls' hostel with the reputation of a tough, no-nonsense lady—a stickler for the rules. Raja was then the bureau chief of a major newspaper, and when a scandal arose about a nude video of a hostel resident in circulation and a report on this was about to be printed in the paper, Agatha took it as a personal affront towards her. When the girl pleaded that it was nothing but a morphed picture circulated by a gang from the men's college—whose advances the girl had stoutly resisted—the college management was not at all convinced. When Agatha was asked to repair the damage by talking to the bureau chief, things did not work out the way she had wanted.

She was disturbed when Raja revealed that such incidents were not unusual these days, and that they would take a serious note of it only when certain other incidents, which had also gone viral in the social media, added spice to the reporter's stand. He had firm faith in the youngster who was one with a high degree of responsibility.

What that sensational stuff was, Agatha wanted to know.

'But there was one such incident in your hostel long ago, too...' Raja said in an attempt to evade.

'Oh, that old story! Are you forgetting that we were the ones who had handed over the culprit, a Nepali boy, working in our kitchen to the police?'

'Yours being such a reputed college, isn't the public concerned about the happenings inside your hostel?'

'Yes, of course. But you should have valid proof for it.'

When the arguments continued, Raja had to concede that the reporter—considered reliable—stood by his version; and so, he also had to stand by him. 'If you could trust your girl, I could trust my boy just the same' was Raja's stance. He pleaded helpless and promised to mask the news to whatever extent possible, instead of 'killing' it totally.

Agatha was sure that Raja was one of those rare journalists who always stood by the truth and could not be won over by vested interests. After that photo incident, he had decided to be extra careful in investigating the authenticity of the stories lodged by young reporters before publishing. He was too concerned about some overzealous cub reporters running after 'scoops' and 'breaking news', which they thought were an essential part of the 'dog-eating-dog' world of media…more so, in view of the deep inroads being made into their space by the visual media. It's true that in that process, he had lost a couple of sensational stories and the reporters were furious, but he had no regrets about it. Half a truth is better than a couple of lies, he had told the youngsters.

The management was also happy that by toeing his line, the overall credibility of the paper had increased.

Raja was quick to respond to Agatha's proposal to set up an organisation for ill-fated girls.

'Welcome, Sister. I would be with you,' assured Raja.

'Thanks, Raja sir. But one small correction, I'm no longer a Sister!'

'OK, then shall I call you Madam?'

Agatha nodded, and that was how Agatha became Madam Agatha—happy that the old appendage has been removed ceremoniously.

'But I'm thoroughly ignorant of the formalities of setting up an organisation,' admitted Raja, jokingly adding, 'As you know, we journos are good at only spoiling institutions, and not starting one!'

Agatha smiled.

'But I can suggest somebody who's an authority on the subject, someone who is worthy of having a final word on such things. Mr Srinivasan of Aiyer, Aiyer & Aiyer Chartered Accountants.'

'But must I approach such a big man for our tiny project?' Agatha hesitated.

'His heart is also equally big. He's a courteous man who has progressed from very humble beginnings. But not so with his partners, son and grandson—real sharks, who won't allow you to get anywhere near him. Things would work the way you want only if you manage to meet the old man himself.'

Then he narrated the peculiar three-tier hierarchy meticulously followed by them. The first contact point would be the grandson, the youngest Aiyer, who sits on the second floor, and only referred cases would go to his father on the first floor. If he could not untie the knot, one would be asked to meet the old man on the ground floor. But such occurrences were very rare. Obviously, the fee also went up, as one climbed down the stairs. The entire fee, including the one for the first visit, would be systematically collected at the front office counter by a traditionally dressed girl. The office had maintained this hierarchy, even in passing on calls. There was no way one could jump this tiered structure and talk to Mr Srinivasan. The old man was weary of using a cell phone as well.

'My god,' Agatha was puzzled.

'But if you could succeed in meeting him, it would be as good as meeting Lord Krishna himself!'

'Still, shall I make an attempt to jump the tiers?'

'Worth it, since it is for a noble cause. Perhaps that old dress of yours would have helped a lot. But still, you have that robe within, I believe—one of love and empathy.'

'Quite so.'

However, despite polite requests, the girl at the reception refused with a charming smile and directed her to the second floor, as was normal. And it was during one of those rare moments when the doorman's attention was diverted by a call on his mobile that she made a slip and managed to barge into the room of the old man. By the time the guard noticed it and started chasing her, she was inside the cabin.

Mildly surprised, Srinivasan asked her with a broad smile, 'How did you manage to jump all those tiers?'

'The Almighty was with me.'

Then she explained about her dream project and how she had decided to take the plunge without the support of any organisation or men of standing. Of course, the finer details were yet to be worked out.

'I understand. But remember, most of the great institutions of the world have sprouted from the dream of a single person—including some corporate giants. Anyway, I could easily sense the nobility of purpose from your face.'

Agatha was quick to thank him, adding that she was looking for the benevolence of great men like him in setting up the organisation.

'Okay, I understand. I'm with you. If you so wish, my boys could take care of the preparation of the trust deed and such other papers for the registration as a charitable trust. I shall also ask them to put your accounting system in place. Meanwhile, please try to rope in some dignified people as trustees so that the credibility of the institution would be well established.'

'Yes, sir.'

'I would have been happy to be one among them, but not now.' After a pause, he confessed, 'My profession demands that I should keep away from such entanglements, and I am also too old for all this.'

While thanking him profusely for his help and guidance, Agatha was about to take his leave but turned suddenly and said regretfully:

'Terribly sorry, sir. I forgot to tell you. Your fee....'

The response was a loud laugh.

'Did I say anything about our fee?' Srinivasan smiled. 'Yes, our charges are high and we do make a lot of money but mind you, this world is not built on money alone. Isn't the world resting on the strong pillars of love, care, and compassion? I often feel so sad that I wasted my entire life for the sake of money and money alone. We have no idea how our liberal donations to the temples and organisations are being used.'

Agatha blushed.

'I'm sorry, sir.'

While seeing her off until the door, Srinivasan bowed gracefully and pressed her hands softly, wishing her all the best.

'My prayers would always be with you. God is only one, be it Jesus, Krishna or the Prophet. You can always count on our advice and support.'

In the evening, when she narrated the whole incident to Mu. Ka. Raja, he found it unbelievable.

'Amazing, what a dream start!' he remarked. 'Certainly, Srinivasan is not someone who can be won over that easily. You have done it, and can now count on him as a well-wisher forever. I'm sure this institution is destined to go places.'

Raja's prediction came true when there was an unexpected call from Srinivasan the next morning. He proceeded to tell Agatha:

'I talked to my old friend, retired Justice Padmanabhan, and briefed him about this noble project of yours. He has agreed to be the honorary chairman of the trust; in case I endorsed the credentials of the people behind it. And trust me, I agreed to do so. You can go ahead with your preparations, Sister, and my boys will work on the deed as promised. Meanwhile, you should be in a position to get a few reputed, non-controversial people as trustees. By repute, I mean gentlemen from different walks of life like academics, ex-bureaucrats who still have contacts with the government, intellectuals, social workers etc. Better avoid politicians and those useless celebrities, who would be good only for photo opportunities.'

'I don't know how to thank you, sir. I had never dreamt of meeting and taking blessings from an amazing person like you... Also, forgive me, sir, but I'm no longer a Sister. You can call me Agatha.'

'OK, Agatha. You can meet Justice Padmanabhan first, and take his blessings to start with.'

'Of course, sir. I will seek his appointment.'

That was how The Nest was set up, and Agatha knew that this auspicious beginning was possible only on account of the right path shown by the activist and journalist Mu. Ka. Raja at the appropriate time.

After getting the consent of Justice Padmanabhan as chairman and Mr Srinivasan as a patron, inducting other dignitaries into the board of trustees was rather easy. Because these two gentlemen were generally considered as tough nuts to crack, many people dared not invite Justice Padmanabhan as the chief guest to their functions, since he was sure to insist on a detailed note on the history of the institution and the people behind it. They might not be able to answer many of the searching queries of the learned jurist.

Professor Abdulla, an English language professor of repute—fondly called Othello Abdulla after his brilliant portrayal as the legendary hero in the Shakespearean tragedy—liked to work with such charitable ventures, irrespective of the community involved. But he was very particular about the sincerity of the people behind it. Incidentally, it was he who had made Shakespeare popular in that part of the country through his portrayal. He was a devout Muslim who performed his namaz five times daily without fail, and was rather liberal with his zakat. His only weakness was about upholding the purity of the language he practiced, viz., English. 'What to do, I couldn't see my dear language bleed', he would say. Apart from insisting on the grammar and spellings, he was fussy about the correct pronunciation, too. In fact, he was the only member who went through the agenda papers word by word, and made it a point to sit with Sarala, the secretary, before every meeting and point out various discrepancies in the papers—including some inadvertent typos.

Both KRR Rao, former additional secretary, and Walter Devanayagam, former director general of police, rarely attended the meetings of the trustees but always made it a point to be on the front row with their spouses on special functions, unwilling to miss the photo opportunities. Not surprisingly, both of them were also regular in attendance in the board meetings of corporate organisations, where hefty 'sitting fee' were being paid.

Ambassador Ravinder Singh, a fun-loving Punjabi settled in the town at the instance of his Tamilian wife, also attended all the special functions of The Nest with his socialite wife. Since there would not be any 'fellowship' on such occasions, he used to devour his usual quota of scotch at home before arriving at the function.

Anita Subramaniam was a known feminist and activist, and was a regular on the prime hour debates of TV channels on matters concerning women.

Although the number of trustees could go up to nine according to the deed, it had only seven members; Agatha was not keen on filling up the remaining two vacancies. Since it was laid down that the board should statutorily meet at least once in six months, both Agatha and Sarala used to struggle hard to ensure a minimum quorum of four. Professor Abdulla, Mu. Ka. Raja, and Anita Subramaniam never missed such meetings but the real problem was to get one more. 'Why do you trouble this old man, why don't you allow this monster to sleep?' the chairman used to ask jocularly. Nevertheless, Agatha was sure that whenever the quorum was doubtful, the jurist would not let them down. Of course, Madam Agatha did not want to be a trustee for her own reasons, but she used to attend the meetings as a permanent invitee and sign the minutes.

Interestingly, very little deliberations took place in such meetings; other than the monologues of some of the articulate members, the chairman was very particular about complying with the legal requirements of the board meeting twice a year.

I'm just a Mother Bird

Having taken the initial plunge, Agatha did not know how to swim thereafter. Always swimming with the tide during her life as a nun, it was going to be just the opposite hereafter—swimming against the tide. Raja had warned her on day one itself that despite her past reputation as an affable lady, she was going to face the wrath of some powerful forces in the days to come. There were many with closed minds and a hidden agenda, uncomfortable with the ones who were trying to champion the cause of tolerance and freedom of speech.

Agatha knew that the world is more complex, much beyond one's own comprehension, and once one was out of the protective cover of the church, it was not easy to fight alone. Still, she set the motto 'Fight, You're Not A Loser' as the slogan for the institution. It was also exhibited at a couple of vantage points. A thumbs-up sign of a closed fist with the thumb extended up—a kind of well done, go ahead sign—was selected as its logo.

At the beginning, Agatha did not have much idea about the organisational aspects. At best, I could only be a dreamer and not a performer, lamented Agatha. Conceiving such a noble project was easy, but to give it proper shape was a mean task. From the drawing board or the blueprint, one has to travel a lot to achieve what one had wanted.

She was dreaming of a nest far above the ground, atop a tree in the midst of woods, which could withstand rains and winds. Tiny birds of different colours and sizes would flock there, fleeing from the prying eyes of hunters. They would chirp and flap their wings—wings that are frail and weak, unsure of flying back into the deceitful world outside. One had to vitalise these little birds by strengthening their wings, so that they could fly out one day on their own, and avoid the eyes of ruthless men. All men were hunters. Only their weapons differed. Whether they used a bow and arrow, a gun, or a dagger—their target was always clear. And rarely did they miss their target.

It was her friend and well-wisher Colonel Ms Fernandez who gave some shape to her hazy thoughts. She wanted a home away from home, much different from the ones which are fancied and talked about, the colonel realised. A nest different from a usual nest. Agatha wanted to name it the Cuckoo's Nest, quite a lovely name. But Colonel Fernandez objected resolutely in the beginning. Cuckoo is a sweet bird which sings. 'This nest would have all kinds of birds—good and bad, heroes and villains, birds of different feathers, shapes and shades, huddled together in a nest... But knowing their strange habitats, it wouldn't be easy; and it would only be for ones which could flock together,' colonel said.

'Yes, they should co-exist. Birds of all feathers should co-exist. And through their chirping and cooing, a new language would emerge—one of co-existence and compassion,' asserted Agatha, adding, 'But I just cannot think of any other name which rings resonantly in my mind.'

'Okay,' Fernandez relented at the end. 'Then Kilikoodu for the locals and Cuckoo's Nest, or simply The Nest, for outsiders,' she compromised.

Agatha quickly nodded in agreement. 'But where will the money come from? I never kept a wallet, because I didn't need one. I've only ideas and no money,' grieved Agatha. While in the convent, there was the powerful diocese behind to take care of all such things.

But as a gesture, it was the colonel who made the first donation. 'I had the reputation of having the Midas touch while in service. My friends used to tease me about not touching them, lest they should also turn into gold!'

Despite being a reputed surgeon, and many of her fellow medicos choosing to practise after leaving the military, Colonel Annie Fernandez had avoided it. '*Bas*, I have had enough of it. No more knives and scissors for me,' she would say.

The colonel had lost her right leg in a mine blast in Nagaland while she was the doctor-in-charge of the Army Medical Corps (AMC) unit when insurgency was at its peak. She had no regrets about losing her limb; she was sad that it did not happen while she was in action though, and that the severed leg did not have the torn army uniform on it. It happened when she was returning with a couple of friends after a late-night party in an army camp. Sadly, there were enough warnings about the mine-laid roads and the driver was also reluctant to take the vehicle through that route, but the insistent doctor had ordered him to do so. When the driver was shattered into pieces, the doctor had no explanation to offer either to the commander or to the bereaved family.

'I learnt a big lesson on that day. A very valuable lesson about my obstinacy and tenacity on inflicting my views on the powerless subordinates,' she had confided later. 'The boss isn't always right!'

Power. Her uniform gave her that power. Despite being in casuals for the party, she always had her uniform and badge hidden in her mind, which the poor driver dreaded. Although she agreed to meet the educational expenses of his elder daughter after that tragedy, the proud wife of the driver declined it politely with folded hands, since she knew that the all-powerful colonel couldn't give back her beloved husband.

Anyway, Madam Agatha took to the colonel easily, for all her queer manners and idiosyncrasies. She loved talking to her and listening to her. Apart from her adventures and escapades, Agatha loved her frank views on the world, more so on relationships. How could a former nun get closer to a woman following a bohemian style of living, Agatha wondered. Then pat came the reply from within: isn't it the opposite poles that attract easily?

'Nobody dared to ask me questions because I refuse to answer the ones I didn't like; no compromises on that. Similarly, I have very few questions to ask others because I don't bother how they live and what their views on the world are. If at all someone wants to inscribe an epitaph on my tomb, it would read "*One who tried to live her life on her own terms*". Who knows, perhaps, I may even keep one ready before I die? Because Annie is one who didn't know what Annie herself would do tomorrow!' said the colonel.

She loved her usual pegs of Chivas in the evenings, not the Indian brewed variety from the army canteen. She had some high profile Goan hippy friends, who ensured a continuous supply of scotch wherever she would be. And she loved good food, all kinds of food for that matter. A known foodie, she had travelled the world over on a culinary quest.

'I am a glutton, a shameless one. I don't mind travelling miles to devour choice cuisine—from choice eateries of Europe and spicy fish curries of wayside joints in Goa to toddy shops in Kerala. But I restrict the quantities I gobble because I cannot do any real exercise these days with this handicap. Earlier, I used to consume a plateful of meat—all kinds of meat without exception. But my workout schedule back then was very strict, much to the surprise of our own PT teachers. They had never seen an army doctor working out like that. But I was cautious about the calories I consumed, and could not be easily carried away by the taste of the food. So now, it's only a question of pleasing my taste buds and not gobbling avariciously as in the past.'

Earlier, she used to drink a lot, eat a lot, and work out a lot—all in excess. But now there are self-imposed restrictions, since she doesn't like the suggestions of others, including some boring dieticians. A senior doctor, who had to sermonise the jawans whether she liked it or not, should not break the rules herself.

And sex.

'Yes, I enjoy sex very much. With agreeable men, of course, even at this age. Because I am reasonably healthy and my biological needs must be met, irrespective of the social taboos and diktats of the elders. But I never have fixed schedules for it. And my close buddy Joe, the Goanese architect, knows my emotional cycles very well. It was he who advised me to stop my evening gulp of Scotch. "You are ageing, Annie, don't forget that. I'll get you some choice French wines, whichever brand you might need. They are mild and taste better," he would say.'

Joe was three years younger than her and she knew that he was madly in love with her. She was considered 'hot', both in her medical college days and while in army service, and there were occasional lewd remarks from some corners about her, which she did not appreciate. However, there were no such comments from him, even during their intimate moments. She could not notice any sign of lust in his eyes…it was only love, nothing but love. A divorcée with two grown up kids who were in college, he was still cosy with his erstwhile wife Mary, and used to dine with her and their daughters occasionally. A good working relationship without any accountability on both sides.

'Tell me frankly, did you ever love her?' Annie had asked once.

'I doubt very much. Neither did she. It was a marriage of convenience, a kind of arranged marriage between the children of close friends!'

She loved talking about Joe with Agatha, who had vowed to maintain absolute celibacy during her monastery days as a devout nun. And she did not find it necessary to break it at this age.

Colonel Fernandez did not want to tempt her either. These were all personal choices. For example, her strange experience at the Artificial Limb Centre (ALC) in Pune where she had gotten her limbs fitted. It was in the ALC that she had met technician Kulkarni, a well-built youngster with real Maratha vigour. She did not know how she had developed a crush on that shy guy, and how she decided to spend an evening with him in a lavish hotel room.

'My God! Who made the first move?'

'Can't you guess? How could I ever allow a man to make the first move!' the colonel laughed aloud.

Then she hurriedly lifted her dress and showed a signature in black ink on her limb designed by him.

'I haven't met him after that, and didn't to want either. But one thing is important… I didn't tell Joe about it. He's quite possessive and jealous.'

Agatha was always in awe of her doctor friend who was insistent on even trifles. For example, the way her name should be written, recorded etc. She did not mind being called by her first name by close friends, on even Ann for a change, but her name should appear always in full elsewhere—Colonel (Dr) (Miss) Annie Fernandez. All correctly spelt and pronounced. Not a single word should be left out.

Kilikoodu took shape mainly due to the support and initiative of the colonel, who had invested the initial funds from her pension and provident fund amounts.

'It would be different,' asserted Agatha.

'Yes, it should be absolutely different,' the colonel, too, agreed.

'It would be a world for women, and men would have nothing to do with it.'

'Quite so.'

'Don't think I'm a staunch feminist, dead against men; no, I'm not. I don't believe in demonising men and deifying women. I have found cases where women were equally at fault. Well,

I just want to be a proud woman, holding one's head high in this cruel male-dominated world... Yeah, I do acknowledge the supremacy of men in certain areas, but I want my space. Every woman should insist on a space of her own.'

'Yes, while dealing with men like Joe, and Kulkarni, the technician. Isn't it?'

Pretending not to listen to this jibe, Agatha continued with renewed vigour.

'Only for helpless girls and women thrown out by their men, whatever may be the circumstances and whosoever might be at fault. But we will stand by their side. We may even fight legal battles on their behalf, if it comes to that... But let me make it clear; this is certainly not a rescue home or a ladies' hostel. We'll provide only launch pads and not couches to relax on. They should be in a position to use them and make a career of their own in areas of their choice. It's nothing but empowerment.'

'Absolutely!'

'No qualms about religion or caste. Rather, I would prefer those who are out of it. They could have customs and practices of their own, not something imposed on them by birth. Again, no such loud practices at The Nest, which might irritate others.'

'Okay. Wonderful!' the colonel nodded and got up hurriedly.

'It's getting late. I should be going,' she said, and Agatha nodded.

Colonel Plays Jester

It was in one of those freewheeling chat sessions on a weekend that Colonel Fernandez happened to notice the sulky girl on the left-hand corner of the last row, with her head lowered down.

Then she remembered that the girl had been on the same seat during the last couple of sessions, too. She did not quite appreciate that; rather, she took it as an affront towards her, since it was meant to be a session for opening up or 'unwinding' among women, irrespective of their age and background. In the initial session itself, she had indicated that despite being a qualified doctor, she was not there to diagnose any ailment or suggest treatment to anybody. It was a friendly chat session to cheer up the girls. Still, if a girl is indifferent with a sulky face, it is a huge insult to the speaker.

Of course, they had all come with their own baggage of miseries, and as a senior person who had seen the world with a different pair of eyes for decades, she had plenty to tell the youngsters.

'You would have seen a war in a Hollywood movie only, right?' she asked once. 'But I have the experience of taking out bullets from the bodies of soldiers fatally wounded on the battlefields, still assuring others that there is a fair chance of survival. I used to curse my role as an army surgeon sometimes, despite being a saviour to many. I have seen many deaths, too. And had to stand unmoved in front of their wailing families and colleagues. After all, the world is so complex, and as one who had seen life and death at close quarters—and after my session if some of you feel that your miseries are nothing when compared to what is happening outside, half the battle would be won. After all, isn't that the motto behind The Nest?'

The colonel observed the girl curiously for some time with her round eyes riveted on her. The girl was unmoved, not knowing that she was being watched intently, while the other girls were enjoying and waiting for the scene to reach an interesting climax. But after some time, the colonel lost her patience, and called out loudly.

'You there, on the left-hand corner of the last row. Why don't you look up and show your pretty face?'

Puzzled and not sure whether the call was meant for her, she hesitated for a moment and then raised her head.

'Wonderful, I'm not wrong. You have a really pretty face, despite the weepy looks. Come on, what's your name, young lady?'

'VP Seetha,' came the meek reply.

'Oh, no wonder you're always weepy. Well, tell me VP Seetha, the weepy, are you by any chance from Ayodhya? The dutiful wife of the great Rama?'

The perplexed girl had no answer. Then came a barrage of questions without respite.

'The daughter-in-law of King Dasharatha? The beloved daughter of King Janaka, whom Rama won in a contest? The ever-dutiful Seetha who accompanied Rama to the forest? His remarkable wife who was prepared to jump into the fire to prove her chastity?'

The initial laughter of the girls turned into a clear gesture of displeasure, which the colonel chose to ignore—of the denigration of a lonely girl who was an introvert and had kept to herself mostly, avoiding to mix too much with the other girls. Was it a motivational chat or a ragging session, they wondered. Meanwhile, Madam Agatha had entered the scene and sensing the mood of the audience, immediately changed the subject.

Kadambari was then slowly slipping into her old Devagiri days. Weepy Seetha was also from there—daughter of Venkiti Annan, a close friend of Appa and Parvathy Ammal. Obviously, her initials VP came from the names of both her parents. But Weepy had not known that Kadambari, too, was in The Nest, and it was a pleasant surprise for both when they met for the first time.

Venkiti Annan's fruit stall was in the same street as the Amman Kovil, a few shops away from Appa's, and was known for keeping a good stock of quality fruits which the devotees used to offer the deity on a shining platter along with the flowers. He took care of choosing the fruits with great care, as they were for offering to Amman. But there were a few others who did not mind keeping pest-ridden fruits on the excuse that, after all, it was for offering and not for human consumption. 'Let the deities also consume some quality stuff for a change!' Annan used to joke.

It was then that certain strange developments suddenly changed their lives and they had to drift apart...

By then, the colonel had changed the mood of the audience by cracking a few quality jokes. And even Weepy, who had occupied a chair on the front row at the insistence of the colonel, had started enjoying it.

Anyway, despite the early awkwardness, it turned out to be one of the liveliest sessions of the colonel, and it ended with a loud applause from the audience. Pleasantly surprised, the colonel was also relieved that she could at least get the cardinal message of The Nest across to the girls.

Later, it was in the lobby after the session that Madam Agatha revealed the real story of Weepy in detail to the colonel. Normally, Madam never bothered to listen to the tear-jerkers from the girls, which were mostly repetitive and often overstated. She knew that in their anxiety to get admitted into The Nest somehow, they tended to be melodramatic, and so, she never used to show any concern about their sobs and frequent use of handkerchiefs. She knew that the real truth would trickle down slowly only after a few days. That was why she used to warn the girls on day one itself that they would always be under a close watch and could be thrown out any at moment.

But in the case of Weepy, Kadambari had requested Madam Agatha that it would be nice if she could listen to the story of the girl from a third party, that too from a family friend and well-wisher. And when she narrated the entire tale, the former nun was stunned and decided to call the girl to her room for a little private talk. When Madam Agatha told her that she had by now assessed her plight in the proper perspective and that she would be absolutely safe and secure inside The Nest, Weepy was unmoved and thanked her without any emotions. Agatha knew that she had reached a stage where no word of comfort would move her that easily. But she could see a visible change on that day after the colonel's lengthy lecture.

'Oh, I'm so sorry,' the colonel was apologetic. 'This is one of those special cases needing a higher level of empathy. I shall also take special care in her case hereafter.'

It was after that that the otherwise reclusive Weepy got very close to colonel Fernandez.

But old memories haunted Kadambari very much after that session, and she wanted to be alone for some time. Feigning a headache, she excused herself and withdrew into the privacy of her room. There, she was at peace with herself and lay on her bed with her eyes closed for some time.

Again, she was slipping back into her old Devagiri days. Oh, Devagiri, my own simple temple town, she cried to herself. It was not easy to erase the dark memories of that huge blaze which had devoured the poor Parvathy Ammal. By the time, she—along with Appa and Amma—had rushed in there, the body of the woman was charred beyond recognition, except for the shining diamond nose ring. Her friend Seetha had already been rushed to the hospital.

In fact, Appa was so close to Annan that they never missed any of the festivals at the nearby temples. Gomathy used to blame Appa for spoiling that good man by his wandering habits. Born lazy, Appa was always on the lookout for opportunities to sneak out of the responsibilities at the shop, and the festivals came handy to him often. On such occasions, it was Gomathy who used to look after the affairs of the shop. Kadambari also used to assist her occasionally. When Annan was also dragged into it, it was a burden on Parvathy, too, who was not at all comfortable with looking after the business at their fruit stall, which was quite a busy one.

Gomathy and Parvathy were close friends, even before their marriage. After the marriage when they started living in houses not far from each other, they used to spend their evenings together in either house, reminiscing their childhood experiences.

Both Kadambari and Seetha used to complete their school homework hurriedly, and wait eagerly for the evenings for these long story sessions in the verandah. Leaning on the shoulders of their mothers and dozing off in between, they used to listen to these stories enthusiastically. They were also eager to pass on the same to their classmates, possibly the next day itself. Since their fathers used to return home quite late only after the temples were closed, it was a big job for the mothers to carry the girls, deep in sleep, to their respective beds.

Later, when the worrying news that Annan had a secret mistress of suspicious reputation in another street fell into the ears of Gomathy and she could not but alert her close friend Parvathy, things took a different turn. It appears that the vivacious pan-chewing woman with full lips was a *harikatha* (a composite art form comprising storytelling, poetry, music, drama, dance, and philosophy) artist earlier. She was allegedly squeezing whatever she could from him for buying jewellery and other valuables. In fact, the neighbours were wondering how she could amass such expensive electronic gadgets and appliances that even Annan did not have at home. This left many wondering how such a nice, God-fearing gentleman respected by one and all could fall prey to the charms of a vicious woman.

Parvathy was sure that her husband would have met the woman during one his forays to the temple festivals. If it was so, Annan would have been in the know of things…and like a loyal friend, he ought to have stopped him from committing such a disaster. When Parvathy's hysterical outbursts gained pitch despite Appa pleading innocent, even Gomathy started believing that there could not be any smoke without fire.

This was how the rift between the two families deepened, and Kadambari was deeply hurt when Seetha stopped talking to her.

Annan had by now reached a point of no return, and the business had also suffered badly due to lack of attention; it was well-known that the shop could close any day now, and that prospective buyers were trying hard for a deal. Meanwhile, Annan's borrowings from moneylenders at usurious rates had peaked, and when he took to heavy drinking and reckless gambling, there was little the helpless woman could do. Disgusted with her husband who did not mend his ways despite her best efforts—and was mostly returning home by midnight in an intoxicated condition—she cursed her fate and threatened to set herself on fire if he did not mend his ways. But having reached such a miserable point of no-return, he was not taking her threats seriously. Poor Seetha had no clue about what was transpiring between her parents. Then it appeared that on one *amavasi* (new moon) night, when Parvathy was on a fast and had kept awake waiting for her husband. Annan had not returned home until the early hours of the morning, which is when the disaster took place. Perhaps, that was the limit to the patience of the dutiful wife.

When Seetha woke up seeing a huge blaze in the bathroom outside and rushed out, it was all over. The body of her mother was charred almost fully, while the half-charred legs were shivering violently. The face was not recognisable, except for that stone shining on her nose, which was half burnt. Seeing the gory sight, Seetha could not cry and swooned on the corridor outside, dashing her head against a pillar. When she regained consciousness she was in the government hospital with a heavy bandage around her head. And Annan was on her feet, crying wildly, begging for pardon and promising not to repeat what he had been doing.

'A typical storyline of a Kodambakkam tear-jerker movie, isn't it?' remarked Agatha.

'Could be,' responded Kadambari. 'After all, movie scripts are also influenced by such gory incidents.'

She was mortally scared to return to that ill-fated home, and could not sleep for a couple of nights but there was nowhere else to go. Annan did not have the courage to go out for a few days for the fear that neighbours would attack him, and had decided to sleep indoors—mostly in an intoxicated state. The wild scene of the fire would have been haunting him in his sleep as well. As the days passed and Seetha was trying to re-group her thoughts and plans for the future, there was a midnight knock on the front door, followed by a mild voice. Someone was calling her name and she guessed that it would be of one of Appa's creditors—that lame fellow who had been throwing lecherous glances at her. Although she did not open the door and had kept a large knife under her pillow, she knew that one day they would break open the door and the inebriated father, kicked into submission, could only groan like a wounded dog—a mute witness to what would happen in front of his eyes.

That was the end of it, and she had no other way other than flee from home. Then the name of Madam Agatha's Nest suddenly came to her mind, as if prompted by the divine powers.

Wasn't it goddess Karumari Amman herself who had guided those two hapless girls into The Nest of Madam Agatha? They were sure that the ardent prayers of both the families to the deities for generations had finally saved them from complete disaster.

'The movie ends here, at last,' sighed Kadambari. 'Not much different from what we used to listen to, leaning half asleep on the shoulders of our mothers during our childhood...only the characters and situations turned different.'

'I agree. Possibly the precious blessings of the Almighty. Anyway, it's good that both of you have landed here, to this safe place. Won't other girls, too, have similar stories to tell?' asked the Madam.

'Surely. Sometimes, weirder. But one should have the patience and compassion to listen to them. Isn't it true that in this queer world, talkers are more and listeners too few?'

Madam Agatha nodded silently.

Parveen, the Mystery Girl

There were 10 residents in Kilikoodu. Agatha had a waiting list, too, but she had kept it under wraps for a while, since she did not want to induct more until the condition of the other residents at the institution stabilised.

The original number was 12. Then two left; one joined an insurance company and the other secured a job of as a physiotherapist in a small hospital. She had done a paramedical course before enrolling at The Nest. She was desperately on the lookout for a job, and was trying hard for it with the blessings of Madam Agatha. Madam was happy that, at last, two of the birds could manage to fly out on their own—leaving a note of encouragement to the other girls. She had indicated time and again that once one gains the strength to fly out, earlier the better…so that another one could take her place.

It was after the departure of these two girls that the colonel prompted Agatha to take a fresh look at her waiting list. 'No, the time hasn't come yet,' she had reacted. Her real dream was to put up a huge nest which could house as many birds as possible, but the infrastructural and financial constraints stopped her from taking such a big plunge.

Then, much to her surprise, some news about another one trying to fly out reached Agatha.

It was Parveen Singh who had escaped from her home, in a remote village in Haryana, a few months back. Quite a secretive girl, she did not mix much with other girls, even with her roommate Apoorva, a local college girl. She preferred to always talk in monosyllables; that, too, in Hindi, and sometimes Punjabi—which her roommate Apoorva could not decrypt easily. Her mischievous attempt to switch over to Punjabi in the midst of a sentence was a deliberate attempt to confuse other girls. After some initial attempts to get closer to her, others left her alone.

Unable to communicate with her roommate, Apoorva had tried a few times to get her room changed. But Sarala had made it clear that she was helpless, since it was as per the orders of the Madam. Agatha was particular that birds of different feathers should join together, and that through their chirpings a common language should emerge—a kind of Esperanto.

'After all, isn't language for communication? Let them mime, if nothing else works,' she had said with a broad grin.

Of course, Apoorva was not unfamiliar with the funny squabbles on language divides through the spat between her Bengali father and Tamilian mother.

But they all listened keenly when Parveen sang the Haryanvi harvest songs in a rustic nasal voice of a village farmer. Even the generally morose Madam Agatha liked her songs very much, and made her sing in the dining room and on festive occasions in the campus. 'These folk songs, particularly from Punjab on the west and the northeast on the, east simply floor us,' Agatha had commented, 'the songs of Sutlej, Ganges and Brahmaputra.

Other areas like Bastar, Jharkhand, etc., too, had ballads of their own. This is the India we all loved—the land of unity in the midst of diversity.'

Parveen had her own sob story to tell Madam Agatha, and the latter did not take her seriously from the beginning, taking it as a clever ploy to wangle an admission. Within a few years, The Nest had earned a reputation of a safe and decent place for deserted girls, far better than the hostels put up by different NGOs and certain community-based organisations. Once, after listening to yet another lengthy tear-jerker from Parveen, Madam decided to call the bluff right on her face.

'Listen, girl,' Madam said with a broad smile, 'you're a definitely a good storyteller, no doubt about it. But remember, this organisation was founded on two cardinal pillars of truth and love. The assumption was that we would love each other as long as we were here speaking the truth, and nothing but truth. Not the usual practice of chanting *Satyameva Jayate* (truth alone triumphs) and then going around telling utter lies. I've pasted stickers at two places on our walls that read 'Fight' and 'You're not a loser'. I expect the girls to do just that, not forgetting the above cardinal pillars.'

Parveen blushed and was speechless for some time.

'Ma'am, you've misunderstood me. I'm from a good family, born of good parents.'

Madam shook her head in disgust.

'So, too, are the other girls. I didn't ask anything about your family and lineage. But I hate lies, even if you think they are innocent and harmless ones. Mind you, the line of demarcation between a blatant lie and an innocent sounding one is very thin, and it depends on one's own perception. As for me, both are the same, and I hate them both equally. Again, we do not normally admit anyone without proper introduction.'

Then Parveen felt that Madam Agatha was in a foul mood, and this was not the time to talk to her. Hence she said, 'I'm sorry, ma'am, I have not made myself clear. Shall I come again at some other time?'

'Fine,' nodded Agatha. 'I shall call when I'm free.'

Agatha did call her later when she was a bit more relaxed, sitting on a bench in the lawn.

'Don't think I was trying to harass you just because you're an outsider. Not at all. All the girls are equal to me. But I have a strange feeling that you're trying to conceal more than what you're willing to reveal. This is the sixth sense I have developed while living with girls in hostels.'

'Sorry, you're mistaken, ma'am,' Parveen repeated in an apologetic tone. 'I was probably a bit too animated when I gave my account initially. But I was only speaking the truth.'

'May be. I would love to believe you!'

Agatha noticed that Parveen had dressed carefully, and had put on elaborate make-up, as if to suit a formal occasion.

'If you need donations, as was hinted by the secretary madam…'

This infuriated Agatha further.

'Did I ask you for any donation? Don't think money can buy everything in the world,' Agatha's voice rose.

'I'm sorry ma'am, I didn't mean it that way.'

'Well, I shall tell your story as I had learnt before listening to your version.'

The girl looked puzzled and didn't know what to say. She just grinned as Agatha narrated the following:

Parveen was the daughter of a Haryanvi businessman Risal Singh now settled in Delhi, who had married from his village. He put up a clothing shop in the busy Sarojini Market, and since the shop specialised in unique Rajasthani cotton saris, they had a long list of loyal customers. Although he lived in Delhi, both his wife and daughter hated the metro life and preferred to stay back in their quiet village. Even Parveen, who had her college education in a city, had returned to join her mother. Of course, they would join him in Delhi during festivals like Diwali, Holi, Navaratri etc. Subsequently, when the business grew much beyond his expectations, Risal Singh planned to put up another shop on the prestigious Ajmal Khan road in Karol Bagh, which was to be managed by his daughter, who had a knack of winning over the customers—particularly women. In fact, they had already taken the space and had done it up, and were waiting desperately for an auspicious date for cutting the ribbon by a corporator who had Haryanvi roots.

Parveen sat motionless for some time. She realised that Madam Agatha knew practically everything about her. Then she took out a beautiful handkerchief with some pink letters embroidered artistically on it, with a heart at the centre. But Madam Agatha was not at all inquisitive about what was written on it. Then Parveen raised it again so that Agatha would read it this time.

A name—Salim.

Parveen's face took an orange hue then, reflecting the setting sun in full glow in the west. They were in the lawn and Agatha was in the midst of her evening stroll. Parveen chose such occasions discreetly to confide in Madam Agatha, away from the snooping eyes of other girls. She knew very well that the girls were too inquisitive about the enigmatic Haryanvi girl.

But Agatha did not show any interest in the name Parveen was keeping close to her heart, and never asked probing questions about it. Still, the truth came out on its own in a disturbing manner within a couple of weeks.

Parveen left Agatha alone, sensing she wasn't interested in the Salim story.

It was a lazy afternoon on a weekend. The girls were either dosing off or chatting in one of the rooms on the top floor. It was then that Karupayyan came with a strange request. A middle-aged man with brown hair and blue eyes, appearing to be a North Indian, was waiting at the gate for admission inside. When he had tried to contact Madam on the intercom, there was no response.

Although Madam Agatha—relaxing on a couch—had heard the intercom bell, she had deliberately avoided lifting the receiver, knowing quite well that the call was from the gatekeeper. She was not comfortable being disturbed on weekend afternoons.

'That man wants to see his daughter.'

'The daughter? Whose daughter?' she asked curiously. So far, nobody had ever come in search of their daughters.

'Not clear. But seems to be from the North. He was speaking broken English with great effort.' As an ex-serviceman, Karupayyan knew Hindi very well.

Oh, it might be that Punjabi girl, Parveen, Agatha thought. According to the information she had, Parveen had run away from home without telling anybody. That itself had raised suspicions about her, even at the time of admission. In fact,

Agatha had taken the help of the Fernandez in this regard, since she happened to be in The Nest at that time; the colonel, in her own customary way, had cross-examined Parveen like a prosecutor—to which the girl had kept crafty replies ready, capable of flooring any senior lawyer.

'Either she was telling the cold, unpleasant truth, or she was a hardened crook!' the colonel had quipped.

'I would rather go with the latter,' Agatha had replied. 'Anyway, having travelled all the way after analysing this organisation thoroughly, I don't want to reject her summarily. I will keep her on watch for three months. Even a minor lapse, and she would be thrown out without question.'

The colonel nodded but insisted Agatha to keep an eye on her, particularly on strange visitors and calls from unknown numbers. It's true that one could not prevent her from using her mobile phone… Still, her roommate Apoorva could be put to use—snoop around and scrutinise the calls, provided she had not erased them forever. Also, secretary Sarala—fondly called Kovai Sarala for her similarity to the well-known Tamil comedian—could also collect as much details as possible. Immensely pleased on being compared with the popular movie actor, Sarala had started aping her mannerisms and way of talking!

'Amma!' Karupayyan was waiting impatiently for a reply; Madam was visibly irritated.

'Give some excuse and send him away.'

'I've tried all! Citing our rules and regulations, for which he was quoting paras from the Indian Constitution. According to him, the father of the girl has the right to meet her, wherever she is. This is what I could make out from his loud abuses.'

'Okay, let me find out whether the girl is interested in meeting this so-called papa of hers!'

Madam then sent Devaki on that secret mission, and she returned within a couple of minutes, boiling with anger.

'That wretched lass says that no such girl lives here now. "There was one Parveen, who had died of heart attack three months back"… She wants me to convey this blatant lie. I wouldn't do it!'

Sensing the bitterness in the girl's reaction, Agatha ordered the gatekeeper to make one more attempt. And if that, too, failed, the intruder should be threatened with a call to the police.

But Karupayyan had tried that, too. And the response was a swear word in colloquial Punjabi, the meaning of which he could not understand. In fact, the man challenged him to call the police so that he could narrate the whole story himself. He then threatened he would go to any extent to get his girl back, raising his bulging purse. Looking at the helplessness of the gatekeeper, Madam knew it was not easy to tackle this tough guy. Karupayyan felt that she should either go to the gate and talk it over with the man herself, or allow him to come inside; she preferred the latter, since it would be too awkward to meet him at the gate. Moreover, it is always be better to talk to a stranger from one's own seat of authority. Then she gestured to the gatekeeper to summon him inside.

Risal Singh was a rotund man with unkempt hair and uncouth demeanour. He reclined on a sofa without being asked to do so, had a quick gulp of orange juice from a yellow bottle he was carrying, and cleared his throat aloud. When some of the fluid trickled down and left a mark on the carpet, Agatha was visibly annoyed. She had been keeping the carpet, meticulously clean all these days.

'Look, Madam, me Risal Singh from Haryana. Now settled in Sarojini Nagar, Delhi. May shift to a good flat in Western Extension area, Karol Bagh, soon. Paid advance also. Waiting for Diwali for house warming. Only one daughter and one wife. This daughter Parveen called Guddi, disappeared a few months back. I put advertisements in newspapers with all India covering, including Tamil Nadu. Now I got a call from somebody that she is here.'

'How do you know that? The gatekeeper would have already told you that's not true.'

'No madam, no lying. A Christian nun, no lying. *Jhooth bole kauva kaate, kaale kauve se darriyo!*'

Madam Agatha had to concede that Parveen was inside her room. But since she had blatantly refused to meet the visitor, whosoever he might be, nothing could be done about it. Obviously, no one in the organisation had the authority to force a girl to come out and meet a visitor.

Unexpectedly, Risal Singh exploded. His voice shook the lobby.

'*Suno* (listen), ma'am. I will complain to the police that my daughter kidnapped by a Christian nun and detained in a convent. For conversion to the church. For getting dollars from America. This is a Hindu country, you can't escape. You can't convert good girls from good family and take them to Europe.'

Risal Singh was grumpy and appeared to be quite vicious. For one who had deliberately kept religion and caste outside the compound wall, this was too much for Madam Agatha.

'Get lost, you rascal!' having waited for long, she shouted aloud at last. 'You are talking like this to a lady who has preached and practised religious tolerance and secularism all her life. It is a rule here that nobody would talk about religion or caste inside the campus. Everyone knows that any such talk would be dealt with severely, and the delinquent would be thrown out mercilessly. And now you are teaching such a person about conversion! Mind you, I'm not a nun anymore.'

Risal Singh was visibly stunned by this sudden outburst from the old lady. Still, he did not want to lose control over the situation.

'Okay,' he retorted peevishly, 'I know how to handle this. If my *laadli beti* (darling daughter) runs away from home with that Islamic rogue who wants to convert her...and then sent to Iraq, Afghanistan or Syria to join a terrorist organisation...you alone would be responsible. Our government will not leave you, you *pardesi isayi* (foreign catholic).'

Madam Agatha was hurt by these uncharitable remarks and felt that there was no point in arguing with this man, and that it would be better to send him out without further arguments.

'Karupayya!' she shouted, gesturing angrily to throw him out of the compound. But having taken the cue quickly, Risal Singh beat a hasty retreat with the parting words of suitable retribution—that, too, merciless ones.

Madam got up quickly and without waiting for him to leave, she went inside, ordering the prying girls to withdraw and go to their respective rooms. Then she called Apoorva, the Tamilian roommate of Parveen, to her room and gave a thorough dressing down.

'Wasn't it rather strange? All this drama happening behind my back for months together, and I didn't get a scent of it? Nobody told me anything about this Salim-Anarkali drama that was being enacted behind my back. Not even you, Apoorva, a daughter of the soil? You stood with that unknown girl from somewhere!' Agatha said, staring accusingly at her.

Poor Apoorva was trying hard to explain to the fuming lady. After all, she was too young to understand the intricacies of such entanglements.

'Frankly, I didn't know much about it, Madam. I had heard her talking frequently to someone in the night, after everyone had slept, but in Hindi. When asked, she used to say that he was an old classmate from her town, and a distant relative, too. And I had no reason to disbelieve her. So far she has been good to me. She used to share her sweets with me; I am perhaps the only person who is somewhat close to her. She is suspicious of others, it seems,' her voice faltered.

'That itself showed she had something to hide. If she had any such plans as accused by her father, then the reputation of the institution is going to be tarnished forever. Once the police enters this campus and starts questioning everybody—from me to all of you—it is going to be a huge scandal. And obviously, the roommate won't be spared! As you might know, there are a few other organisations who were jealous of our activities and fame, and our stand on certain issues'.

That night Agatha had a long chat with the colonel on the phone. The colonel mumbled at the end.

'Don't take this casually, Agatha. This could blow up into a major issue for many reasons. Times are bad and one has to be careful on such matters. Even otherwise, it is not easy to run a girls' hostel, whatever name you might give it to, because girls are highly explosive material in the present social context. It's a clear label—handle with care!'

That was somewhat intriguing to Agatha, who was once the matron of a college hostel for girls, decades back. Although times have changed significantly, have the girls changed that much, to be dubbed as 'explosive material', to be handled 'with care'? Isn't it the one-sided view of an ex-army officer, who used to measure everyone on a scale of discipline alone?

'I know, colonel, but what should I do in this case? Succumb to those scoundrels, father of the girl and the so-called boyfriend, whose intentions are unknown?' Agatha was confused thoroughly.

'Don't worry. Let me put on my thinking cap. I shall come tomorrow morning. Meanwhile, I need to have a little chat with that Parveen girl and her roommate. Incidentally, I have a close friend, a retired major who runs a security agency. They do some private detective work too. Often, he used to say that he ought to have been in the police as an investigative officer. I shall request him to locate this Salim guy and trace out the details of his relationship with our Anarkali. Hope it doesn't turn out to be a *Mughal-e-Azam* type, where the poor girl Anarkali had to be sacrificed on the altar of an unforgiving Akbar. I have seen that movie half a dozen times in my younger days in Mumbai's Maratha Mandir, and wouldn't mind seeing it again—provided it is not enacted in our campus, with you playing the role of a killjoy Akbar, a female version, of course!'

Thoroughly enjoying her own joke, the colonel laughed aloud. Her usual hollow laugh. Almost like a guffaw, which Agatha did not quite appreciate. She was not at all in the mood to join the laughter.

That was a sleepless night for Agatha. All kinds of weird dreams disturbed her sleep. And it was the cool early morning breeze through the open windows that fanned and soothed her. And when she woke up again, it was bright dawn and the sun was blazing mercilessly on the lawn.

An early riser, she jumped out of the bed apologetically and started her morning rituals in a hurry.

A Strange Call for Seetha

It was an unusually warm and humid evening, and dark clouds were gathering on the western corner of the sky, indicating possible showers late in the evening. A day on which the chat session of the colonel was scheduled and the girls were looking forward to it. Then Agatha suggested that they might as well relax in the lawn rather than sitting in the stuffy hall. The colonel readily agreed. Fernandez always preferred to have such sessions under a village banyan tree or on a water front, with cool breeze blowing around. And she asked the girls to arrange the chairs suitably.

It was then that a strange telephone call came to The Nest.

The caller was looking for one Sujatha, a lanky girl with a slight squint in her left eye. The phone was picked by the housemaid Devaki—a close confidante of Madam—who was busy doing her evening housekeeping chores.

'May I know who's calling?' Devaki asked.

'I don't have to tell you that,' a curt and authoritative voice on the other side irritated Devaki. She was quick to retort.

'First of all, we don't have any Sujatha here. Moreover, we don't allow strangers to talk to the girls here.'

'Don't teach me your bloody rules. Give the phone to that girl from Devagiri, the daughter of a fruit merchant near the temple compound!'

'Oh, you mean VP Seetha?' But he was partially incorrect, since Seetha was not squint-eyed.

'Possibly, that might be her real name. I want to talk to her for an urgent personal matter. Does she have a cell phone?'

'I don't know whether she has one or not. Even if she did, we wouldn't give you the number. Those are our strict rules.'

There was a shout on the other side, probably followed by a filthy expletive. Devaki shuddered for a moment. It appeared she was threatened with dire consequences if she did not pass on the call to Seetha. Dazed, she could not retort immediately, and covering the mouth of the phone, she called out to Madam that somebody wanted to talk to V.P. Seetha. Agatha was busy overseeing the arrangement of chairs in the lawn, and she could see Seetha talking to Kadambari in a corner. For a moment she hesitated in giving the phone to Seetha, and called her to ascertain who it could be.

What followed was a bizarre scene. Immediately after Seetha had taken the phone hesitantly and listened to the tough voice on the other side, Kadambari heard a loud cry from inside. It was Seetha shivering, mortally scared, unable to utter a single word. It was clear that the man on the other side was threatening her with severe consequences.

Visibly perplexed, Devaki called out again to Madam Agatha, who was in the lawn. It was Kadambari who ran inside first, followed by Madam Agatha. Closely behind was the colonel, who could easily sense there was some serious problem. Kadambari had never seen her hopping on her walking stick with such speed, not caring whether she would trip on the uneven mounds hidden under thick grass, overdue for mowing.

She surveyed the scene for a moment and yelled.

'What happened? Why is Weepy really weeping?'

Nobody could answer. Even Madam Agatha. Weepy Seetha was sobbing with a puffy face and swollen eyelids. All were looking at Seetha for an answer. Then it was Kadambari who answered rather meekly that an unknown phone call was the real reason why Weepy was weeping. She was still holding on to the telephone. Onlookers could clearly hear a man shouting from the other side at the top of his voice: *'Hello, hello, you bitch, are you there? Have you gone away? But I'm not going to leave you like that.'*

It was then the furious colonel grabbed the phone and took control of the situation.

'Who's this bastard on the other side?' she yelled aloud. To this, there would have been a filthy rebuttal from the caller. Madam could see the colonel's face turning crimson red. She was quick to shout.

'You son of a bitch, don't you remember the names of the guys who slept with your sister last evening? Have you forgotten to collect your dues from them?'

Then she gestured to all the girls to move as far away as possible so she could let her full steam out.

It would have been real hell let loose. After some time, Madam Agatha could see a thoroughly exhausted colonel sinking to a nearby couch with a bottle of water and a deep sigh.

'So relieved, so relieved, Agatha,' she murmured. 'After so many years, I was reminded of my youth and the old *fauji* (army cadet) days. *Jawani yaad aayi* (remembered my youth). And I really enjoyed hurling those choice Punjabi expletives on that scoundrel. He would have been dumbfounded, because his stock was nothing compared to this rare *fauji* collection. In service, I had to interfere in some dirty brawls between the jawans. After exhausting their stock abuses in Hindi, they normally switched over to their native Punjabi and exhibited the flourish of their vocabulary. Anyway, that guy wouldn't dare to make another attempt to call our poor Weepy.'

Madam nodded peevishly. Although relieved, a former nun could not appreciate a woman hurling such foul abuses at a man, however bad he may be.

That is the life of a *fauji*, the colonel wanted to tell Agatha, but left it that.

After swallowing a tablet for her blood pressure levels to come down to normalcy, the colonel relaxed for some time. She felt that this was not the time to ask Weepy for the reason for all that chaos, since she could burst into an uncontrollable cry any moment.

'Well, well, I know who it was. It could be one of the lenders of her papa.' The colonel said calmly, 'Since they couldn't lay a hand on the old man—who had apparently vanished into thin air—and since his wife chose to take the ultimate step which she had been threatening for long, they had found a soft target in this weepy girl. But it's surprising, Agatha, how could they locate the number of the girl and call her without any difficulty?'

Madam was still looking angrily at the housemaid Devaki, who had disobeyed her strict orders and passed on the call from a stranger to the girl. She could have easily bluffed and got away with it.

'That's nothing, colonel,' Madam replied coolly. 'I had heard about similar cases elsewhere. These village moneylenders use all kinds of tricks to recover their dues. They threatened the women folk at home at odd hours, and even employ musclemen to handle their targets physically. After all it's money, you know. Money borrowed at usurious rates in desperate situations.'

'Then why should this poor girl suffer for the misdeeds of that scoundrel who ran away, leaving her in the lurch. *Darpok... Gadhe ka baccha* (Coward... Son of a donkey)!' yelled the colonel.

Kadambari did not want to correct her that it was Seetha who had abandoned her father, and not otherwise. Any way, it would have made little difference, since Annan was no way in a position to restart the business again and repay the debt.

'As I said, the lenders have their own bag of tricks. Even well-known institutions took law into their hands and used musclemen for such purposes, I have heard,' commented Agatha.

'What law!' colonel muttered. 'Although not a student of law, I know a bit of law. I have appeared as a principal witness in many medico-legal cases, both in service and in criminal courts outside. But I know that these lenders unlawfully take a whole bunch of documents from loanees like pronotes, guarantee agreements, and even signatures on blank papers, etc. In dire situations, where they have nowhere else to go, the borrowers would sign on any papers, not even looking at them. I don't know whether this girl has also signed any such documents herself.' To this, Seetha shook her head vehemently. She was thoroughly unaware of the transactions entered into by her inebriated father, who was mostly under the influence of a high dose of liquor.

'If the old man was still alive, the lenders would have to proceed against him first. Even if he had disappeared, the situation would not change as long he was alive, until proven otherwise. But if the crook has gone forever, then you have a real problem on hand. Since the mother is no more, the daughter would be responsible for assets and liabilities alike...'

Weepy's sobs, which had a little respite for some time while the discussions between the elders were on, now came back with double the vigour. But the colonel was quick to console her, ably supported by Madam Agatha. Kadambari was holding her close to her body, patting on her back.

'Don't worry, Weepy, it's my problem now. I have already told you once that you're my favourite weeping doll, one who wails on pressing anywhere! Anyway, let me see to what extent those rascals can go. Ruthless *bhenchods* (sisterfu***rs), As if they didn't have mothers and sisters! From today onwards I'm your patron and local guardian, take it from me,' the colonel declared aloud.

'No doubt,' Agatha agreed. 'When the colonel says something, those are the golden letters inscribed on a silver plate. She would go to any extent to keep your honour. I have many such instances to narrate.'

Although pleased immensely, the colonel stopped Agatha.

'*Bas*, *bas*. Enough, Agatha. This guy is not going to call again. But he won't leave it. From his words I could understand that there were a few other creditors in the line. He would even provoke them into action, perhaps a more severe one. Anyway, let's see. Having started the war, we won't retract until we have reached the logical end. After all, I'm a *fauji* and proud to be one. A *fauji* would never retrace her steps in the face of a few barks from stray dogs.'

Madam Agatha was aware that Fernandez took great pride in calling herself a *fauji*, and used to repeat it often.

Somewhat relieved, Seetha thanked the colonel with folded hands, and the latter hugged her with all the warmth she had.

Colonel was aware that a brilliant student and a topper in all her classes, Weepy's lifetime ambition was to become a doctor, that too a reputed gynaecologist—and she would have been one but for the blunders committed by her father during the crucial period of her life. In fact, she was a year junior to Kadambari in the school, and both had planned to tread similar career paths.

Madam Agatha nodded in the affirmative and assured that something would be done in this regard.

That day's chat session in the lawn ended with an unusual discussion on Weepy's tale in an open forum of the residents. Normally, Agatha would ensure the privacy of the girls. But on that day, she thought of baring it all in Weepy's case, and did not mind even if the girls asked probing questions. And Seetha could respond to them for the benefit of other girls, if she chose to do so. But nothing of that sort happened. The girls did not have anything to ask, and Seetha sat in a corner with a sullen face in the company of a consoling Kadambari. At the end, the girls expressed their solidarity with her and pledged to support the colonel's attempt to help Weepy.

Lady on the Wheel Chair with a Third Eye

The lady on the wheel chair refused to divulge her name. 'After all, what's in a name?' she asked. 'If you are so particular about it, you could call me Miss X, a female version of the proverbial Mr X of the movies, who did the amazing vanishing trick at inopportune moments.'

Puzzled a bit, going by the quiet nod of the Madam, Sarala entered the name as Miss X in all the records.

'What about your ID?' Sarala asked.

'I don't have one,' she replied curtly. 'Not even a passport.'

A disgusted Sarala shook her head and proceeded with her work.

But the girl was to tell Madam Agatha later that she had a tiff with the secretary, since she had refused to enter her name as Miss X. She had casually scribbled 'unknown' in that column in block letters, with a red question mark in the bracket.

When Madam tried to laugh it off, she commented tersely.

'Be careful with that woman!'

'Why do you say that?'

'Haven't you looked at her eyes straight?'

'Why?'

'An evil eye, which would glow in the night!'

'Oh!'

'It could bring bad luck to the birds in The Nest. Meanwhile, does she sleep here?'

Madam shrugged her shoulders in disbelief.

'Mind you, I have a third eye,' she said with a twinkle in her eyes.

'A third eye! Amazing,' Agatha chuckled.

'I can see the past and the future alike,' the girl appeared to be serious. 'This property has been let out to you by a rich guy who is away. That, too, without any remuneration. Don't you know, why? There was a burial ground on the southern side long back, and evil forces still keep an eye on this property.'

'Nonsense!'

'I don't want you to believe it, but just a note of caution. Mind you, the man has not been able to sell this property, despite his incessant efforts. He even did some *homam* (a ceremonial ritual) here once, which was of no avail. That's one reason why he gave it for free, thinking that charity might purify the place. Of course, there may be some builders interested in buying the place, but he is not inclined, since he doesn't want his ancestral building to be demolished for putting up a skyscraper or a mall.'

'Okay, okay,' Agatha wanted to dispose her off quickly.

Miss X was in her early thirties. A lean woman with a rosy face, long nose and deep blue eyes, she was unusually agile in her movements, despite the handicap. Obviously, she was a misfit, compatibility-wise, among other residents—which had left Sarala wondering about the queer ways of Madam Agatha. Later, the lady told Madam Agatha that she would be like an elder sister to all the girls, and might as well be called *Didi* (elder sister), as they did in the North, or *Akka* as was common in this part of the country. Perhaps *Didi* would sound better for her looks and behaviour. Although originally from a village near Kochi in Kerala, she had completed her college education in Mumbai, and hence, was reasonably comfortable with Hindi and Marathi. Madam also liked *Didi*, as she did not want her to remain nameless among a group of girls. And so, she asked Sarala to correct her name in the records as Miss Didi. Sarala was also relieved that, at last, she had a name to address her with.

Didi had come armed with the strong recommendations of two well-known people, one being none other than Anita Subramanian, one of the trustees. 'Please don't compare her case with that of other girls who were all victims of a miserable past,' she had warned, adding, 'You must not take her as a "runaway girl" like others, since she is a lady of her own standing. Further, she does not need any support; having heard a lot about you and your noble activities at The Nest, she was too keen to be associated with you.' Anita also told Madam Agatha that she had felt for a while now that she needed someone like her to lend a helping hand in her activities at The Nest.

Incidentally, her parents were long settled in Australia, with her father having a very successful business there. But this lady, on account of her peculiar nature, did not want to settle down in another country. She was happy living here in the company of her favourite wheel chair. 'As one born and brought up in this ancient country with a great heritage, why should I migrate,' she asked, adding, 'Were they in anyway better off than us? All those tall claims about world leadership are nothing but *bakwas* (gibberish). Didn't the Britishers become rich by looting us? Weren't we the ones who had showed them the light of knowledge when they were in the dark, thousands of years ago?'

When Agatha was initially reluctant to take her in, considering the compatibility issue, she was assured by Ms Subramaniam that she would be a rare asset to the institution, that she would meet all her expenses in addition to making a substantial donation. It's not about the money but the overall compatibility, Agatha had pointed out.

'Don't worry, dear, she would mix freely with anybody, and with her crazy comments and childish pranks she was going to be a huge hit among the girls,' assured Anita, adding, 'Further, she can talk on any subject under the sun—from history and geography to anthropology. She is a born prodigy who can take on some of the scholars even, if it comes to that.'

That was proved beyond doubt on the day of induction itself. When Sarala asked her sympathetically as to what had happened to her legs.

'Oh it was nothing serious, buddy,' she spoke as if to a pal, in a serious tone 'I slipped and fell while running the women's marathon in Rome Olympics. Wasn't it splashed on the front page of all our English newspapers?'

'Oh, I see. Sorry to hear that.'

Sarala sympathised with a sigh. Little did she know that the lady with the polio-ridden legs was not even born at the time of the 1960 Rome Olympics, and that the women's marathon was introduced in Olympics only 24 years later.

'Again, this wheel chair was much shorter when I had started using it. But it grew taller along with me. That's why I love it so much.'

'Oh, how odd, Muruga...' Sarala thanked the almighty for such miracles.

Having scored the first point, Didi felt abundantly confident about her eminence in The Nest. She could take on anyone!

Later, she amused Madam Agatha by greeting her with a rare self-introduction, too.

'You might be wondering why I'm not revealing my name. The answer is simple, just because I don't have one. This namelessness makes you so light that one can even fly in thin air without any fuel. Many of the problems in this country would be solved if you didn't have a name or surname of your own, which reveals much. Shiv Prasad Agarwal should be a Marwari and Uday Shankar Shastri a Brahmin from the Hindi belt. Similarly, a Walter Anton D'Costa is bound to be an Anglo-Indian, possibly from Mumbai or Goa. What about this ABCD (American-Born Confused Desi) Rama Reddy? Why does one carry the whole pedigree record—including the name of the village and all the ancestors one could think of—on their shoulders? And when the poor boy lands up in the Silicon Valley, they would mercilessly shorten it to Ram. The valley is full of such funny names, like Erapally Chandrasekharan becoming Chanks. How funny, and I'm sure no parents would approve of it!'

An interesting argument indeed, Madam nodded. In this country, one is easily identified by the name or title they carry—a Hindu, Muslim, Parsi, Jew, Sikh or Christian. Even castes and sub-castes are reflected in the names, like Rajputs, Jats, Kayasthas, Yadavs, Marathas, Lingayats, Khammas and, of course, the Brahmin—who are a class of their own.

'Exactly,' beamed Didi. 'Now there is no way one can identify my religion or caste.'

Madam Agatha agreed quietly.

'So let us have more of such Mr As and Miss Bs. Wouldn't it sound better?'

Again, Madam nodded approvingly. But the manner in which the girl amused the usually tough colonel was more interesting. Having heard a lot about her from Madam and the other girls, the colonel wanted to pull her leg. But she easily floored the colonel with her unique thoughts.

'Don't think I am awfully...doctor...' she could not complete when the colonel interrupted.

'Call me colonel, lady. I'm no longer a doctor.'

'Okay, okay. Don't think I'm awfully handicapped, colonel.' She completed the sentence. 'I could have easily run half marathons if I had wanted. But I avoided them because I'm deeply in love with this wheelchair which, incidentally, has given me amazing privileges—like that of a star. I get preference in all types of queues, and sometimes I wheel forward, jumping the queue while winking at others...much to the disquiet of some. But my only regret is that I can't become a lady goon—I badly wanted to be one!'

'A lady goon! But why?'

'So that I could break the legs of all those corrupt politicians, irrespective of their party affiliations. But I would never kill them, since I want to see them all on wheelchairs—a party meeting with all the leaders on wheelchairs, in place of chairs of authority; a swearing-in ceremony with the governor standing tall amidst a row of ministers on wheelchairs; and a cabinet meeting without chairs, but only wheelchairs! Of course, there may be some who could boast of legs of their own, but wouldn't they try to express their solidarity through a wheelchair? Again, a warning for the future.' She was reeling out her peculiar thoughts effortlessly while the dumbfounded colonel sat unmoved.

After a long chat with this interesting girl, the colonel enquired, 'Aren't you a Jew, possibly a Cochin Jew, if I'm not terribly mistaken?'

The lady nodded in appreciation.

'Wow! Spot on, colonel!' she applauded. 'Then guess my name, as recorded in the synagogue records, which I have conveniently renounced…'

'Renounced? But how?'

'Published in the gazette, since I found it too heavy to carry. But what about a passport, you might ask. But I didn't need a passport, since I had no plans to go out of the country. If people want to meet me, let them come down…as simple as that! Then guess the original name, as was recorded in the synagogue records, of this nameless me!'

The colonel thought for a moment and announced firmly, 'Miriam. Or at the most, a Rebecca!'

'Not wide off the mark! Possibly, eight out of ten!' cried Didi. 'Okay then, I should be going now, since I have bored you enough.'

While saying bye, immensely pleased with her maiden performance at The Nest, she revealed that all those claims about participating in half marathon etc. were bunkum, and that she had been polio-ridden right from her high school days. When her parents wanted to take her with them, it was she who had wanted to remain here.

'I guessed so,' smiled the doctor, 'both as a doctor and a *fauji*. A *fauji* can spot a lie earlier than a doctor, since the doctor needs all kinds of tests for back-up!' When she asked Didi why she did not migrate to Israel like many others, she was clear in her mind. She was happy that at last the colonel had opened her favourite topic.

'Why should I?' exclaimed Didi. 'They claim it was a return to the Promised Land. But I couldn't agree. When I was born and brought up here in a small village in Kerala, this was my land and I spoke the language of the land. Why should I learn Hebrew now, since it is not my mother's language—the language I was born into. Moreover, how can you know that it would be a "return", since one could never be sure as to whether all their ancestors had migrated from Jerusalem? My parents also agreed on this point, and migrated to Australia instead—a place of their choice.'

'She's nuts but sensible,' the colonel mumbled.

In fact, the colonel was greatly interested. 'At last, we have a Jew in The Nest to make it really heterogeneous,' she complimented Madam Agatha, adding, 'She has a streak of madness within her though!'

Madam Agatha allotted Miss X a corner room on the ground floor—shifting the earlier occupant to the first floor—so as to make it easier for her movements and accommodate her wheelchair.

'You've been promoted upstairs on account of my wheelchair, darling. Say thanks to my chair!' she congratulated her, and the poor girl did not know what to say. 'Anyway, you can call me Didi or Akka, whatever you wish!'

Her roommate was the ever-devout Sabeena, who never missed a single namaz. On the first day, Didi tried to impress Sabeena with one of her tongue twisters.

The poor girl sat amazed with her mouth wide open for a moment. It was left to Didi to pat her on her back and bring her to normalcy.

'Nothing to worry, dear,' she assured. 'Not mine, lifted from somewhere.'

Anyway, since there was very little space left to share her wild thoughts with Sabeena, she left her in her own domain of prayers, religious books, and Arabian Nights.

That evening, she e-mailed her parents in Australia about her first day at Madam Agatha's Nest. It's a wonderful place, she affirmed, where a Jew could co-exist with a devout Muslim in a small nest on a treetop without a Gaza strip in between.

It was true that the rooms at The Nest were not uniform—with a few large rooms and the rest comparatively small, and with very little space between the cots.

How did the girl get the old story about the burial ground on the southern side? What's this third eye she claims to have, Madam Agatha was left wondering. Anyway, since the story was true, her claim also might have some stray elements of truth, she concluded.

'Yes, the lady on the wheelchair, who had a third eye, could be an asset to The Nest, as assured by Ms Subramanium,' she told the colonel, who also nodded in agreement.

The Khap Panchayat and the Missing Parveen

What's disturbing Madam Agatha, wondered Apoorva. What's the reason behind her spending sleepless nights and wandering alone through the corridors late in the night? Was it her roommate Parveen Singh, an outsider who came to The Nest to disturb its peace and tranquillity?

Apoorva was right. After the return of that rustic Risal Singh, Madam's worries seemed to have multiplied. It has become her responsibility to see that this little bird doesn't fly out unnoticed.

That was why she called the gatekeeper Karupayyan and threatened him again.

'No boozing during duty time, mind you. Times are bad!'

'I know that ma'am.'

'That girl's father is quite tough. A ruffian, you know.'

'I know ma'am. Didn't I see so on that day?'

His way of talking, keeping his palm against the mouth was only to ward off the foul smell of liquor and not to show respect, Sarala used to say. And even though Agatha was also aware of that, she was ignoring it in consideration for his family. She also knew that Sarala was keen on seeing the back of that man on some pretext or other.

Nevertheless, Agatha repeated her warning that he would be the first target if something untoward was to happen. It's known to all that as the one doing all kinds of odd shopping for her, Parveen could easily win him over by exploiting his weaknesses.

There are many birds in my nest, but this one alone is the cursed one, Agatha used to lament.

That's why she started roaming around alone in the night. But when Apoorva, sitting late with her studies noticed it, Madam had to discontinue it reluctantly. But much to her dismay, that duty was later to be entrusted to the girl herself. When Madam reiterated that Parveen is a valuable 'commodity', Apoorva was left bewildered. She didn't quite understand the import of that word.

But this surveillance on the part of Agatha and her roommate did leave Parveen amused. She questioned Apoorva later, 'Why should I run away from this place, dear? I came here since we considered it to be the safest place. Still, why this high-profile security? Am I a leader or a convict? Which category of security is this? Why don't you explain this to Madam Agatha?'

Poor Apoorva did not have the guts to face the tough lady and talk. She tried to explain to Parveen rather meekly, 'Why don't you tell her yourself? Madam was not like this earlier. Isn't your baba responsible for all this chaos? After all, times are bad and if a charming girl like you falls in the hands of hooligans outside, what will happen to the reputation of The Nest?'

Parveen nodded understandingly.

'I'm prepared to apologise to Madam Agatha on behalf of baba.'

'What use is that? The damage has already been done.'

Still, Parveen could not fathom why Madam Agatha was so flustered. After all, didn't she have a well-known organisation behind her?

The colonel was also aware of the worries haunting Agatha. As one not familiar with the life up North, she had too many questions to ask on various matters. That's why the colonel found it necessary to brief her on certain vital issues.

'Have you heard of the Khap Panchayats?' asked the colonel.

They were sitting on a bench in the garden. It was the beginning of winter and a cool breeze was blowing. The colonel was quite relaxed. She took a long puff of the cigarette and coughed a couple of times. Normally, she did not smoke inside the campus but that day she badly wanted to, to lift up her mood. In fact, she loved smoking an ornamental pipe. 'Like a man,' she used to say with a chuckle. Like an Earl relaxing on a couch near the fire place, with a pipe in hand and a glass of scotch on an ornamental table nearby—in true Victorian style.

'Have you heard about the Khap Panchayats?' She repeated the question, as if Agatha had not heard it.

Agatha nodded.

'I have seen some news reports.'

'Of course, they are in the news mostly for the wrong reasons. But these Khaps were started as a Union of Panchayats with thc good intention of settling important issues relating to the people of the community. But later, some of them fell into wrong hands and became power centres, and started functioning like self-appointed village courts—even summoning innocent villagers for unsubstantiated charges and awarding them with severe punishments. Investigator, prosecutor, judge, and executor—all rolled into one. Later, their area of surveillance widened and sensitive issues like man-woman relationships etc., too, were scrutinised closely. Even love affairs and marital alliances became a bone of contention, and offenders were punished severely.'

'In the case of our Parveen....'

'Yeah, I'm coming to that... It's a very serious issue, Agatha. No doubt about it. A pretty girl from a reputed family, for whom there would have been many eligible suitors from the same area, falling for a faraway boy—an unknown Muslim at that. That's not something they could have imagined. In a society where even marriages outside one's own caste or sub-caste are taboo, an abnormal violation such as this must be blasphemous! Mind you, even a marriage alliance with a boy from a faraway village is not allowed, even if he is from the same caste, gotra etc. At some places, there are other funny arguments like marriages among the same gotra and village are taboo, since they are like siblings. There are cases where the girl's father is ordered to shoot down his own darling daughter, and they have to obey meekly. They label it as "honour killings" in the name of the community!'

'Jesus! In which age are we living?'

'Stone Age, possibly. But mind you, these are stray cases, whipped up by media, too. Still, it is significant that despite a few strict court rulings against such practices—particularly where the offenders were killed brutally—nothing substantial has happened. Strangely, even some politicians support these illegal practices, and state administrations slow pedal them. At the same time, it is true that there are many panchayats who are doing really good work, and only a few are seen misusing the newfound power. So one can't really generalise it easily.'

'What would happen in Parveen's case?'

'It's quite possible that the Panchayat would have considered this contentious issue, a love affair between a Haryanvi Hindu girl and Tamilian Muslim boy. They would have even ordered a trial, and that's why Parveen chose to run away from the area in the middle of the night.'

'Couldn't she have approached the local police here for protection?'

'They'll coolly pass on the buck to her own state. They would ask the girl to appear before their police, since by all possibility "a girl missing case" would have already been lodged there.'

'Then what will we do?'

Madam Agatha was getting panicky. She realised that they had a knotty problem on hand. That guy Risal Singh had threatened to come again, possibly with some goons or a court order. As the girl's father, he had every right to take her back. Perhaps, only that Salim could save the situation and protect Parveen by marrying her—if he was really serious about the relationship, that is.

It appeared the colonel was also thinking on those lines.

'That Salim guy appears to be quite enterprising. He is working hard and through the lorry business, he has developed contacts all over—even in the North-eastern sectors. According to that major, my friend, he has purchased a new flat here recently and had done it up beautifully... Anyway, let's watch the way things develop,' she consoled Agatha. 'It's quite obvious that it was Salim who told the girl that our Nest was a safe haven. All other claims are false. However, for now, let's lie low but keep an eye on that girl. She should not run away; if she does, a Habeas Corpus petition would follow, and you would be the first to be questioned. Their contention would be that you were behind this illegal detention, in collusion with that Tamilian boy.'

'Jesus! Anyway, I'll ask the gatekeeper Karupayyan to be more vigilant.'

'How good is that old dude? He appears to be a lazy bum.'

'As you know, he is here only for the night duty... Appears to be quite loyal and honest. He's an ex-serviceman himself, but does not seem to have acquired any of the good qualities from the service like discipline and obedience. Of course, he has all those bad qualities like drinking and use of swear words in abundance. Here, he is used to listen only to me, and does not care about the secretary who is responsible for running the administration. After selling the military quota of liquor on double the price, he drinks the cheap country stuff. So he gets a bit out of whack when the dosage of arrack exceeds his tolerance level. Indeed, he has reduced it after my repeated warnings, but yet to stop it fully... To be frank, whenever I have intended to take some stern action, his wife has come wailing and touched my feet, pleading that this was the only source of income for their family of six.'

As a hardened military person, the colonel was least impressed. A security guard should always be a guard, come what may, and the pleas from his wife is another matter.

'It is sad that I have to remind a former *fauji* about the basic principles of sentry duty,' the colonel moaned.

'Ok, let's hope that nothing untoward happens. Take as much care as possible. Meanwhile, I wanted to have a private chat with this Parveen girl again, who wanted to be another Anarkali.'

Madam Agatha nodded in agreement.

'Anyway, let me put on my thinking cap again…something ought to emerge,' said the colonel.

Having arranged for this private talk, Madam Agatha withdrew to her office. She wanted to make a couple of urgent calls, one to an old friend in the convent who had remained her advisor on all major issues. Agatha knew that the first question from the old sister would be 'How's your health, sister?'. Her concern was that Agatha was someone who always worked hard, wherever she might be, without caring about her health. As one who had issues regarding palpitation of the heart, she ought to be a little more careful about her health, she might warn again.

She would also reiterate her earlier instructions to the secretary, that complete details of all residents should be obtained and recorded meticulously. Moreover, she must try to collect as much details as possible about the family details of the girls, including photographs, contact numbers of close relatives etc.

Meanwhile, there came a late-night call from the colonel. It appeared, that the girl was quite cool about the developments in her village. 'Why are you people unduly worried about my case,' asked the girl with a nonchalant smile. 'Might be okay in the case of Madam, since she was a pious nun with a soft heart once, but as a former senior military officer, you ought to be a tad bolder,' she scorned. On being reminded about her father's visit to The Nest and his threat, she laughed it away. 'Let the old man inform the police and let them take me to the police station for questioning,' challenged the girl, adding, 'I'm just waiting for that, so that I can finally speak my heart out to them.' According to the colonel, she was quite confident that the police wouldn't interfere in such matters, since she was a not minor anymore, and had every right to take her own decisions in such matters.

'Was that boy behind all this?'

'Not really. A very strong-willed girl,' she smiled.

'When I asked pointedly about Salim, she had reserved a rare bouquet of exquisite words for him. Quite a charming boy, claimed the girl, capable of winning over anyone, including the usually tough colonels and ex-nuns. Ultimately, when the police would allow the couple to go their way, she said that she wanted the gracious presence and blessings of the colonel and Madam Agatha for their marriage... What a clever girl, eh?'

'Quiet so.'

With that, Agatha was relieved to some extent, and relaxed enough to share a couple of old jokes with the colonel.

Kadambari's Revelations

In the wee hours of the morning, Kadambari was floating within layers of sleep. Flowing within non-linear time and unable to fathom the depth of the stream, the flow of currents were taking her forward to the point to which she was destined... Would there be some wild shrubs to latch on to, jutting from the shores?

But she could clearly place the pavement of Devagiri, the one that led to Gopuram—the tall tower in front of the ancient Karumari Amman temple. The long path up to the steps was paved with ancient granite meticulously kept clean, quite unlike many other temples frequented by a large number of devotees. After climbing the steps, one reached the mandapam. The devotees who had not observed due penance and had not kept their body clean stopped there, and worshipped the Amman from outside with closed eyes and folded hands. Although there was no such stipulation from the temple authorities, it had become an age old self-regulation by the worshippers. The temple was religiously visited by hundreds of ardent devotees, irrespective of the seasons and schedules. It was not a question of belief or blind faith, but a soothing comfort that the Amman was always with her faithful followers; never to desert them in bad times. The real power of Amman was visible when contagious diseases like chicken pox and measles spread disastrously. It was believed that the seeds of the chicken pox were sown by none other than the Amman herself—when she was infuriated over some wrongdoing and had remained within the infected person for more than a week, depending on its severity. The patient then normally slept on a mat on which neem leaves were spread thickly. After the illness was cured, the patients normally visited the temple in remorse and gave generous offerings for their past sins.

In fact, it was one of the few temples where the doors of the *sreekovil* (sanctum sanctorum) were not closed to the devotees for unduly long periods. Only for the noon puja where the deity was offered her *naivedyam* (offering to God), and for the usual evening rituals like *archana* (personal, abbreviated puja done by temple priests for individual guidance/blessings) and *aradhana* (the act of glorifying God via prayers), where the idol was decorated and worshipped with the traditional *aarti* (Hindu prayer ceremony during which lights made from camphor-soaked wicks are offered to God). Of course, the rituals varied from place to place. The pujaris took turns in such a way that the worshippers commuting long distances were not inconvenienced anyway.

Kadambari heard the bells ringing in unison from the Kovil far away, indicating that it was time for the evening *aarti*. Sitting alone in the veranda of her house, she waited for the temple bells to stop and the eventual dusk to fall, engulfing the entire area with a pall of gloom—the temple, the pavements, the busy streets with the devotees rushing back to the nearest bus stations—yet another nightfall in the temple town, when the bustling town was allowed a much-needed rest, only to wake up to the next morning's buzz. A temple town has its own schedules, matching the activities of the temple, and all the residents had to structure their timings according to it as well.

It was then that the bats had flown in, flapping their wings loudly and shrieking wildly. Kadambari could sense their shadowy movements in the thickening layers of darkness, trying to devour the trees avariciously. And there was yet another group flying low over her head into the thick darkness, looking for their nests. Loud flaps of the wings and shrieking cries again...

Kadambari woke up with a loud cry and fell out of the cot with a loud thud. Opening her heavy eyelids, she still could not convince herself that it was all a dream, and that she was safe inside a room in The Nest. It was still dark outside, and her body was shivering with an unknown fear. Her roommate Gouri was fast asleep, snoring occasionally, not knowing what had happened. Kadambari was really thirsty and desperately wanted a glass of water, but she did not have the nerve to climb down the steps. Neither did she want Gouri to be woken up from her deep sleep.

Later, while completing her morning chores leisurely, Kadambari knew that she had no escape from the memories of Devagiri—the temple town that made her who she was now. An unknown girl, possibly the daughter of a street beggarwoman, had attained this level in life due to the kindness of the beloved Appa and Amma. And she might have to take several births to repay that debt to them... Then a wild thought came to her mind: Was I right in abandoning them and running away from home, without giving any clue to anybody? Were the reasons so disquieting so as to take such a desperate decision?

Why? Why?

A barrage of never-ending and tormenting questions that might not draw an answer easily. At last, she decided to break the ice and reveal everything to Madam Agatha.

And Agatha was willing to hear the story. After the Parveen episode, the atmosphere at Kilikoodu had changed substantially. She knew that the apparent calm outside was deceptive, but really, it was as if a wild stone had been thrown into the middle of a pool of clear water. Who had thrown it? Why did he do it? Would it happen again?

Was it waiting to happen?

As clearly indicated by the colonel, in such an institution where girls of all shades and colours from different backgrounds with hidden baggage of their own congregate, anything can happen any moment. This episode could even be the tip of the iceberg. While registering the trust, the government officials concerned had indicated that all the possible records of the residents should be obtained and preserved meticulously. Later, the local police officials had also emphasised the need for asking pertinent questions and recording the available details. Nobody should have access to the data, which could even be tampered with, they had warned. Obviously, since all of them would have sob stories to narrate—probably straight from a popular soap opera on the TV—it is for Agatha to sift the grains from the chaff. One had to be tough for it. This was what the colonel had also underlined the previous night. She had also doubted whether a former nun with a soft heart straight from the convent was fit enough for that.

Thereafter, she had also decided to put all those stories under a powerful scanner and learn to 'sift the grains from chaff'.

But Kadambari indicated right in the beginning that she had no sob stories to narrate. It was all hard facts and nothing but facts. But please don't be surprised if truth turned out to be odder than fiction, she had urged.

Madam Agatha was attentive as never before. In fact, she had wanted to listen to Kadambari's story mainly because she had claimed that her Appa had also maintained a Nest comparable to this, and so this was only a simple relocation from one branch of a tree to another. But no ugly bats flying in from bottomless nights to hang on the branches.

Another nest, one branch of a tree to another! Agatha was curious.

The story of an abandoned child, possibly stolen by a beggarwoman from another village and another family, taken possession of by a childless couple from a festival ground... It was all fate, nothing but fate. The festival had ended and Shankararaman and his wife Gomathy were resting on the ground on their palm leave mats after, watching the late-night *Harikatha* that was being performed by a well-known troupe. When they woke up suddenly hearing the temple bells, it was time for the first bus to leave. They hurriedly folded the mats and washed their faces. And when they were hurrying to the bus stand, a little girl approached them, and before Shankararaman could understand what was happening, she clung to his dhoti... refusing to leave him.

Although Gomathy shook her head, gesturing to leave the child there itself, he hesitated for a moment. When he looked at her innocent face, he felt she was possibly stolen from a good family. Anyway, since nobody had come to claim the child, despite a couple of announcements on the public address system, he did not try to separate the child forcibly from his body. When he asked the little girl to wash her mud-smeared face at a tap nearby, she was unsure for a moment, hesitating to leave the tip of his dhoti. And he had to accompany her to the tap and stand there, watching her clean her face and mouth with one hand, while holding on to his dhoti with the other.

Not recollections from the vague memories of a four-year-old but vivid accounts of Appa and Amma, who had been repeating it over the years incessantly without getting bored. And how Amma used to curse the moment she even tried to persuade her husband to abandon the child there itself. While inside the bus, she was still thinking whether they could get off at their stop unnoticed by the weary girl.

That was how the deserted girl became the darling daughter of Shankararaman and Gomathy. They became her Appa and Amma instantaneously and she was named Kadambari, a name the girl herself was happy to be christened with. Appa was from the family of wholesale and retail dealers of temple flowers and their shop was located in a prime area, right in front of the Amman temple. It was his father Anantharaman, during whose time the family business had thrived to this extent—from a small shop handling flowers and garlands for offerings to the deity to a major business outfit, entering the wholesale trade. Anantharaman loved the flowers very much, and knew the subtle details about the origin and behaviour of each variety of flower. He was also an ardent researcher on the subject. He could deliver a lecture or two on it to the well-known professors and floriculturists.

Much later, fed up with the flower trade, he wandered a lot in the forests and valleys in search of wild flowers unknown to the civilisation outside. He firmly believed that there might be one, unique on its own and a gift from heaven, and was always in search of that isolated divine one. From a successful trader, he had turned into a keen lover of flowers, who earnestly believed that flowers should not be plucked, and that they were meant to remain on the plants for radiating their fragrance and beauty to the onlookers.

Although lazy by nature, his son was an astute businessman and went ahead with his mission to open another shop near the Muruga temple on the hill above. But Gomathy's worry was regarding the servicing of that unit, as one had to wake up early and carry the loads up through an uneven track before the temple opened for the early morning *aarti*. It was not easy to get a dependable employee, as most of them had no qualms about swindling money right in front of the deity! But knowing his lazy nature, Gomathy was not in favour of taking this additional burden, and hence the project was shelved with a vow that he would do it one day or the other in the future.

Kadambari used to sit at the flower stall sometimes, but her attention always gravitated toward the anteroom behind the house, which was a later addition. It was in this room that the garlands meant for the temple were prepared. Girls well-trained for the job would assemble early in the morning to string together the garlands with long needles and deft fingers.

It was often said that a flower man's family never slept. By around 2:30 am, Gomathy would get up, and by the time she lit up the gas stove and prepared black tea, Shankararaman would be up brushing his teeth. No change in the schedule, be it torrential monsoons, searing heat or chilly winters. By around 3:30 am, driver Muniswamy would arrive in his pick-up auto with the loads of flower cartons that would have arrived by the morning passenger train. The name 'A.K. Shankararama, Amman Koil Street' written in bold with a black sketch pen was easily identified by the porters from the packed bogie—a daily consignment that arrived by the same train. After all, they were all ardent devotees of the Amman, and were also well taken care of by Shankararaman for their prompt services.

By that time, the five girls from an orphanage would have arrived in a horse cart. After sipping a cup of hot black coffee Gomathy had prepared lovingly, they started their work. All were handicapped—partially blind, deaf, dumb, differently-abled, polio-ridden, etc. After some time, Kadambari also wanted to join them—as the sixth girl. Why don't I join as well, am I also not an orphan, she used to think, and it was with great hesitation that Amma grunted her approval. Wasn't she a gift to the family from unknown parents, with the blessings of Amman, Gomathy used to grumble... Appa had named the girls after flowers—*mullai, chempakam, kanakambaram, jamanthi, rajamalli* etc. Apart from the usual garlands, bouquets, wreaths etc., they prepared all kinds of decorative works with flowers as well. Sometimes, they would also hire some workers from outside for putting up and decorating the ceremonial pandals which was a big business but had to be stopped later, since the commitment was too big and pressurising.

Of all the girls, Kadambari had a special liking for Kanakambaram. She was partially deaf and had left her house after a bitter quarrel with her father's second wife. A drug addict, her father would return from work in the evening, and listen to his wife's pillow-talk complaints and thrash the girl mercilessly. One day, a fierce push from the veranda to the courtyard ended up damaging her tympanum and ear drum alike, which had made her partially deaf...

Like that, every girl had a story to tell, all culminating in the atrocities of men—mostly close ones, like father, uncle, brother etc.

But your case is totally different. You had loving parents. Then what was your problem? Why did you run away from such loving parents? Any other tragedy? Madam had these questions on her lips. Kadambari, too, had expected such painful questions from her. But Madam Agatha did not ask. After listening attentively, she sighed about the curious ways of the world.

To some extent, Kadambari was relieved that Madam did not ask those embarrassing questions. She had only one regret—that she could have dropped a vague hint to dear Kanakambaram, who used to bare her heart out to her. She had not kept a single secret from her, even some of the blunders she had committed—including a love affair with a boy, and the way she had once succumbed to his amorous advances in a corner in the park.

After the long narration, strangely it was Kadambari who had a question to ask, something which had been lingering in her mind for quite some time.

'Madam, shall I ask you something? Something silly that might make you laugh. But please listen carefully and give me your view.'

Madam Agatha felt a kind of motherly affection towards the girl for the first time. She had met many girls during her stint at a women's college run by the diocese, but none of them had charmed her so much…Kadambari felt like an estranged child, a close blood relation.

'Okay, go ahead,' she said softly.

'Don't take it as a joke. I want your frank opinion…'

'Why all this? Go ahead, ask already!'

'Do I have serpentine eyes that would mesmerise men by a mere gaze? The evil eyes of a *Naga Kanya* (daughter of the serpent), cursed by the *Naga Devta* (snake god)?'

'Ridiculous! Who told you all this nonsense?'

'Amma used to say that I was very pretty. My classmate Pavizham, envious by nature, had accepted that I was reasonably beautiful. And those two jealous daughters of Ayya Sastrigal, Vasundharamma and Yasodharamma, knew I was really charming but did not want to acknowledge. But whenever I looked at the mirror, I felt that I was just okay, nothing more, nothing less.'

'But why all this now?' Agatha was puzzled. She could not understand what Kadambari was aiming it. But Kadambari was not listening. She was in a kind of stupor.

'The men who had looked at me were hypnotised, irrespective of their age and position, as if I had some mystical powers.' Kadambari was continuing in a voice which was not hers. 'That dance master Nattuvan Sivamani, who had pedalled all the way on his old bicycle for 18 kilometres through the uneven muddy roads to coach Shankararaman's daughter some basic steps on dancing—the famed guru who ran a *natyavidyalaya* (drama school) in the town and was so busy that he had stopped admitting beginners, readily accepting Appa's request to teach a novice, that too pedalling all the way… Why? The middle-aged man's face looked somewhat odd; cat's eyes on the left and crow's eyes on the right. And a thick golden bangle with a serpent's hood on it, between many coloured threads on the left hand. Hardly had he struggled for about three months did I notice that he was visibly distracted. His eyes were eager to convey some hidden message to me, not a good one either... Then I had to put my foot down. "Enough Appa, no more dancing. That man is not okay". Appa was puzzled. "What are you talking dear, he is a famous guru, and a middle-aged man, too". But I was stubborn.'

'Jesus!' she heard Madam Agatha saying.

'Then came another well-known guru, Ponnayyan Bhagavathar,' Kadambari continued. 'He agreed to teach me classical music after looking at me with admiration. Appa's friends could not believe it. Bhagavathar, a known stickler to rules, riding all the way on his old Lambretta scooter, 12 kilometres through the same muddy road to teach Shankaraman's daughter Carnatic music. That, too, thrice a week. But it did not take me much time to start disliking the new teacher. He had this bad habit of touching me here and there needlessly—including at some unwanted places with an innocent look on his face, as if it was a show of parental affection. Another dirty old man, I murmured. After three months, still struggling with the basic *swaras* (notes), I said enough was enough, no more *swaras*, no more touching. When the old man rode the scooter back, he felt the distance doubling.'

'Oh, my!' Madam Agatha groaned. 'Yet another insult!'

'When the tuition classes in art stopped, then entered the science teacher Vedanayakam, who agreed to teach me mathematics. It was the head mistress, a matronly sister who had felt that with some coaching in mathematics I might bring top rank to the school. She was the one who had a reckoned a 'rank' in the public exam as second only to the Almighty,' chuckled Kadambari.

'Vedanayakam reminded us of maestro Gemini Ganesan, the eternal romantic hero of Tamil filmdom. He had a gloomy face of a loser hero deserted by his sweetheart. Very rarely did he talk to other teachers, least with his own students. It was true that I had some special liking for that teacher because he was so very different from the other ones. It's true that there were a few girls fascinated by his sleepy eyes and the thin, drooping moustache, but it was clear from his occasional glances that it was me who had caught his fancy. For me, he was the ideal teacher, too, who had made the once unconquerable Mathematics look fairly simple—and we scaled the great heights together, hand-in-hand. When I scored full marks in the math paper, Amma invited him home and treated him with some of her choice snacks. It was then that the inevitable thing happened... In the guise of taking a look at my bookshelf in the attic, he managed some private moments with me. While pretending to search the shelf, he was unusually tense and was shivering unnecessarily. It was then that he tried to hold me close to his body and kiss me forcibly, much against my resistance. When I slipped away sobbing, Vedanayakam was stunned for a moment. Anyway, that incident strengthened my fear that I have serpentine eyes—an eternal curse of the *Naga Devta*, from which I could not escape, neither would the onlookers.

Kadambari sighed.

Madam Agatha was astounded for a moment. She could not say anything to calm the girl, who was lost in her memories. Agatha was also thinking of all such bizarre instances where an evil eye could lead a good man to bad deeds, from the days of Adam.

'Now tell me ma'am, do I have serpentine eyes that charm men?'

'What do you feel?'

'Possibly, the curse of the *Naga Kanya*.'

'Not at all, nothing but the excesses of some dirty old men.'

'Then what about that Vedanayakam sir?'

'Tell me frankly, didn't you love him?'

Kadambari was silent. But Madam had read her mind clearly.

'Probably. He, too, loved you deeply. But unable to read the mind of a teenager, he was a bit too aggressive unnecessarily—as is the wont with many men.'

'Then what about the serpentine eyes?'

'Nonsense! Better grow up from the level of comics and cartoon movies. You're indeed a pretty girl and there may be many who would have been charmed by you, but it's not your fault.

'But ma'am,' Kadambari was still not satisfied and was repeating something she had said sometime back.

But it appeared Madam had not heard her. She was muttering to herself.

'The kiss. The precious kiss!'

As if she was guided back to her days in the convent amidst a group of nuns who were secretively exchanging bad jokes amongst themselves, many of them strictly forbidden within the four walls of the convent.

'The cherished kiss! The first kiss from a man whom you had loved deeply could never be forgotten by a virgin,' Madam Agatha got up suddenly and told Kadambari curtly. 'Enough, young girl. Enough for the day.'

Kadambari, too, was dazed. She could not understand the sudden change of mood and the rush of blood to her face on hearing the word 'kiss'. Did I say anything vulgar to the venerable Madam, she thought for a while and repented uneasily.

By that time Agatha had withdrawn quickly to her private room, and a puzzled Kadambari also thought it was imprudent to remain there any longer. Having been relieved of her burden to some extent, Kadambari was a bit more relaxed. After gulping a glass of cold water, she returned to her room to complete the latest issue of *Kumudam* she had half-read.

There was a late-night call to Madam Agatha from the colonel. The major's group had located the boy. He was a lorry broker called Salim from Nagapattanam, now operating from here. Indeed, the team could not meet him as he was away on tour, but they had met a close friend of his and procured all the required details. Salim travelled all over India and spoke chaste Hindustani. He was an authority on Urdu ghazals and had a good collection from Mehdi Hassan and Begum Akhtar to Ghulam Ali, and sang well, too. He had told his friend that he was deeply in love with a Haryanvi Hindu girl now hiding in Tamil Nadu, who was also a keen fan of ghazal maestro Ghulam Ali. She even sang the old ghazals of Parveen Sultana, her namesake and favourite, soulfully. Music was possibly the thread that had bound them together.

Parveen used to refer to herself as Anarkali—the name she was going to adopt on conversion, and it puzzled Salim very much.

'Did anyone ask you to convert?'

'No.'

'Did anyone ask you to change your name?'

'No.'

'Then won't it be enough to carry one religion and one name in your life?'

Anyway, since Parveen was a name quite common among many communities, she did not have to change it at all. Anyway, both Salim and the girl were aware that the orthodox villagers would not spare them. That's why Parveen had cut all contact with her parents, despite her love and longing for them. According to the colonel, the situation was too complicated because those villagers were very rigid about their lineage, customs, and practices, and would not spare either, more so since the boy was from another community altogether. She promised to come the next morning and chalk out suitable strategies together.

'Anarkali! So Apoorva was right. When Parveen had consulted her about that name, it was a good signal that the couple had planned their future life together. Possibly, she might elope from the place one day, unnoticed to join the boy in some secret place,' Agatha said.

That was another sleepless night for her. All along, she was too proud of the institution she had founded, the quick progress it had been making and the impressive media coverage she had been receiving. But for the first time she cursed the moment she had taken the final decision to take the plunge, much against the warnings of some of her conservative friends from the convent days.

Anyway, the only way now was to fight in a manner suggested by the colonel and other well-meaning friends, with the support from the local police and the government administration.

In trying to console herself, she remembered the advice of her old grandma—that nothing was truly good and truly bad in this world. There would be good and bad in everything and the problem lies in measuring the ratio of plus and minus, depending upon each situation; that success lay in taking on the bad with the good. Ultimate success would be yours if your intentions were clean.

Ultimate success would be mine, since my intentions are clean, Agatha murmured to herself.

Not a Couch but a Launch Pad

If some have taken this as a rescue home for 'runaway girls', they are sadly mistaken, Madam Agatha had warned the girls right on day one.

'For heaven's sake, don't consider this as a permanent shelter, a home away from home. This is just a branch to perch on for some time when you really need one. It's only a nest for you to rest for a night. In the morning you're expected to fly out, and The Nest doesn't expect you to return always. You might return or not, it's a matter of least concern to all of us here.'

Madam Agatha had plenty to reiterate.

'All of you have off-loaded your baggage on me. Some have even confessed under oath, on the belief that as a former nun I would be impressed. But to tell you the truth, I have learnt from experience that these stories are meant to be stories alone, and one has to take them as they are. There is no point in swearing that they are true, and nothing but truth. I consider human existence as nothing but a work of fiction concocted by a crafty creator. It is a clumsy mix of myths, legends, facts, and pure imagination—full of unexpected twists and unseen turns. If you venture to detach any of this from your life, you might not exist as you are now.'

Madam Agatha distinctly remembered that she had once argued with Father Andrew about the confessions in the privacy of a booth in a church. When she bluntly said that she did not believe in confessions in the presence of a vicar, he had taken it as a big joke.

'Not that I don't know that it would contain as much bran as grains. But the earnestness to confess and repent is the best way to atonement.'

When Agatha continued to argue, he chuckled with a mischievous twinkle in his eyes.

'You wicked sinner, you probably have plenty to hide.'

Agatha chose to keep quiet, since she didn't want to misuse the freedom allowed to her by the learned priest.

However, Agatha wanted the girls to realise that they had a long life ahead, and had to pave a distinct path of their own. Now that they have a shelter for the present, a safe one at that, they had to identify where their real passion lay. She convened a meeting of the girls in the presence of the colonel and reiterated that her aim was to empower the girls who were in The Nest. That such assistance at the right moment should not be taken as a couch to rest on but as a launch pad for future.

As usual, the colonel took the lead.

'Each one of you have a hidden passion of your own. Either you don't know it, or you don't have the resolve to pursue it assiduously. We are here to guide and support you should you need it. Which one to choose, you may be wondering. Of course, the ultimate choice would be yours. Suppose you want to start a self-employment project like tailoring, garment-making, manufacturing curry powders or condiments, catering on a small scale, even setting up a small tuition centre or undertaking some computer-related job etc., you might need financial help.

Here, I could be of assistance to you since I have some friends in the banking industry. They do have schemes for it and the government also extends subsidies in some cases.'

She added that she could even arrange a guest talk by a friend who was a much sought-after career guidance expert, without payment of her usual fees.

Madam Agatha was happy that the colonel had made a good beginning. She had opened the topic effectively and the girls also seemed impressed by her talk. Then Madam started with her opening remarks:

'What we mean is that we don't want girls of your age, bustling with energy, to sit idle and waste their time on trifles. You should all be in a position to carve out a life of your own, despite the setbacks you have had in your past life. I remember the success story of-three middle aged widows who got together and started a project of supplying lunch boxes to office staff. After starting on a modest scale three years ago, they are now one of the leading catering companies of the area—capable of executing orders for marriage feasts even. There was another case where a couple executed a roaring business from the dickey of their ambassador car. They used to park the car in front of college campuses with a container full of home cooked biryani.'

Excited by Agatha's encouragement, Kadambari decided to set up a tuition centre in a small room on the first floor of a tailoring shop. When someone suggested that they should invite a corporate for lighting the traditional lamp and cutting the ribbon on the opening day, Kadambari was adamant. 'None other than Madam Agatha!' she declared. After all, it was Madam Agatha who had given the idea to her.

Parveen was unhappy she could not join the venture despite being a qualified Hindi teacher. She knew that many Tamil and Telugu-speaking ladies were very much interested in learning Hindi; that, too, with the correct pronunciation of a North Indian. Madam Agatha also knew that since Hindi was her mother tongue, Parveen was ideally suited to become a Hindi teacher. But how? In the present situation nobody had the guts to allow her to go out of the campus—more so, after the visit of her father Risal Singh, who had vowed to pursue the matter further, possibly with the help of some other bullies.

Anyway, Kadambari was the first to start a tuition centre on an auspicious day, where she could teach housewives English. Although started on experimental basis and quite unsure of the future, the venture grew very fast because many college girls who were poor in spoken English were looking desperately for such a coaching centre. They were, indeed, mortally scared of appearing for interviews where they had to speak in English. They were particularly concerned about their awkward diction. A girl was even scoffed by a member of an interview committee, by being asked whether she was speaking in Tamil or English.

'Why should one be ashamed of her diction?' asked Kadambari. 'Every country speaks English in a way akin to speaking their own language. Germans, Americans, Japanese, Chinese—all have their own way of speaking another language. Even within a single country, the intonations vary from place to place.'

Kadambari was not a qualified teacher but she was confident that she was quite strong in English, particularly in her pronunciation—thanks to the insistence of the English teacher of the convent school where she had studied. In fact, the teacher was so impressed by her diction, both in English and in Tamil, that she was the automatic choice for anchoring various programmes in the school until she left. Overjoyed by this unexpected recognition, Gomathy had stitched special dresses for her befitting each occasion.

She still keeps the photo taken in a studio where she was seen in a black blazer with the school's logo on it, proudly keeping her hands on the shoulders of her parents.

Having made a good beginning through her English tuitions, Kadambari decided to familiarise the housewives with the basics of computer operations—just the elementary lessons on word processing, handling of emails, and apps like Facebook, YouTube, WhatsApp, etc., which had become immensely popular among the housewives. Some were very happy that they could see some clippings of old movies on the YouTube. Further, when a grandma opened a WhatsApp account and sent her selfie to her son in Boston, and got an appreciative reply from him, a kilo of ladoos were hurriedly procured from the nearby sweetmeat shop and distributed in The Nest. And when another lady opened a Facebook account on her own, she could easily connect with her old classmates in the US and Europe, and exchange pleasantries and share the group photos with their grandchildren.

Even a grandma, the first one to take a degree from her village five decades ago, admitted that she was only semi-literate until now in front of her grandchildren.

Agatha was equally happy. Immensely pleased with the success of her initial efforts. 'Now that I have tried to empower you, you are in turn empowering the aunties around. That's how the system should work,' she commented.

Anyway, Kadambari's initiative prompted other girls to look for better opportunities. At least they realised that they were not here to stay forever, as it was a charitable institution run entirely on donations from well-wishers, known and unknown. They are aware that the cost of living is on the increase, and that Sarala had been trying hard to balance the budget. Further, there was a long waiting list and once someone vacated, there would be many to grab it. Agatha had also reminded that those who were once the beneficiaries of this institution should not forget it once they left, and should reciprocate the favour through appropriate gestures, if only they could.

Incidentally, one of the earliest residents, possibly the first to sign the admission register—a Telugu girl called Ranjini long settled in the area—came out successful in a recruitment test of an insurance company, and managed to get placement in a nearby town. Leaving The Nest forever, the sobbing little bird embraced all the resident girls one by one, touched Madam Agatha's feet, and while departing in an auto rickshaw and still unable to control her emotions, promised that she would set apart a portion of her monthly income as donation to The Nest. After a month, when she made the first donation, Madam thanked her profusely on the phone. Although meagre, it was a great gesture…and Agatha had tears in her eyes when she received the cheque. She exhibited it in front of the girls at the dinner table, and remarked in a choked voice that it was worth a million.

That was a good beginning that made Agatha beam, and she was hopeful that there might be more girls who would follow the enterprising girl, who had been preparing studiously for achieving her lifelong ambition.

Swamiji Visits the Nest

The saffron-clad Swamiji in his early sixties was quite tall and thin, with a clean shaven head. His face was silky smooth with rosy cheeks. Despite his stooping stance, his sparkling eyes and booming voice made him an imposing figure. In fact, Madam Agatha was made to wonder how such a thin man could have such a voice. He must have been a good orator right from his student days, she thought.

Madam Agatha stood up in reverence with folded hands and guided him to a prime seat on a thickly-velveted couch, which was normally reserved for important guests. Relaxing on the couch and surveying the surroundings with a broad smile, Swamiji said, 'Impressive, very impressive. I understand it's practically a one-woman show. Your grooming at the convent probably helped you immensely!'

Madam Agatha smiled softly. She bowed her head and replied courteously, 'Not really, Swamiji. It's a collective effort of a few well-meaning people, generously supported by a good number of well-wishers from all over. How could a penniless former sister start such a unique venture? Of course, the convent days could not be easily forgotten but frankly, I'm not a Sister or Mother anymore. I left all those labels behind long ago.'

'Yes, I'm told,' Swamiji nodded with the same smile.

Although Swamiji spoke in chaste Tamil and carried his distinct features, he did not look like a Tamilian. Agatha was to learn later that he hailed from a village near Rohtak in Haryana, and had been in this area for the past two decades. Then something snapped in Agatha's mind. Instead of asking him plainly about the purpose of this unannounced visit, she asked him something entirely different politely.

'Swamiji, I'm surprised. You have chosen to drop in alone; that, too, without a call. Had I known you were coming, I would have received you at the gate,' she said.

'No issues, I'm not bothered about such formalities. Aren't we all ordained to be in the service of the Almighty? Now, I'm not alone. I have a devotee with me, who is waiting in the verandah. He's too scared to come inside. He has come all the way from Haryana to offer pranam to me.'

It was then that Agatha was convinced that that the guy outside was none other than Parveen's father, and that Swamiji had come with an obvious mission. Then her stand hardened.

'Just a courtesy call from the esteemed Swamiji, I suppose…' she muttered, avoiding his sharp gaze.

'Not entirely a courtesy call,' Swamiji's tone took a serious turn. 'I've come for a noble cause.'

'A noble cause? Please be specific, sir. What can I do for you?'

'It's about a girl from our area who got entangled with a local boy from another religion. I don't remember her name. The man outside is her father. Shall I call him inside?'

'Not necessary. Now I understand the purpose of your visit. But there is nothing I can do, since the girl is legally an adult and has the full liberty to do whatever she wants,' Agatha stated firmly.

'I know, I know,' hastened Swamiji. Pausing for a moment for emphasis like a typical orator, he continued in a low voice, 'But we are all concerned on another front... Haven't you heard of the movement "Love Jihad"?'

'Not yet.'

'It's nothing but *their* boys trying to lure *our* girls in the guise of love and convert them into *their* religion. There is a big conspiracy going on behind it, and there are reports that some of these girls have even landed up in the terrorist camps of Syria, Afghanistan, and Iraq—among the insurgents in Kashmir even!'

Madam was unhappy to hear objectionable terms like *ours* and *theirs*. She knew that the practice of 'othering' had been gaining strength in this country, soiling the fabric of India's communal harmony propounded in the Constitution.

'I am sorry, Swamiji,' she retorted tersely. 'If you're thinking that this a rescue home run by Christian missionaries, you are sadly mistaken. It's true that I believe in Jesus, but you can't count me as a Christian alone, like the ones you would have come across. And this institution is quite profane in its outlook and practice—it is an accepted principle here that nobody must talk of their caste and religion inside this campus.'

'That's your rule,' Swamiji smiled, 'but I am a visitor.'

'It applies to visitors also.'

'Oh, I'm sorry then.'

The whole conversation was leaving a bad taste and Agatha was anxious to close it as early as possible. Then came another unexpected move from Swamiji.

'Have you heard of those Khap Panchayats, active in some parts of the North?'

'Yeah, I've read media reports about some of the crude practices followed by them.'

'Please don't be led by media reports. They're mostly one-sided and coloured,' Swamiji chuckled.

'Might be, but we can depend only on media reports, since we are based down South. But I believe they still live in an ancient age and practice cruel laws.'

Swamiji's face reddened.

'Sorry, you're sadly mistaken again.'

'Possibly.'

Swamiji did not want to prolong this argument with Agatha; in his opinion, she was basing all her comments on certain coloured media reports appearing from that part of the country. Hence he came straight to the subject, and continued in a serious tone.

'I understand that their Panchayat has taken up the case of this girl in all seriousness, and has summoned her to appear before them immediately. It was then that she disappeared suddenly in the dead of night and surfaced here. If she does not appear there now with that guy, the consequences could be disastrous. I am afraid even the fair name of this great institution would be sullied unnecessarily,' Swamiji's voice rose, as if he was sounding a note of caution.

That irritated Madam Agatha beyond comprehension and the rebel in her—who once boldly took on the powers to be in the convent where her pastor could not take it any longer—took the front seat. If not for his saffron garb, he would have been asked to leave the campus, she muttered to herself. But she controlled her temper with great difficulty and replied tersely.

'Look here, Swamiji. I never knew that this so-called Panchayat had judicial powers. If they do, let them bring the police and take the girl away without her consent.'

When she got up from her seat discourteously, Swamiji could see the rage on her face and felt it improper to continue the conversation. Then, with a parting missive, he said that he was trying to advise her as a senior sanyasi from that area. Due to the long tenure in this place he had developed a special liking for the simple people of this area, and did not want any of them—more so a former Sister—to get into such knotty problems. And then, even without a formal goodbye and trying his best to conceal his annoyance and dismay, Swamiji chose to leave the place in a huff.

While withdrawing to her private room, Agatha realised that this issue cannot be ignored easily and that the matter had to be tackled properly in consultation with all; if necessary, the chairman, too—an eminent jurist himself. He was a no-nonsense man and did not mince words while giving his professional advice. Meanwhile, she waited for the colonel's views, since her visit was due the next morning. She didn't want to trouble the jurist unnecessarily for such silly things. Meanwhile, she wanted to caution Parveen and advise her not to go out alone, since the goons from her area may be on the prowl. It was then that she heard a shrieking noise at the door. It was the girl on the wheel chair.

'Be careful of that Swamiji,' she warned. 'He might bring bad luck to the institution.'

Madam did not like this unwanted interference. She retorted angrily, 'Why do you say that?'

'Don't you know that I have a third eye?' the girl replied calmly, and then quickly turned the wheelchair back.

Weepy Seetha Weeps Again

'I want to cry!' said Seetha.

'Thinking of Amma?'

'No.'

'Appa?'

'Not at all. I don't want to hear anything about him.'

'Then about your good old days of Devagiri?'

Seetha was silent for a moment. She was probably thinking of those days, good and bad. Then she suddenly turned around and asked, 'How could the world be so cruel to us?'

'Not to us alone, but to so many people. Human life is full of misery and happiness, light and darkness. You did have your golden days when Venkiti Annan was highly prosperous, and you got whatever you wanted.'

'Yes, I did get more than I wanted in those days. Until that wretched woman cast her evil spell on him.'

'That's why I said the world is full of light and darkness. Good ones and bad ones. Only bad ones make us see the goodness in good ones. Ravana was born to glorify Rama. Without Kaikeyi we wouldn't have seen the greatness in Kousalya. And weren't Krishna and Kamsa born in the same family?' Kadambari was talking like a philosopher.

Weepy was not pleased with these sermons. Does she think that she is Lord Krishna herself, and was it a kind of *Geethopadesam*, wondered Seetha. They were standing at the long corridor of the upper floor, leaning on the wooden railings. Outside, the traffic was picking up and the road was to be crowded with people and vehicles soon as the day advanced. When Kadambari was standing there alone—as she often did in the morning, lost in her own thoughts, Weepy Seetha had joined her unexpectedly. She was probably looking for her to talk to, because she was the only one with whom she could confide in freely.

Not that Kadambari did not empathise with the plight of poor Weepy; she had wanted to cheer her up somehow, as encouraged to do so by the colonel. In fact, Kadambari was the one who knew the entire family history of Venkiti Annan, and how good and kind he was during his good days. For him both Kadambari and Seetha were like his two eyes, as he used to claim openly, and he had never returned empty handed after the festivals he had attended along with Shankararaman. While Appa never bothered about buying things for his daughter, Annan always had two big packets with him, one each for both the girls without distinction, containing glass bangles of different colours, kajal, kumkum, gold covered ornaments etc.

Before that mistress came into his life and started extracting all kinds of favours from him, the income from his earlier savings had kept him afloat. Later, when he fell into the company of gamblers who used to assemble for their card game under the big banyan tree adjacent to the temple compound, Appa had tried his level best to pull him out of the gang. The stakes were small initially and Annan had always won, but the picture changed later when professional gamblers, too, joined the group; by that time, he was hooked to the game and started losing money heavily. The man, who had not known the taste of liquor until then, started drinking, too. Getting the scent of the disaster, his mistress started squeezing more out of him… And then there was no other way other than borrowing money from village moneylenders—that, too, at high interest rates. Meanwhile, the shop had to be closed down despite the best efforts of Parvathy; even Seetha, who used to sit at the stall during the long absence of Annan in the festival season.

'Remember, Seetha, bad days don't continue forever. After all, had the world been that dark, none of us would have survived.'

'But not in my case…'

'Why do you say that? Didn't you know that all the girls here have some sad story or the other to narrate?'

She had no answer to that and Kadambari continued:

'You should be happy that at last you were lucky enough to have reached a safe and peaceful place, like all of us, and your good days are going to start now. Didn't you see the joy on the face of that Telugu girl Ranjini—one of the earliest residents who was a rape victim, who was brought in here in a hopeless condition after having tried to commit suicide twice and failed? She was also so gloomy and withdrawn always, refusing to talk to anybody. She even used to curse God for not allowing her to die. It was Madam Agatha who changed her thoroughly and instilled a ray of hope in her.'

Seetha came to know of her case after she had left The Nest. Although Madam had decided initially that the institution would not be like a rescue home—having already turned down few such cases, but looking at her condition she could not but accept her request. A qualified person on the lookout for a job, Ranjini appeared to have been cheated by a young man—a relative of her uncle who had the liberty of visiting them often, and their marriage was about to be fixed. It was then that he took the liberty of taking her for a movie and then to a hotel room, roofied her with a glass of orange juice, and raped her repeatedly for a week. Later, his friends joined him, too.

A familiar story—similar to what one reads in newspapers fairly regularly. Somehow, she managed to escape but did not want to inform her parents or lodge a complaint with the police. She wanted to avoid further embarrassment of a police case. Of course, the whole history of the girl had been kept under wraps by Madam, since Ranjini was averse to any kind of sympathetic gestures from other girls. 'I want only empathy, not sympathy,' she had commented. Even the over-inquisitive Sarala came to know about it only after the girl had left.

'Didn't you see that when she was about to leave for taking up a job and the so-called uncle and auntie had tried to enter the auto rickshaw, she had refused to even look at them. Thank god she did not push them away, as many had thought she would,' Kadambari said.

Seetha was listening carefully to that episode and appeared relaxed to some extent.

'Anyway, please see whether you can find a way to make a living or not. Forget the past and think of the future...try to find some work that would distract you from your worries and generate some income, too. As for me, the tuition centre I had started on a modest scale now keeps me engaged, and I am sure that it would grow steadily.'

Seetha smiled.

'Let's hope that things would turn better in the days to come. I'm sure that Madam had founded this place on an auspicious day and her intentions, too, were noble,' assured Kadambari.

Then, suddenly looking at her watch, she noticed that she was getting late for the tuition centre.

'Sorry, I should get going. It's getting late already. If you want you can come with me to avoid the boredom here. It's not far away.'

'No...sorry,' replied Seetha. In fact, she did not want to admit that she was too scared to step out of the safety of the compound, however close the centre might be—a petrified bird that preferred to stick to its nest always.

Actually, her roommate Lisie had also been soothing Weepy very much, to the point of being repetitive. On the day when the colonel took a harsh dig at her in the presence of others and she had cried out after reaching her room, Lisie had gone to her help—like a true nurse she was going to be one day. She embraced her closely and calmed her to some extent via her soothing words. Talking about the colonel, she said that she was 'one without any bone in her tongue', as they used to say in local parlance.

But the tough exterior was deceptive because she was so soft at heart, consoled Lisie. 'As a former army doctor, she has seen the harsh realities of life and is prepared to face any kind of hardship. Having seen the miseries of the world, she would go to any extent to help the suffering people, and does not have any selfish motives behind anything she does or says. Now that she has been briefed about you by Madam, she would be different in her dealings with you hereafter.' Weepy was not willing to narrate her story to Lisie, but occasionally she would to drop some hints about the kind of bizarre experiences she had gone through. And Lisie had always tried to lighten it by saying that such things did happen in the world, and that as a young girl she could only put up with the ways of the world and get on with her life.

Lisie, of course, did not have such stories of misery to share since she had left her home in totally different circumstances; with the knowledge of her widowed mother, who was living with her brother in a remote village in Kerala after the sudden death of her father. In fact, she had wanted to see the world on her own, without anyone's help. While she did have some relatives who could be of help to her, she had set out on a daring journey without telling them anything, since she was sure that they would have stopped her from doing it. It was an aimless journey without much money in her wallet, but she had planned to take the help of priests and sisters in monasteries and convents wherever she went. When the local vicar, who had got a wind of it from her lonely mother who had gone for her Sunday Mass, had tried to stop Lisie, she evaded a direct reply and excused herself from the situation cleverly... And she did wander a lot, covering many areas of South India.

It was during one such trip, a journey in a night train, that she happened to come in contact with Madam Agatha—that, too, in a bizarre situation. She was fast asleep on the middle birth of a sleeper coach and it was pitch dark inside but for the dim blue night lamp burning in a corner. The train was picking up speed and the coach was shaking vigorously. Suddenly, she felt the presence of a dark figure close to her face, emitting foul smell of liquor. When she woke up shouting for help, that man's hand was caressing her body, trying desperately for a wild kiss. It was then that Madam Agatha jumped out and switched on the light. Meanwhile, the other passengers had woken up suddenly and tried to apprehend the culprit but they could not do it, since he had pulled the chain and made good of his escape from another compartment. Then, only Lisie had remembered about that old man, staring at her from a side seat a few rows ahead.

Then the girl narrated her whole story to Agatha, who turned a patient listener. Thus started the valuable connection with Madam, which made Lisie terminate her journey at The Nest.

When she heard this, Weepy, too, realised how valuable their connections with Madam and The Nest really is. As Kadambari would remind her often, they ought to thank the Almighty that despite the initial miseries, they could all reach a safe haven eventually.

Lisie was proved right later, when there was a visible change in the attitude of the colonel towards Weepy. Having known her story, the colonel took a lot of personal care in Seetha's affairs, and even motivated her to start some project of her own from within— preferably making some homemade articles like condiments, curry powders, pickles etc. She could take the help of the cook, Janaki, and also use the kitchen for the purpose.

Seetha profusely thanked her for the lead, and promised to think further on it. But she did not reveal that judging herself by the bad experience of managing Appa's fruit stall for some time in the past, no self-confidence was left in her now.

The Curious Case of Apoorva Majumdar

It was Professor Abdulla, alias Othello Abdulla, who had introduced Apoorva Majumdar to Madam Agatha. He himself had come along with the girl—quite unusual in the case of dignified trustees, and Agatha was pleasantly surprised.

'Surprising! A mere phone call would have been more than enough, professor,' she remarked. 'I'm sure you wouldn't recommend any undeserving case.'

'Okay, but had I sent the girl to you alone and you had rejected her case on some technical ground, that would have been very painful to me, since she was the daughter of one of my brilliant students who was very close to me during her college days.'

Othello was right, thought Madam. In certain weak moments she had taken some crazy decisions in the past—like those taken by some Shakespearean characters, which she had regretted later. She used to concur with the colonel that she was quite moody and unpredictable, like a typical English summer, where it rained suddenly in the middle of bright sunshine—why Londoners always preferred to carry an umbrella with them.

When the girl introduced herself as Apoorva Majumdar, Madam was perplexed.

'Say that again,' she asked, and the girl repeated.

Was she not a Tamilian, since she was speaking in Tamil fluently?

'She is,' smiled the professor. 'Her father is a Bengali, Partho Majumdar, and mother is a local woman, Fathima.'

'An inter-caste marriage, then!'

'Yes.'

Directing the girl to wait in the office, they moved to the lobby and the professor chose his favourite couch—the best piece of furniture in the whole building according to him, on which he could relax for long.

'Yes, it was an inter-caste marriage. An odd one, too, as it emerged later,' he continued.

It appeared both Partho and Fathima were working in a textile mill in the nearby town, Partho in the plant as an operator, and Fathima in the office as an accounts clerk. And it was in the canteen that they had first met and exchanged pleasantries. Since Partho hated chapattis and Fathima, too, loved to devour a plateful of plain rice or curd rice if available, it was the bountiful rice grown in the paddy fields of Tamil Nadu that united the disparate couple. Initially, Fathima was pleasantly surprised when she saw Partho picking up rice from the buffet table…that, too, in two helpings. She had heard that all North Indians preferred chapattis and ate rice only when their stomach was upset.

'I'm not a North Indian, but a Bengali,' Partho retorted, as if he was insulted.

Fathima could not believe him. How could a Bengali be other than a North Indian, she wondered. But Partho babu was stubborn. 'I'm from the East, not from the North,' he insisted.

Anyway, that was the first lesson the girl learnt about the man whom she was destined to marry a couple of years later. It was almost love at first sight. That was why he always chose to sit opposite her at the lunch table in the canteen.

Soon, the news of their affair spread far and wide, and became a point of discussion within the factory.

'Things are getting serious,' commented one.

'An inter-caste marriage… I smell a conversion now,' replied the other.

'Either this way, or that way,'

'Only one way, since it's Partho on one side!'

'Let's watch the fun!'

When these comments reached the ears of Partho, he was furious—as expected.

'So what?' shouted Partho. 'If I'm going to marry her straightaway?'

When the news reached the girl, she was stunned beyond comprehension. She had not even dreamt that things would reach this level one day. Then, the love-struck girl was forced to face the reality—like the disparities in religion, region, language etc. She had never thought of the apparent compatibility issue, as the society around them did. She also knew that she could not wish away such realities in a marital alliance, where the families of the couple, too, are involved to a great degree. Her parents were devout Muslims, originally from Nagapattinam.

Partho's parents were settled in faraway Midnapore in West Bengal, and the matter would have meant very little to the father since he and his son had already decided to live their lives on their own terms. The father was sure that his son would do just the opposite of what he would ask him to do. If he asked him to go left, he was sure to turn right. When the father managed a job for the textile technology diploma-holder in a mill in Ahmedabad through a friend, the son decided to work in a mill in the South. Again, the father came to know of it only after Partho had finished packing and had gone to him for touching his feet, which was a customary ritual for him. Whenever, the son had stretched his hand towards his feet, the venerable old man knew that he was up to some mischief. As was normal, he laughed aloud because it was nothing new to him.

But when he heard, that too from a friend, that Partho had decided to marry a Muslim colleague from South India, he could not laugh for some time. Later, he did realise that he should not miss such a rare opportunity and laughed merrily, worrying his wife. The family doctor had already advised that *dada* (big brother in Bengali) should not be made to laugh too long—to which he had responded with 'What to do when you have such hilarious sons in the family?'. Although the doctor had nodded in agreement then, he had cautioned his wife privately to take care of him.

Later, he found it difficult to console his weeping wife. And when the first photograph of the couple arrived, he remarked that the girl was quite pretty, which did not please his wife. When she continued sobbing with 'after all the girl is Muslim', he had countered it by a stern 'so what?', with the obvious conclusion that she was the girl selected by his son and that they were a good match. To tease his wife further, he went on to say that he had planned to take his *bahu* (daughter-in-law) to some prominent mosques of their area when they would come to visit for Durga Puja festival...

Mighty well pleased with his performance, the Shakespearean character was in full form, and was continuing with added enthusiasm but for the untimely intervention by Madam Agatha.

'What happened then, professor?'

But the professor was not concerned about the intrusion and continued with the same verve.

'And then they got married,' he concluded. 'And the problems began when they started living together in a modest house with neem trees all around. Indeed, the high-quality rice grown in the nearby paddy fields was a gelling factor initially, yet they realised later that other opposing factors were beginning to surface, too. When a casual remark by Partho about his sweet language was scoffed at by Fathima, he was infuriated. While Fathima was dead sure that Tamil was the oldest language in the country, Partho was equally confident that Bengali was equally old and one could always boast of their rich literature. "What about Rabindranath, Bankim Chandra, Saratchandra, Tarashankar, Bibhutibhushan etc. whom the entire country adored," his voice rose. "But didn't we have Thiruvalluvar, Subramonia Bharathi, Kambar, Ilanko Adigal, Kalki down up to Puthumai Pithan." retorted Fathima. "What about Rabindra Sangeet," asked Partho. "It cannot be compared to Carnatic music, which is unparalleled in the world of music," countered his wife.... It went on and on until they reached the popular dresses people wore in both areas. When he referred to a scene in a Bollywood movie where the popular comedian Mahmood was seen wearing a lungi, mimicking a Tamilian with words like *"ayyayyo"*, etc., she had plenty to comment about his way of talking, as if a *rossogolla*

(Bengali sweet) was thrust into his mouth. This enraged Partho further. "Don't talk about our *rossogolla*, you *idli sambar* (South Indian meal)", he shouted. "Then don't talk about our *idli sambar*," yelled Fathima... It went on and on like that until both of them were thoroughly exhausted. Ultimately, a temporary ceasefire was called in. That too, at the instance of a friendly neighbour.'

'It was then that the contentious issue of beef came up. "I'm prepared to eat the meat of an elephant or a leopard, but don't talk of beef," said Partho. "Isn't *gau mata* (mother cow) sacred for Hindus?" he raised his voice. But when did Partho become so religious, wondered Fathima. As one who had grown up relishing various concoctions of beef, she insisted on visiting her choice of restaurants for it, and Partho agreed hesitantly. "But beef would never be cooked in my kitchen," asserted Partho. However, the usage "my kitchen" was the height of tolerance for the poor girl. How could this hot-headed *moshai* (fellow in Bengali) who could not prepare even a proper cup of tea claim it as "my kitchen"? Wasn't she the one who always used to toil in the kitchen, she wondered.'

'"Enough. It's nothing but the hegemony of the male," she muttered. She could now see the kitchen as a strong political symbol, where the husband wants to establish his supremacy. Then she had to react again. "If you don't want to cook beef in our kitchen, so be it, I don't want to cook fish either." She knew quite well how it would hurt a Bengali babu!'

Thus, a new war front was opened between them. Beef vs Fish.

Obviously, the fight intensified, and when the neighbour also excused himself from mediating, poor Apoorva was forced to face the brunt of the conflict.

'Then what happened, sir?' asked Madam. She was getting a bit fidgety. 'Now that you have recommended, we will take that girl in, 'she agreed.

'Thank you for that, but please listen to this last bit... I will finish it soon,' assured the Shakespearean character, always conscious of the reaction of the audience. And so, he continued.

'When a pretty girl was born to them, both were very happy. Their parents were equally happy, too. In fact, it was the grandma who had wanted a picture of the baby first. Things went on smoothly until they came to the process of naming. The name had to be given to the hospital desk before discharge so that it could be communicated to the municipal authorities for registration. Fathima had two names in her mind, Vani or Aishwarya. If Partho did not agree for Vani, he might easily settle for Aishwarya, she had thought. But, "over my dead body" was the curt response from Partho. He had already selected the name and had given it to the hospital authorities, and it was nothing other than Apoorva. It's true that Fathima liked the name, but she did not like the way it was selected by the father of the child arbitrarily, without even bothering to consult the mother.'

'Then, some of the long-settled issues surfaced again. Bengali vs. Tamil, Tagore vs Tiruvalluvar, Carnatic music vs Rabindra Sangeet, *rossogolla* vs *idli sambar*, etc. It was also to flare up again later, when Partho started calling his daughter "Opu". "Why not 'Apu', if you had wanted to call that way," asked Fathima. But Partho was visibly surprised. "How can Opu be one other than Opu herself," he asked. And the fight continued even though the girl started growing. But strangely, they did not argue on which religion the girl should be inducted into. "Let Opu decide that when she grows up," said Partho. "Yes, let Apu decide it herself," agreed Fathima. Hence, this was the only area where there was no squabble between the couple...'

Thus, the professor concluded his long and impressive performance, and was thoroughly exhausted. Agatha was exhausted, too. She brought him a glass of cold water, fresh from the water cooler. Then, when she brought him some coffee, the professor declined it politely, saying that he was surprised that she had forgotten that he always avoided both coffee and tea—supposed to be dignified poisons of modern-day life.

'Wasn't it rather silly?' she asked, 'fighting over trifles...'

'Of course, it was childish. Those with king size and queen size egos shouldn't get into such alliances,' pointed out the professor. 'But when it had reached the stage of exchanging blows, both being highly argumentative and physically strong, too, the family of the girl had to interfere with the support of the Ustad at the local Masjid. This intrusion by a religious head obviously worsened the situation further, and made Partho question the credentials of the Ustad in his affairs. As they had reached a point of no return, the couple had started sleeping in separate rooms. In fact, like fighting cocks, they were waiting for an opportunity to pounce upon each other.'

It was here that Fathima, a dear student of the professor, wanted him to interfere so that their dear daughter would be saved from further embarrassment. The professor agreed. 'This is not a conducive atmosphere in which a girl should grow up. At this impressionable age, kids could be tempted to pick up bad things first. Hence, it would be better to shift her to a hostel like The Nest, which is quite safe and secure,' he suggested. While Fathima nodded approvingly, Partho resisted initially—he had the impression that girls could get into bad company in hostels. But, when he was told that this was being managed by a former Sister, he agreed immediately. Having seen the service rendered by Mother Teresa in Kolkata, he had a high opinion of such institutions.

That was how Apoorva, a college girl, was admitted to The Nest as its youngest bird, much to surprise of others. Incidentally, she was the only girl to have joined with the consent of her parents. Being the juniormost, all other residents were *Akka* to her, except, of course, *Didi*—who was *Didi* to all. At the first glance itself, Agatha knew that she was like her mother—a typical Tamilian teen in a *davani* (South Indian attire) and not in a *chooridar* (typically North Indian attire), which was quite popular all over the country.

Professor Abdulla was extremely happy that by his association with The Nest he could save a poor girl from near ruin. He was least bothered about the plight of Partho and Fathima; let them fight until either of them get exhausted, he thought. But he felt that they should be undergo proper counselling by an expert. And if it still didn't work out, it would be better to get separated at the earliest, since they had nothing in common. After the initial fascination had gone, they had reached a stage where one was waiting for an opportunity to score a point over the other.

But as a last-ditch attempt, he called the couple and asked like a vicar in front of an altar.

'Partho, do you love Fathima?'

'Yeah,' replied Partho.

'Then let her eat beef?'

'Yeah!'

'Fathima, do you love Partho?'

'Yes, of course,' replied the girl firmly.

'Then let him eat fish?'

'Why not?'

Then he was reasonably assured that the couple was still in love, and that this could be an ideal case for a competent counsellor.

When the colonel heard the story, she was amazed.

'Rather strange,' she commented. 'I've heard of all sorts of mismatches, but this seems to be a rare package. Strangely, it is not the religion that makes them fight!'

'Obviously, there are too many ways of picking up a fight.'

Agatha nodded in agreement.

Kadambari Falls Sick

It all started with a loud sneeze, followed by yet another. Many more followed later, making Kadambari feel like her head was whirling. A cool wind was blowing across. Holding the headrest of the cot firmly. she requested roommate Gouri to close the windows on the western side.

'Don't you feel the chill, Gouri?', she asked, shivering. Gouri was surprised, since it was yet another pleasant morning and the dawn was about to break.

'You have probably caught a bad cold after the late-night bath yesterday. I had warned you then itself to avoid washing your hair in the night. That, too, in this unpredictable weather,' said Gouri.

That was correct, Kadambari realised. The weather had suddenly turned murky last week. While the days were unbearably warm, the evening breeze blowing from the mountains cooled the air and the temperature came down suddenly. Such variations in mercury levels during the day and night are usually treacherous. This is the season when all kinds of contagious diseases spread, ranging from viral flu to conjunctivitis and chicken pox. Gouri did warn her when she was about to go the bathroom with a towel and soap that it would better for her to avoid wetting her long hair at night.

But Kadambari was quite sweaty after a long stroll in the lawn, and wanted a shower badly. While going for a shower she felt it would be better to go for a full bath, so as to cool her head and get some sound sleep.

'I stink when I perspire and you were the one who always complains about my bad body odour, don't you?' she quipped.

That did silence the usually lazy Gouri, and she knew that Kadambari was trying to make a dig at her for her reluctance to have a daily bath.

Kadambari felt that her throat was parched and wanted a glass of warm water. Without disturbing Gouri—who had now started snoring loudly—she climbed down the steps and went past the cook Janaki sleeping on the kitchen floor peacefully, and lit the gas stove. A cup of hot black coffee did lighten the heaviness of her head, but she realised the weakness her body was feeling.

Back in her bed after some time, she could feel the fatigue and could not sleep any longer. Although the dawn had broken, she was not inclined to get up, brush her teeth and start her daily routine. Normally, she used to go to the tuition centre before 10:00 am.

Meanwhile, the bell in the assembly hall had rung, and Kadambari heard a few footsteps hurrying down. But she lay in her bed with her eyes closed, trying to dose off for some more time.

But it was Gouri who woke up first and placed her palm on Kadambari's head. Gouri could easily sense that Kadambari had high fever. Quite a sensitive girl, she ran down the steps and alerted other girls. A small crowd had assembled around the cot by the time the weary Kadambari opened her eyes.

'Nothing, just the usual flu,' she tried to assure the crowd around her. But when the girls took turns to feel the temperature on her forehead, they were worried. Meanwhile, one of them had fetched her thermometer and forcibly thrust it into Kadambari's mouth, making her speechless at least for a couple of minutes.

'Oh, it's 104 degrees!' she shouted.

'104!' other girls exclaimed. Someone ran down the stairs to inform Sarala, since they were sure that Madam would be busy with her morning rituals.

But it was Madam Agatha herself who rushed in.

'What's all this *gallata* (mischief in Tamil) about, girls?' Madam shouted.

Then the girls narrated their anxiety about Kadambari's illness, particularly how such a fever could be contagious, stressing the need for quarantining the patient immediately.

'Quarantine, phew!' Madam scoffed. 'Don't be panicky, I know how to handle such situations. Get back to your rooms and continue your work.'

When the crowd dispersed reluctantly and she was alone with the anxious patient, Madam Agatha tried to take the advice of the colonel, who was then on her morning walk. Normally the colonel avoided carrying unnecessary appendages like cell phones while on her long morning walks. But it so happened that she was in the middle of a long chat with an overseas friend, and did not want to cut the call nor delay her daily routine. Despite getting frantic signals of the incoming calls on the phone, she ignored them since she was on a long-distance call.

It was only after a few attempts that Madam could succeed in getting the colonel on the line.

'Oh, shit,' the colonel said, gasping for breath since she was walking fast. 'It's just a common cold. The normal cleaning schedule of the system when all the dirt inside is cleansed automatically. It would go on its own. One week with a doctor and seven days without him, as they used to say.'

That did not satisfy Agatha. She knew that the colonel was one who took such cases too casually. Moreover, she had been avoiding any kind of consultations on medical issues lately.

'I'm not a practitioner any longer!' she had repeated curtly.

'But you were one not very long back,' reminded Agatha.

She reiterated the exact same stand she had when someone would contact her for medical issues: 'One who does not practice anymore and has not updated her knowledge for quite some time is unfit to be called a doctor. I am just a medical degree holder, a post-graduate so to say, and that does not qualify me to be called a practising doctor. I was a famed surgeon once with a very high success rate, but I'm no longer sure of my hands now. Moreover, the world is changing fast and so is the medical science. One who does not keep pace with it is almost a semi-literate—a quack out to make fast bucks, and I don't want to be one among them.' And that's why the colonel had avoided giving any kind of advice on any issues, even common fever. Madam did not need it either; it was just by way of abundant caution.

'Agatha, there's nothing to worry. It's common cold. Give a paracetamol with a bowl of *kanji* (rice gruel) and she would be all right. If that doesn't work and the temperature does not subside, then further investigation might be required.'

'No need, Madam,' Kadambari interfered in between. 'I have my own medicines.'

Agatha knew that Kadambari was totally against any kind of allopathic treatment. Her Appa had warned her against the use of paracetamols and antibiotics. Normally, they would drink hot black coffee mixed with dry ginger and pepper, and after a couple of sweating sessions the fever would come down. Sometimes, when it was a little more serious and the eyes had started burning, they used to put drops of the juice of black Tulsi leaves in the eyes. All along the entire family had been using natural remedies, carefully avoiding all forms of allopathic treatment.

To a certain extent, Madam was also wary of allopathic treatment, particularly any kind of steroids and surgery. But she was more inclined towards homeopathy. Ayurveda was all about bitter *kashayams* (water decoction of a single or multiple herbs) and *choornams* (powder form of herbs), and it was much nicer to swallow the sweet pills given by the homeopaths! A later convert to vegetarianism, she had given strict instructions that only vegetarian food should be consumed in the campus. Janaki was also quite good in cooking vegetarian dishes. While the local girls had accepted it with suppressed murmurs, Parveen was vehement in her protest. A compulsive meat-eater as true Haryanvis are, she was uncomfortable missing her plateful of biryanis and the occasional taste of chicken kebabs or kormas.

'You wouldn't cook meat in the kitchen, agreed,' she was to argue later, 'but why do you object to our getting food from outside? That, too, at least once a week. The ever-obliging Karupayyan is waiting for your green signal.'

'No way. Order is order. No concessions for anybody. If you wish to go outside and eat meat, it's your problem.'

'Please, ma'am. I feel miserable without it,' she pleaded.

'If you're miserable here, you are free to go elsewhere—where you can get your usual stuff.'

That was enough to subdue the vulnerable girl and she had to withdraw, hanging her head in shame in front of her mates...

Kadambari knew that if her fever did not subside, she might have to go for her usual *kashayam* along with the *vettumaran tablet* (ayurvedic tablet for fever), a generous stock of which she had always kept with her.

When Madam wondered how *kashayam* might be prepared here, Kadambari assured her that Janaki, hailing from a nearby village, knew the ingredients and could prepare it without any difficulty. She had been enjoying a cosy relationship with Janaki all along, and used to help her occasionally in the kitchen when she was unusually busy as well. Janaki was also happy that unlike other girls, Kadambari knew a bit of vegetarian cooking, picked up from her Brahmin parents.

But Kadambari's ayurvedic medicines did not work. And when the fever could not be controlled, Agatha was very worried. 'Better take allopathic medicines, girl,' she advised. 'Don't take chances with fever. After all, this is a hostel and I have to worry about other girls, too. But Kadambari was reluctant as she was mortally scared of those drugs.

Madam then remembered the words of wisdom from the colonel. Times have changed, she had cautioned Agatha once, during a private talk after a couple of pegs in her cosy drawing room. Madam had just had some red wine, which she used to take rarely—on festive occasions like Christmas and Easter with other sisters, and very discreetly at that.

'Fever is no longer an innocent ailment as it was once!' the colonel had cautioned. 'It's treacherous and can even turn fatal sometimes. It might branch out in any direction and no doctor with all the modern gadgets at his disposal might be able to diagnose it at the right time.'

'It could be malaria, typhoid, pneumonia, jaundice, meningitis etc.; or could just be plain viral flu,' she continued. 'The doctors normally try to zero in on one such category, purely by the process or elimination or pure instinct. Sometimes the drugs administered for one ailment can go against the other. If the patient is lucky enough, the illness can be diagnosed early. The problem is that when the medical science progresses fast and develops more and more new drugs, the bacteria and viruses also became more and more aggressive. Some of these strong antibiotics and steroids they prescribe can have serious side effects. A patient who gets cured fast compliments the doctor, not knowing that the latter has administered a steroid. It's well known that it's obligatory on the part of the doctor to brief the patient about the steroid being used, but it is a fact that some of the doctors—particularly those in small towns and villages—ignore it for the sake of quick recovery and for impressing the patients.'

When the colonel continued her lecture on this with an obvious disclaimer that she was no longer a practitioner, Agatha made it a point to change the subject quickly. She did it cleverly by pouring another drink in the colonel's glass. Still, those alarming warnings continued to echo in her mind...

Kadambari's condition worsened, and Agatha's worries increased. She did not know what to do as her main advisor—the colonel, was out of town and could not be reached on her cell phone either.

When Kadambari started blabbering something incoherently, Gouri came running crying aloud.

'She was talking all sorts of things... She did not recognise me, calls me Marathagam sometimes... or Pavizham...' she was on the verge of breaking down and could not complete the sentence properly.

By the time Agatha shut down her laptop and was scrambling up the stairs, the colonel's call came. Alerted by half a dozen missed calls within a span of 10 minutes, she wanted to know whether the Nest was on fire.

When she heard Agatha's voice she was relieved that at least the Nest was not on fire. But as a seasoned doctor, she had realised that they did have a serious problem on hand.

'Nonsense,' she thundered, 'why the hell didn't you admit the girl to a hospital? Haven't I warned you that if the fever did not subside, one has to be cautious? Why did you allow the girl to go after those *kashayams* and *choornams*? Was she not under your care? Aren't you the person who has to answer one day?' pausing for a moment, she lowered her voice 'Anyway, rush her to an ICU immediately. She has to be on fluids and drugs. I am flying down tomorrow morning. Take care.'

Madam Agatha was shocked. She could not answer for a minute. By the time she had arranged to take Kadambari to a hospital, an ambulance rushed in blowing its horn. It was the ambulance arranged by the colonel from her friend's hospital.

The staff at Dr Geetha's hospital were waiting anxiously on the porch with a stretcher, and she was rushed to the ICU straightway. Although Gouri volunteered to be at the hospital as a bystander throughout, Agatha said it was not necessary. She could return by evening and they would arrange with some other girl to be on night duty.

Once the patient was inside the ICU and tied with tubes, there was next to nothing Agatha could do in the hospital. After making all the preliminary arrangements, she returned to the Nest. Later, Gouri informed over phone that after the initial check-up, the doctor suspected pneumonia; but further tests were to be conducted. The doctor was visibly irritated about the delay in admitting the girl. However, she had assured that there was nothing to panic about, and that the patient could be shifted to a room after the fever was brought under control—possibly within a couple of days. Agatha was also relieved that the colonel would be in station the next day, and that her friend Dr Geetha was bound to take special care of Kadambari after that.

Meanwhile, Lisie had volunteered to be on the night shift at the hospital, since she was trained to handle such eventualities as a qualified nurse-to-be. In fact, Lisie could not complete the course a few months before the final examination due to the sudden death of her father. All kinds of suspicions were afloat about this unexpected death at that time, and the main anxiety of the girl then was how the bank loan taken for her studies would be repaid. Since they had mortgaged their house and papa was no more, she was worried that one day the bankers would take the property and vacate them forcibly. She was sure that in such an eventuality, her mother wouldn't have any other option but to take the help of her younger brother and move to his house. She knew that her mother would only be a domestic help in that house, since his wife was quite rude and selfish. But there was very little that she could do about it. It was in this situation that her mother herself forced her to get out and look for a better life outside. Thus started her aimless journey with very little money in her wallet...

It was well known to all that it was Madam Agatha who had brought Lisie to the Nest and provided the protective umbrella when needed. One of the earliest residents, her ambition was to complete the course one day, pass the examination and secure a job in a hospital—possibly in a well-known hospital like that of Dr Geetha's, so that she could save her mother from slavery at her uncle's.

But what surprised the girls most was that when Kadambari was shifted to a private room within a couple of days, it was Madam Agatha herself who had volunteered to be there in the night. There was a separate bed for a bystander and she could sleep there as well.

'But why, ma'am?' Sarala asked, surprised. 'There are other girls eager to take the turn. It would have been an opportunity for them to be out of the campus for a while.'

'So, too, for me!' Agatha giggled. 'I also wanted to be out of this Nest for a whiff of fresh air!'

But it was Kadambari, who had since gained consciousness, who was profusely apologetic about the inconvenience caused to all, particularly the elderly lady. She also pleaded with her to return soon, since there were sufficient number of nurses in the hospital and there was no need of a bystander. She was insistent that Madam might as well depute one of the girls from the hostel.

But Agatha shook her head vehemently, indicating that it was her problem, too, and there was no need to worry on her count...

The situation continued for a couple of days more, and Kadambari recovered faster than expected—more so, since her general health conditions were good. And she told Madam, who had continued her night vigil on those days, with a beaming face that she was sure to be discharged next day, as assured by the duty doctor.

'I'm sorry, I've to struggle hard to catch up with the lost time at my Adarsh Centre, particularly the computer classes.'

She was indeed worried about it, since the elderly housewives were anxiously enquiring about the condition of their young teacher. It was a wonderful piece of empowerment to some of them.

On all those days at the hospital, Kadambari was wondering about sudden change in the attitude of Madam Agatha. Right on the day when she had fallen ill, Kadambari could sense the apparent worry in the mind of the lady. She was visibly disturbed. Inside the tough exterior there was clearly a very soft heart, which could not easily control her emotions. Despite taking charge of the situation, and trying to calm the girls, it was evident that there might still be a few situations where even she would panic—and this was one. Possibly, she was banking too much on the strong shoulders of her friend colonel to lean on in a crisis. More than that, was there a tinge of motherly affection towards the helpless girl... She had heard of such suppressed emotions in the case of elderly sisters and mothers in convents and orphanages—a daughter who ought to have been incubated in my womb-syndrome.

It was then that she remembered her early days in Devagiri. She distinctly remembered that initially Gomathy was thoroughly uncomfortable with the orphan, who had deliberately clung on to the dhoti of her husband. She loathed whatever she touched—the dress she wore, the vessels she used and even the floor she had dirtied like any other four-year- old... But an innocent soul that he was, Shankararaman took it as the rare blessing of Devi Karumariyamman for their continuous prayers and penances. After all, in this *Kalyuga* (Dark Age) when injustice and sin were on the increase, it was on the prayers of none other than Lord Shiva and Narayana that the Devi Karumari wielded all her weapons, seen and unseen.

When the child fell ill and was unconscious due to high fever, it melted the tenacious mind of Gomathy, and she made it a point to attend to her by sitting by her bedside throughout the night without closing an eyelid. While continuing to wet her forehead with a damp towel and administering the medicines at prescribed intervals, she thanked Amman profusely for her invaluable gift, and begged her pardon for not acknowledging it in good time. Hence, it was but natural that the family had observed fast for a day and prayed at the temples of Amman and Lord Muruga atop the hill and offered flowers and fruits as a token of their respect.

There was a dramatic change in the attitude of Gomathy thereafter, and Kadambari found it rather amusing that high fever and connected miseries could prove to be a unique weapon to refine the obstinacy in human beings.

She was right. Madam's attitude, too, softened considerably after that event, and she took more care of her after that—much to the envy of other girls. She would even ask about the present position of the coaching centre and whether she had been able to make it a real 'Adarsh' centre, as the name suggested. She was mainly concerned about the fees she had charged. She had been told at the time of lighting the lamp that there was nothing wrong in having a different fee structure at the centre, with poor but deserving ones getting a concession. And Kadambari has been meticulously following her advice.

Anyway, the relationship with Madam took a curious turn, when once in a private moment, Madam admitted rather emotionally that she now felt like she should have married in good time and given birth to a child, that too a girl child—like Kadambari, obviously.

'I know, I'm contradicting myself, of a mother choosing a child etc. Probably, things are little clearer to me now. The world has changed a lot, and we now live in a totally new world. It's you who taught me the present notion of motherhood. I have since realised that motherhood is not a biological concept alone, that it can be acquired and nurtured by love and compassion. I thank your presence for changing my opinion.'

Stunned for a moment, Kadambari ran towards the lobby gasping for breath. She did not know what to do. A mother, again, she tried hard to convince herself. She wanted to tell the whole world, or at least her close friends, that she was no longer an orphan. She had another mother, possibly a second mother. She rushed to the office and sat at the computer table with the consent of Sarala, the secretary. When she eagerly opened her old Facebook page which was unattended for several months, she was greeted by a host of emotional posts from many friends like Maragatham and Pavizham (she never knew they could operate a computer)—and strangely, a WhatsApp message from Vedanayakam.

Too many queries. Where are you now? Are you okay? Why did you leave without telling anybody?

All were pleading with her fervently, wherever she might be, to return at the earliest. Vedanayakam had even commented that Shankararaman was in the hospital and that his flower stall had been closed after her departure. It appeared Venkiti Annan, too, had committed suicide by pouring kerosene over his body, as his wife had done.

Although moved for a moment, Kadambari controlled herself immediately. The secretary was curious to know about the sudden change on her face but she courteously thanked her and rushed towards her room.

Later, she realised that it would be better to not tell the other girls about this, since all had been vying with each other for gaining the attention of Madam Agatha.

'Thank you, ma'am. Thank you, mother!' she told herself with a broad smile.

Gouri's Big Secret

Despite sharing a room with her for many months, Kadambari did not know that Gouri was a divorcée. It was by a rare coincidence that she happened to stumble upon her staring at a wedding photo hidden in her suitcase. Although she pretended it was nothing important, Kadambari managed to steal a glance and then snatch it from her hand forcibly. Fearing the picture would get ripped apart, she released her fingers reluctantly.

It was young Gouri in a glittering Kanjeevaram sari, bejewelled with antique gold ornaments and decked with a thick crown of jasmine flowers. By her side was a young man appearing to be the bridegroom, quite masculine, and with sharp eyes.

Kadambari looked at her questioningly, and Gouri nodded reluctantly.

'A one-night relationship! That's all,' she explained hurriedly, and grabbing the photo from Kadambari's hand and hiding it safely in her suitcase, she moved away to the window, averse to continue the conversation further.

That was probably the reason why she always had a grim face; of course, not the kind of a weepy face like Seetha. True, only very few in The Nest had pleasant demeanour, as most of them had some kind of unhappy past or the other. Some of these miseries would have been of their own making which they did not want to concede, always having some handy scapegoats to name. That was why Madam Agatha used to say that she was tired of those sickening sob stories, many of which were repetitive and nothing but over-exaggerated narratives of weaklings. She had a feeling that present-day girls did not have the guts to stand up to situations boldly, but preferred running away from it all at the first opportunity.

It was in this backdrop that Kadambari started brooding more about Gouri. If she hated that guy so much that she decided to sever the relationship after a one-night stay without giving a second thought, why was she still keeping that wedding photo? And that ring on her finger with a man's name clearly engraved on it… Kadambari had her own suspicions about it in the beginning and had believed that an estranged lover of hers would have put it on her finger in their good times, and that she might be keeping it in memory of those beautiful days.

Kadambari had noticed that of all the girls, the colonel had shown special interest in the affairs of Gouri from the beginning. In fact, some of the remarks she had made during the chat sessions were seemingly directed at her. On all those occasions, Madam was seen nodding in approval. She possibly knew quite a lot about her.

In one of the sessions, the colonel was emphasizing on the need for the girls mixing freely with the boys during their student days, particularly at the college level. She explained that what she had meant was a healthy friendship and not 'dating', as the new generation kids would love to call it. In this highly complex world with sex-starved guys hanging around, there was paramount need to give the girls some kind of sex education in an appropriate manner. There should not be any mystique or religious taboo around it, and the girls should certainly know more about their organs, which would have an important role to play during their subsequent conjugal relationships. Ideally, this should come either from the mothers and elders or female teachers, and not from porn books and videos—much in circulation among the youngsters. While the present-day mothers took care of it, those of the earlier generation had very conservative views on such things. Discussing sex in front of their children was considered a sin for them, and they had objected to their daughters watching movies under 'Adult' category on the television or at the theatre.

While the colonel was discussing these issues in detail and the girls were quite attentive, it was only Gouri who sat there unmoved, lowering her head as if the subject did not relate to her at all...

Anyway, after that wedding photo incident, Kadambari had vowed not to ask Gouri anything more about her unhappy marriage, divorce and the eventual escape. But more details about her background trickled in later from the indications given by Sarala. Quite talkative and nosey about the affairs of others, she had full details of each and every resident. She used to boast that she knew more about the colonel than Madam Agatha herself. Knowing her nature, particularly the inclination for loose-talk, Agatha had warned that nothing should leak out of the four walls of the campus. Sarala, an unfortunate widow with two small children, also knew that in case of any delinquency, she would lose her job—which she could not afford in the present conditions of her family.

'Haven't you heard of the great Subbaraman sir, the well-known orator?' asked Sarala. 'Gouri is his only daughter.'

Of course, Kadambari had not heard about him and she hesitantly shook her head. Then Sarala explained that on retirement as the head master of a school, Subbaraman Sir, the well-known mathematics teacher, took to conducting discourses. Within no time, his fame spread far and wide and he was in high demand, particularly during auspicious periods. His discourses were mostly on classics and epics, and not on religious subjects. His discourses on *Kambaramayanam* were quite famous; he was known more for his expositions on the classic *Thirukkural*. He had the rare ability of leading the audience to different ways of reading the *Kural*, particularly in the contemporary context. What poet *Thiruvalluvar* had scribbled centuries back gained relevance as the days went by, and Subbaraman had plenty of interesting anecdotes in support of his findings. Of course, Sarala did not have the good fortune of listening to any of those discourses, but some of her friends have confirmed their unquestionable reverence to the great man.

And now, look at the plight of his darling daughter, lamented Sarala. This indicated that certain sayings of *Valluvar*, as expounded by the narrator, could even recoil into one's life.

What about her marriage? What went wrong?

Sarala also did not know much about it, except various rumours that were in circulation then. But having seen herself how innocent the girl was, even a gossip-monger like Sarala was in no mood to listen to them. But it was true that the girl was married into a good family, and that boy with a decent job in Dubai was a good match for her. In fact, it was his mother, charmed by the looks and manners of the girl during the evening *aarati* at a temple, who had taken the initiative of locating the whereabouts of the girl and had asked her hand in alliance for her son. *'Mahalakshmi polirikku antha pon!'* (the girl looked like Goddess Mahalakshmi), she was said to have remarked to her husband. When it was discovered later that she was the only daughter of the famous Subbaraman, the boy's family and relatives were immensely pleased. And the horoscopes of both had also matched. It was in this context that all were puzzled about what went wrong in the alliance.

Strangely, Sarala did not know that it was only 'a one-night' alliance, and that Gouri had run away from the boy's home the very next day when he had gone to the town with his parents for some shopping. Once Kadambari had shown some interest in Gouri's story, Sarala promised to collect more reliable information on her weekend visits to her home town. In fact, Gouri's village was not far from hers, and in view of the fame of the great scholar, news about his family did spread very fast. And she did have a few relatives who had married into some families in that village.

A week after that, Sarala was excited to give more details of Gouri's family. It appeared Gouri's mother Revathi was just the opposite of the highly religious and orthodox Subbaraman. Having passed out of an English medium school in the nearby town run by a convent, she was quite proficient in English, and knew a bit of French, too. A voracious reader, she had read all the classics—from Thomas Hardy, Tolstoy, and Dostoyevsky to her favourite author, Kazantzakis. She was keen on sending her daughter to an English medium school so that she would be familiar with the events of the outside world; but Subbaraman, the scholar, was stubborn. 'No way,' he had asserted, 'my daughter should know more about Tamil culture first, and then Indian culture at large.' Thus, she was admitted to a Tamil medium school and was administered a liberal dose of Tamil classics during her school days. In college her staple diet was the works of Sri Ramakrishna and Swami Vivekananda. Referring to the famous Chicago speech of Vivekananda, he earnestly believed that no orator anywhere in the world could match that speech.

And strangely, the scholar was very particular that the girl should be admitted only to a women's college, preferably run by a Hindu institution. In these troubled times, he wanted to ensure that the innocent girl born in a reputed family and brought up in a traditional way with high principles should not fall into a bad company. He was not happy about the morning prayers in Christian colleges in particular, and wanted the girl to sing the well-known bhajans instead, as was done in Hindu colleges. Moreover, the yoga she had been practising right from her young age would also be continued in the traditional manner, without any hindrance.

While the poor girl had obeyed her father's wishes assiduously, it was her mother Revathi who was thoroughly unhappy about the manner in which her darling daughter was being brought up. It was a fact that there used to be occasional tiffs on this issue, but ultimately the wish of the father would prevail, and the lesser-known lady was made to withdraw, cursing her fate.

As such, when the proposal from a Dubai-settled boy came, that too from a good family, Revathi was happy that at least after the marriage Gouri could escape from this suffocating atmosphere, breathe the fresh air of a foreign country and lead a life of her own. Subbaraman was not comfortable about the girl crossing the high seas, but he was convinced by his close relatives that such a golden opportunity should not slip out of their hands. Fascinated by the girl's charm and quiet manners, the boy's parents had not made any specific demands on dowry, including money and gold ornaments, leaving it entirely to the choice of the girl's parents. They could gift the girl whatever they wanted but there will not be any demands from the other side.

'What happened then?' asked an anxious Kadambari.

But Revathi was shocked beyond description later, when it was known that the groom would not be able to take the girl immediately on return. According to the revised regulations, there were certain conditions to be satisfied for getting a family visa. Of course, he was hopeful of managing it within a couple of years, if not earlier. That meant he would have just 21 days to spend with the girl after the marriage.

'My God!' cried Kadambari, 'what a curse on the poor girl!' But Sarala did not find anything strange in that. There were any number of cases where the boys had to leave their wives behind but made annual visits. The wives would also join them occasionally on tourist visa. Further, since there have come up so many online mediums to communicate, girls can easily settle down after the initial discomfort.

'Nonsense!' Kadambari mumbled, 'married life is for living together and not for such make-shift adjustments.' She did not want to listen more. Even otherwise, Sarala's information was patchy. Also, her informant could not sense what had really gone wrong after the nuptial night. Didn't the great scholar look for a sacred *Shanthi Muhurtam* (auspicious nuptial time) for the young couple? Sarala had wondered.

Kadambari did not want to ask her roommate more on this issue but she found considerable relevance in certain references of the colonel in one of her chat sessions. While talking of marriages, she had pointed out that in Western countries, they have something called 'pre-nuptial agreements' which the couple signs before marriage. It was a kind of contract or vows they took before entering a wedlock. Nothing like that in our country. Here, it is dependent more on the reputation of the family and the background of the couple. It's a fact that families do take great care in matching the horoscopes, but there are any number of cases where the marriages have failed, despite the horoscopes matching 10 out of 10. Then, the colonel supplemented her earlier statement that more than the written contracts, what was needed was a proper pre-marriage counselling, particularly to girls from conventional orthodox families. The old concept that talking of sex was bad and nothing but sin, should be dumped in a dustbin. The girls should be educated about such things, without any misgivings, instead of their picking up bits and pieces from wrong sources.

'Enough, girl' Kadambari muttered to herself. She could easily guess what would have happened to the poor girl during her first night. As one groomed with such care, any impatient advances from that guy would have been scary to the girl, who would have been nurturing rosy romantic dreams about her nuptial night, where the prince charming would have entered, riding a white mare.

This was confirmed by Gouri herself without Kadambari asking about it. She would have felt herself guilty of keeping her close roommate in the dark about it. In fact, in a weak moment, Kadambari had confided in her all about the happenings in her life.

'I was attacked by a beast in the night,' without asking, she burst out. Kadambari was shocked.

'Where? In the courtyard?' she asked anxiously.

'No, inside the house.'

'Weren't there others who could have stopped the beast?'

'They couldn't, since it had happened inside the bedroom, where we were alone!' the girl said calmly 'And the beast was blurting "only 21 nights, only 21 nights…" The only words he had spoken during our short life together.'

Twenty-one nights! All are concerned about the girls' nights and not days, wondered an agitated Kadambari.

Scarier than the famed 'One thousand and One nights' to which the famed Scheherazade of Arabian Nights was exposed.

Kadambari was stunned.

Parveen Escapes

The dawn did not break that day; it burst instead. Unable to gather the splinters of the Sun's rays outside, the girls had assembled in the lobby.

As a habitual early-riser from her Devagiri days, it was Kadambari who had woken up first. And then Lisie, the nurse-to-be. But it was Apoorva, the Tamilian girl, who broke the news first. Her roommate Parveen was missing, she announced tensely. Then she was flooded with uneasy queries—how could she escape from this protected campus? When did it happen? When did you see her last? Are you in the habit of sleeping early? But poor Apoorva had no clue. When she had woken up to go to the toilet, the cot was vacant. She would have escaped any time after midnight, since Apoorva—a college student—had plenty to study, and had the habit of reading late into the night.

Madam was in the lobby pacing the floor at a furious pace. Since all her efforts to get some clues from the gatekeeper Karupayyan proved futile, she was waiting anxiously for the colonel to take charge of this nasty situation which had erupted all of a sudden. Since managing the girls' hostel in a college for a pretty long time, she had not faced such a piquant situation so far.

The colonel rushed in and her SUV came to a screeching halt at the porch as usual.

When Karupayyan tried to salute the colonel in his own clumsy style, she did not even bother to look at him, and hurried inside looking for Madam Agatha.

All the residents were asked to wait in the lobby until the colonel finished questioning the gatekeeper. The gatekeeper, flustered about the serious blunder he had made, was sure that he was going to lose his job.

'What did you drink last evening, the usual arrack or some other unfamiliar country brew?' colonel started in a coarse tone.

'Believe me, colonel ma'am,' Karupayyan pleaded, 'I didn't drink last evening. It was a Thursday and I don't drink on Thursdays. I swear on my two children,' he said, almost bursting into tears.

'Yet another lie, unadulterated lie!' Agatha interfered with uncontrollable fury. 'How many times have I caught you in a drowsy condition even on Thursday nights? Don't lie to a colonel, she has handled many such rogues in service!'

Meanwhile, the colonel raised her hand and stopped her, indicating that she would do all the questioning herself.

'Look here man, better come out clean. You know you can't lie to a *fauji* of all the people. Think of your serious lapse and dereliction of duty. If a sentry on a sensitive post slept while on duty, even the country's security could be in peril. Don't you know that as an ex-*fauji*? It's immediate detention and court-martial in such cases! Who knows whether you are not an accomplice? You might not see the daylight again. Here, it is a serious case of a girl missing from a hostel, where Madam

Agatha had specifically cautioned you to be vigilant in her case. Anyway, the police is not going to leave you just like that. You would be apprehended as an accomplice. They might charge that you had taken money from that boy, or perhaps liquor—your proven weakness. Even your innocent family won't be spared.'

Karupayyan burst into tears, and was about to fall on her feet when the colonel moved away hastily.

'I hate such theatrics,' she remarked scornfully. 'Ask this man to go away. Let him face his fate in the hands of the local police. They are better equipped to handle such rogues,' the colonel told the secretary. Unsure of what to do next, the gatekeeper looked pleadingly at Agatha, who gestured him to get out of the building fast.

Later, Agatha admitted that he was an alcoholic and languid, but not dishonest. He was like a faithful dog, one who was prepared to die for his master. The colonel knew it, too. But judging the seriousness of the lapse, she was sure that he would certainly be one of the prime suspects in the eyes of the police, that they would not mind unleashing their infamous third-degree methods on the defenceless fellow. How did the girl escape without his connivance, they would ask. It was clear that the girl had planned the entire escape plan meticulously. She was probably planning and patiently waiting for some time for this D-day, or D-night, as one might call. A Thursday night would have been chosen deliberately, since Fridays were off days for Salim and nobody would have looked for him on that day. She would have kept a long vigil on the balcony to ensure that the old man had dozed off, and had managed to escape by scaling the compound wall quietly. It was clear that she would have got out of the building through the back door, since that door was found open in the morning. The front door had been bolted and locked by Madam Agatha herself.

Then where did she meet that Salim? Was he waiting by the roadside with the escape vehicle? Or was she trying to escape alone?

There were unusual wrinkles on the colonel's forehead. This queer situation made her razor-sharp mind work faster. Relaxing on her usual couch, she ordered a cup of steaming hot tea. 'Whosoever is the rascal behind this plot, I am not going to leave him—be it a man or woman,' the colonel muttered.

The colonel knew very well that questioning the girls would only be a mere formality and she might not get any useful clues from them. But she wanted to do it before the local police subjected them to their usual rigorous grilling. From whatever she had understood, Parveen was quite a secretive girl, and the language barrier and the peculiar plight she was in would have stopped her from mixing freely with other residents. Thus, cautioning the girls that they should be prepared for a severe grilling at the station individually or jointly, not necessarily in the presence of their Madam, the colonel left hurriedly. Having got involved in the case as if it was her own, it was clear that she might take the help of that private detective friend on her own, since the organisation did not have the money for paying her fees.

When all the residents withdrew to their own private world speechless, it was an edgy Sarala who chose to take Kadambari to her room for a little private talk. It seemed she was brimming with some spicy stuff, and was keen to get it of her system as early as she could. As usual, Kadambari was a person in whom she could confide safely. She did not want to tell the Madam first, since she was not sure how she would have taken it.

It appeared two strangers with brown hair and blue eyes, seemingly North Indians, had been seen loitering around the campus during the last couple of days. A friend of hers who ran a fancy women's store in the street had noticed their suspicious movements. It was clear that they had not gone to the gate, which is why Karupayyan didn't notice them at all. Kadambari knew that this would be a very valuable clue to the police, and asked Sarala what the point was in keeping it a secret. After the visit of the Swamiji and the threat of Parveen's father, Parveen's story was no longer a secret in the campus; rather, it was a hot topic for discussions. Hence, Kadambari advised Sarala to rush to Madam Agatha without any further delay.

But that new piece of information found Agatha in an awkward situation. Who were those two guys? Were they on the lookout for Parveen? Were they from her town or family? The whole story took a curious turn and the colonel was indeed fascinated by it. But her only complaint was why Kovai Sarala hid this from her. She had told the girls to part with all the available information, howsoever insignificant it might be.

Sarala was visibly tense. She admitted that she was new to such kind of situations and was scared of handling it—more so, since the police was involved. Right from her childhood she was frightened by the very sight of the khaki uniform, and the elders had often used this as a ploy to discipline the little girl.

Later, Apoorva came to Kadambari's room with more information, some of which she had shared with Madam Agatha in confidence sometime back.

That was about Parveen's affair with Salim. Now that everybody in The Nest knew about it, she did not want to conceal it any further. It appeared Parveen was quite tense about something the past few days, before making her final escape. She used to wake up suddenly in the middle of sleep, sometimes with a suppressed wail, thus waking up her roommate, too. The usually jolly girl—at least inside the four walls of her room—and always waiting for an opportunity for singing the rare ghazals of *Begum Akhtar* and *Parveen Sultana*, was avoiding that, as if she was frightened of her own voice. Suddenly, she appeared to have changed the tack. She now preferred to sing another one of her favourites sung soulfully by Lata Mangeshkar in the unforgettable film *Anarkali*, the parting lament of the imprisoned Anarkali.

Yeh zindagi usi ki hai jo kisi ka ho gaya
Pyar hi mein kho gaya...
Yeh zindagi usi ki hain..
Yeh bahaar yeh samaah keh raha hai pyar kar
Kisi ki arzoo mein apne dil ko bekarar kar...

It was the eternal lament of the immortal Anarkali, which used to make the women in the audience weep. Similarly, she had started to recite the lines of *Heer-Ranjha* and *Sohni-Mahiwal* songs in her nasal Punjabi style, portraying the romance of young couples, all of whom had tragic ends.

'How come all these love stories had ended up as tragedies?' she once asked Apoorva. 'Isn't it the heroine who is always made to suffer?' But Apoorva had a clear answer to it: only tragedies drew sympathy and were remembered forever. Had those couples united and lived happily forever, who would have bothered about them? Wasn't Shakespeare known more for his tragedies than the comedies he had written? Parveen had no answer. She nodded with a deep sigh.

However, Parveen was sure that Salim was quite serious about his love, despite his entire family being dead-against their younger son marrying the daughter of a *kafir* (an insulting term used by some Muslims for non-Muslims), even after conversion. Boasting of their high lineage, they had planned for an alliance with a girl from a well-known family. After all, a *kafir* is always a *kafir*, they would say. And then, there were problems in her own family....

Kissing the diamond studded silver ring, she had indicated that it was none other than her lover Salim who had put it on her ring finger ceremonially in a corner of their mosque, without being noticed—she was in a purdah, like a devout Muslim. Salim's gesture was a firm assurance that under no circumstances would he ever leave her. Interestingly, it was she who had insisted that the ring should be in silver and not in gold, with a green stone at the centre. She would have been willing to share a bed with him even, had there been such a request from his side. After all, my mind and body belonged to him; so why should I grudge, she had told herself. But the thorough gentleman that he was, Salim couldn't even think of such excesses with his sweetheart he was to marry later.

Despite his tough exterior, she knew that her papa was soft inside and loved her so much that he would have forgiven her later—if it had come to that. But what about her uncles and the *mukhiya*, the village Panchayat chief? Her uncle, the father's younger brother, was a tough man with strong political connections. For him, even a murder was justified if it was for upholding the honour of the community, since he had to stand in the elections. Thus, despite a couple of charges for kidnapping and even murder registered against him, the police dared not touch him. According to the police records he was reported to be untraceable. Further, he had a gang of loyal goons who accompanied him wherever he went. Even the usually obstinate *mukhiya* was scared of him.

Did that mean that those two men on the prowl were the goons sent by Parveen's uncle?

Quite possible, Agatha agreed later. So, too, the colonel and the police inspector. The inspector, a handsome man in his early 30s, had visited the campus on the first day itself for surveying the scene of action. Well-educated and suave, he was not like the usual cops with big moustaches; he was quite affable in his approach. The law degree that he had taken had equipped him with the basic skills for questioning any suspect in a professional manner. He informed Madam Agatha that they had already registered a case, and that all concerned would be summoned to the station for interrogation within a couple of days. When Agatha asked why the police station and not here, he smiled softly. Let the girls have a feel of the police station, too, since they might not get such opportunities again.

And the girls waited, keeping their fingers crossed.

Meanwhile, the private detective friend of the colonel had tracked down Salim even before the police could do it. He was on a trip to the Northeast and had crossed Visakhapatnam. Normally, he did his cargo business purely on commission basis and never travelled with the trucks. In this particular case, since the party was one of his close friends and the cargo was of special interest to him, he had decided to oblige him.

This information put the colonel and Madam Agatha in a fix. This had clearly indicated that Parveen had not eloped with Salim, who, incidentally, was found travelling in the opposite direction on the fateful night. Then what had happened to her? What prompted her to get out of the campus on her own? Or was there anybody else with her?

The whole issue was becoming more and more intriguing and when the police was also done collecting similar information from their own sources, the inspector rushed to the campus for completing the process of questioning the girls. In view of the recent developments, he thought it would be better to do it in the campus itself, since the girls might not open up in the intimidating atmosphere of a police station. It would be better to be friendly with them and extract as much evidence as possible, he had cautioned the team accompanying him. This had already developed into a sensational case and the national media had blown it up beyond all proportions, possibly on two significant counts: community divide and North-South divide. The regional language channels from the North were following up the case closely through special correspondents, since the girl involved was from Haryana and the South-based boy was from another community. They could easily sense some spicy stuff in this incident. The police officers at the HQ had also started monitoring the situation closely, so as to brief the ministers periodically.

Things have gone out of our hand, Agatha, lamented an exasperated colonel. The TV crew who was after Madam Agatha until now had started chasing the colonel as well. Ultimately, she decided to be very tough with the female TV crew, and it was decided to keep a security guard on temporary duty at the gate of The Nest during the day, too. Strict orders were issued to him that nobody should be admitted inside the campus. Whatever information they needed could be collected from the designated authorities, viz. the police.

The sessions with the girls had proved futile for the police and the inspector felt that it would be better to take their counterparts at the girl's place into confidence, as the girl would possibly be somewhere around there.

The police did have a photo of Parveen which they had used for putting up the advertisements in the papers but it was an old one, and not clear either. Hence they wanted a couple of better pictures from Madam Agatha. But Madam pleaded helplessness, since she had already parted with the only image she had in the office records. Then they had to turn to her roommate, where they succeeded unexpectedly.

A couple of selfies extracted from Apoorva's phone did help the police in having a good look at the missing girl and for updating the records at the police station. Meanwhile, there were unconfirmed reports that Salim would be flying back from Kolkata, and the police was ready to nab him at the airport itself.

And more than anybody else, the TV crew were also waiting anxiously for Salim's arrival.

Twins from the Slum

When Mu. Ka. Raja sought an appointment with Madam Agatha, she was surprised.

'Why all these formalities, Raja sir? You could have walked in any moment. After all, it's your organisation,' she said.

'It's not about that. I wanted to meet you for a very urgent matter of importance. I wanted to check whether you were free.'

'Okay, sir, please do come.'

Obviously, Raja had a long story to tell. With the flourish of an accomplished journalist, he narrated the sad story of the twins Kamatchi and Kamalachi from the slums as follows:

They were all living in the slums for years, since the textile mill nearby was closed. When all the efforts for reopening the mill proved futile, the banks and other creditors had no other option but to approach the court. After protracted court battle, they succeeded in attaching the prime land and bring it to the auction table in the presence of a court-appointed receiver. By this time, a narrow slum with small huts housing around a dozen families had come up behind this land parallel to the main road. The roofs of these huts were thatched with palm leaves, tin sheets, etc. The adjacent vacant land stretching up to the railway track was government property and, practically, there was very little activity there for a long time. Then the local boys put up wooden poles on both sides and started playing football in the evenings. Slowly, it became a popular joint for youngsters to gather in the evenings.

Things took a dramatic turn later, when a Marwari group from the North which had taken possession of the property in court auction wanted to put up a five-star hotel on the site. On completion of relevant formalities, they influenced the politicians to get the adjacent vacant land on a long lease on the assurance that they would convert the plot where football was being played into a lovely children's park with all the modern facilities. They could sell this idea easily, since the town did not have any such play areas for the kids.

However, protracted public agitation and legal battle followed against this dubious deal for a fairly long period. Meanwhile, Palaniyappan, one of the local boys from the slums who was a regular on the football field, had managed to play for the state in the Santhosh Trophy. Subsequently, he joined the Railways as a Travelling Ticket Examiner (TTE) under the sports quota, which gave him a much wider exposure. But as bad luck would have it, when he was preparing hard for the national selection trials, he was injured in a train accident while he was on night duty in one of the coaches. Recovery after a few months of treatment could not improve his plight, and it was doubtful whether he would be able to come back to competitive football and make it to the national level football. Nevertheless, the boy became an icon for the locals in their protest against the encroachment of public land. Many flex boards and banners carrying the photos of the player were put up at vantage points. There were also serious allegations against leasing of the open land. It was also alleged that the permission to put up the hotel was issued, flouting certain norms in force.

When it became clear to the company that acquiring the vacant land would be a difficult proposal and the local politicians were also becoming jittery in view of the oncoming general elections, their eyes turned towards the slums, which was growing slowly. How to get them evacuated? The local politicians were visibly wary of such an action in view of the possible public outrage, which could affect their vote bank equations.

It was then that a major mishap occurred.

One *amavasi* night, when the street lights had also gone off and it was pitch dark all around, a small blaze was noticed in a heap of garbage near one of the thatched huts in one corner. It appeared in the beginning that the fire could be doused easily by pouring a few buckets of water; but the situation changed quickly when the flames spread to one hut, and then a strong breeze fanned it across to all the huts nearby. Sensing a real problem, a small crowd had assembled in front and the rescue operations started. Since the only fire engine at the local fire station could not do anything useful, urgent messages were sent to the nearby stations. Still, they could not contain the fury of the fire. The second engine at the station had been out of order for a long time, and was not repaired despite repeated requests. Since it was peak summer and thatched roofs were dry, the fire spread fast and huge clouds of smoke engulfed the whole area, followed by occasional explosions caused possibly by gas cylinders. Heaps of inflammable waste dumped in the vicinity and tins of kerosene stored in some of the kitchens fuelled the inferno. Pandemonium prevailed and hearing the loud cries of women and children, the passers-by also rushed to the spot hurling conflicting instructions, thereby adding to the confusion. The rescue act was short and disorganised, and occasional explosions deterred many from daring to douse the blaze. By the time more fire engines had arrived from other stations, much of the damage had already been done.

The scene of action then shifted to a rescue shed put up in a nearby compound, and a few social workers had reached the spot to take stock of the situation. While resettlement of the victims would be a long-drawn process, some NGOs distributed cans of water and food packets by way of interim relief.

Meanwhile, a huge crowd had gathered there, hurling questions at each other.

'Have not come across such a huge fire in my life,' commented an old-timer.

'Me neither...'

'How did all the street lights go off just as the fire started?'

'What happened to the other fire engine? Why was it not repaired despite repeated requests?'

There was nobody to answer these uneasy questions, and the wailing and thumping of chests of the victims' families continued.

A few political leaders had also visited the spot and assured that actual casualties were being estimated, and that interim relief would come shortly. They would also be accommodated elsewhere. While most of the slum-dwellers did not trust them, there were a few who felt that since the elections were fast approaching, some foundation stones are sure to be laid in some open lands. Meanwhile, a youngster even threatened that if it came to that, they wouldn't mind fielding Palaniappan as an independent candidate in the next assembly elections. Of course, they didn't take that threat seriously, since they knew that he was not one to quit the prestigious railway job. Still, they knew that the popular player was capable of diverting a few crucial votes, which could tilt the balance—more so, since this was one constituency where the margin of victory was always narrow.

Meanwhile, the police chief visited the site and ordered a detailed enquiry, too. But their initial findings, however, were that the mishap would have been caused by a lit cigarette butt, thrown carelessly into the heap of waste. It was in line with the normal police theory that behind any fire, there could only be either an electrical short circuit or a lit cigarette butt thrown casually by a drunkard.

Too shocked to assess their own personal loss, womenfolk gathered in a corner to mourn aloud, thumping their chest and cursing their fate. It was discovered later that an old man had been shifted to a local hospital with severe burn injuries. Seemingly, he had rushed into the neighbouring hut after salvaging whatever he could from his own hut, much against the warnings from the crowd. As he went in, the entire roof collapsed with a loud thud and the inferno swallowed the poor old man.

He was the father of the twins Kamatchi and Kamalachi, who were the darlings of the slum-dwellers. Although uneducated, they were prolific singers and dancers, hugely admired by the residents. Hence, when the news arrived later that the old man had succumbed to the burns, there was a huge uproar in the area.

Raja's visit was solely to present the sad case of the twins from the slums. In fact, this was the only case activist Mu. Ka. Raja had presented to Madam Agatha so far.

'That old man, a former mill worker rendered jobless when the factory was closed, was managing the household by selling lottery tickets,' Raja explained.

It appeared his wife had died years a few years back during an outbreak of cholera. She was working as domestic help in the nearby homes after he had lost his job, and was earning a steady income. More than that, the family could sleep on a full stomach because of the surplus food she used to carry home. Bringing up the girls in such a situation was a huge challenge to the poor man; he could not even give basic school education to them.

Listening patiently for some time, Agatha asked, 'What should I do, Raja sir?'

'Isn't The Nest meant for such girls?'

She sat speechless for some time, since she was so preoccupied with the pressing problems Parveen's escape had caused. With the funds dwindling, she had decided to take a short breather for the time being and stabilise first, before venturing into more projects and new admissions. Taking two girls from the same family again would have been an unusual move, too. At the same time, she could not say 'no' to him, considering the invaluable support he had been giving to The Nest right from its inception.

'Okay, sir. This is an odd case, so please give me some time,' she mumbled, to which Raja nodded rather reluctantly. He was probably expecting a positive response straightaway.

A strange objection came from unexpected quarters.

'Over my dead body!' shouted Mrs Lalithambal, wife of the chairman, who was totally different from her husband in approach and outlook. 'Twins from the slums, no way,' she thundered.

For a moment, Justice Padmanabhan was startled. He could not remind the lady that normally the trustees did not interfere in the routine administrative matters of The Nest, which were entirely within the domain of Madam Agatha and others. He also did not want to remind the lady that she was not even a trustee!

Madam Agatha did not care about this news when it reached her, since she knew that Lalithambal—a member of many social clubs—was a known socialite, a typical 'Page 3' lady of the nearby city. They were called so mockingly, for being a regular in the partying circuit, taking care that their photos appear regularly in Page 3 of the city edition of the papers. She did not mind motoring down to the city exclusively for this purpose, and had a faithful driver who used to take care of all her requirements.

It was learnt later that some within the campus, particularly Sarala, was also not comfortable with the proposal.

'Wouldn't people outside mock us? Have we been reduced to that extent?' Sarala appeared to have told some of the girls. Sadly, a few girls were also unhappy to be in the company of such destitute kinds, but they did not have the guts to say that openly.

But as usual, it was the colonel who was unusually firm on the topic. So, too, was trustee Anita Subramaniam.

'Why are you vacillating on such issues!' she exclaimed. 'Money, or no money, these girls are the ones who should have been taken in first. Thank God, at least our activist friend Raja decided to take it up at the right time. And I am glad your colleague on the board, Anita Subramaniam, supported it.'

When Agatha did not reply, the colonel raised her voice.

'Is the slum the symbol of a caste or a caste in itself?' she shouted. 'Have we cared to analyse how Asia's largest slum came up in this country and a Brit could glamourise our slums and win Oscars and what not? Are we aiming for the topmost spot in the world on this count?'

Inclined to consider the request somewhat, Agatha was emboldened by the strong support extended by the colonel.

'Good, colonel,' she quipped. 'I'm happy that we are on the same page.'

'Didn't you know that we were always on the same page? Since I believe you can never go wrong because your intentions are always clean, this hesitation on your part really hurt me. You didn't have to consult all and sundry, let alone a person like me who is not even a trustee.'

When the diffident girls in old and worn out clothes stepped into the building with a puzzled look, Madam Agatha was the only one to receive them with a warm smile. Sarala was conspicuous by her absence. Thoroughly unhappy with her boorish gesture, Agatha asked Kadambari to complete the formalities. They had lost the ID card and other such records in the fire, so Agatha asked Kadambari to collect whatever data the girls had. The case of issuing duplicate IDs to the victims would be taken care of by the authorities later. Their rehabilitation was also of the government's concern.

When the girls were formally ushered into their room by Kadambari, they were on the verge of tears. They did not know what to say and whom to thank first, the Almighty or Madam Agatha; for a moment, they were even doubting whether there was any difference between the two. They had never seen such a comfortable room nor been in such atmosphere, and were still unable to believe that they were to live there from now on. Deeply grieved on missing their dear father who had toiled hard to bring them up, they were somewhat relieved that they could get away from those horrible surroundings of a rescue shed with a shaky roof and no walls. It was another slum, and all the dwellers were finding it very hard to put up with it. However, having passed through the gory scenes of the night when the whole area was gutted, they were reassured, at least, of a strong roof which would not catch fire easily.

When Kadambari was looking curiously at the clumsy attire of the twins, Kamatchi, the elder of the twins by 30 minutes, blushed.

'Don't worry. I shall arrange to get some clothes from our girls for you until we get new clothes for you. Hope they would fit,' Kadambari reassured them.

The girls thanked her with folded hands, and Kadambari hugged both of them lovingly. In fact, Kamatchi was carrying all their belongings in a huge bag, which was also pretty tattered.

While Kamatchi was dark, slightly taller, and well-built, with two of her front teeth jutting out, Kamalachi was somewhat fair, with a slight squint in her left eye. Anxious about what was in store for them, they were relieved by the warm welcome given by Madam Agatha and the affectionate embrace by Kadambari.

'Think of me as your friend... I'm also like you,' assured Kadambari. 'But we're not orphans here. We have a mother and a few sisters... Of course, of different temperaments. Be friendly with all.'

The twins nodded in agreement and hastened to put their things in order.

But a curious development in the dining hall later disheartened Agatha to some extent. It was an old stipulation laid down by her that all the girls should meet at dinner time and eat together in the dining hall. This was the only time when everyone is together at home, since the main gate was shut by evening. One could enter the campus after that only with the prior permission from Madam Agatha. This was meant to be an occasion for unwinding and the girls were free to crack jokes and be silly. The usually rigid Madam used to be quite informal at the dinner table. But she had cautioned that all the comments and jokes should be civilised and without malice.

On that night, when Madam Agatha was the first to enter the dining hall in her anxiety to introduce the new girls, as was her wont in the past, she noticed that three seats were vacant. Since Sarala had excused herself on the pretext of going home, who could be the other two girls, Agatha was wondering. While the girls watched silently without naming the absentees, Madam herself found out it was Weepy Seetha and Sabeena.

'Aren't they in their rooms?' she asked aloud.

While others kept quiet, Kadambari chose to nod reluctantly.

'Oh, I see,' Madam mumbled. Then she ordered Janaki that no dinner should be served to the girls if they came later. The dining room should be closed immediately after everyone had eaten and left.

Of course, the twins did not understand the cause of confusion. But they did notice others exchanging embarrassed glances, unable to raise their head and meet the furious eyes of Madam Agatha. They ate silently sensing the mood in the room, and were deeply hurt when Agatha got up without finishing her dinner and left in a huff.

It was yet another disturbed sleep for Madam Agatha. Have all my attempts gone awry, she grieved. As the colonel had remarked, was the slum a caste in itself? Are those girls untouchables? How could those two girls Weepy Seetha and Sabeena, who have miserable pasts of their own, could be boorish like this? Aren't those twins also God's creations? Was it their problem that they were born in a poor family and rendered homeless by the sheer irony of fate? The sole aim of Kilikoodu was that birds of all feathers should flock together in a single nest. The Nest could not have two tiers…

Agatha felt miserable that all her pep talks with the girls, individually and collectively, had proven futile, almost like some of the hollow sermons of the vicar at the Sunday morning mass. On many such occasions, she had noticed inattentive parishioners exchanging texts among themselves on their smartphones. They were probably too eager to get back in time for their favourite TV programmes.

She decided to keep it to herself, unwilling to brief even the colonel. It was her ardent hope that Lord Jesus will not allow such dust to collect at unwanted places too long, and it had to settle somewhere, earlier the better.

She was proven right when both the absentee girls came to her room the next morning and apologised profusely with tearful eyes. They had since realised that even the Almighty would not pardon them for such grievous sins. In fact, Weepy Seetha wanted to have a private word with Madam Agatha, so Sabeena was asked to wait outside. It was then that Seetha admitted that she was also one who had to flee from home when her mother had died of fire. After that traumatic event, even the very mention of fire had scared her. The very sight of the twins would have reminded her of the charred body of her mother, which she was cursed to see. But she was to realise her folly soon and when she rushed to the dining hall, it was already closed. However, Kadambari took her to introduce the twins next morning itself, when she held them close to her heart and wished them all the best.

Greatly relieved, Agatha called Sabeena inside and advised both the girls to be cautious in future, and to be more friendly with the new girls. They agreed, and Sabeena even offered to present some of her *chooridars* to the girls, provided they would accept them.

'They would. Their innocent minds have not been polluted by the so-called civilised society,' commented Madam.

Deeply ashamed of themselves, the girls left.

When Agatha got up the next morning and was about to take a round, Didi hurried in on her wheel chair.

'Ma'am, just a moment,' she pleaded and Agatha stopped. Didi was panting, 'I wanted to compliment you on your bold decision. Wanted to do that at the dinner table last night but you were terribly disturbed. And take it from me, those twins would bring good luck to The Nest and are going to be quite prosperous one day.'

'How do you know that?' taken aback, Agatha retorted.

'I have a third eye. Don't you know that?' the girl smiled.

'She's nuts but still sensible…', Agatha remembered the words of the colonel.

Sarala Gets Jittery

For quite some time, Sarala, the secretary, was getting nervous about certain arbitrary decisions taken by Madam Agatha without keeping her informed. Possibly, at the insistence of her friend, Colonel Fernandez. After all, I had been taking care of the entire administration of this organisation from the beginning, she grieved. Never to have taken credit for it, she was happy that the institution did reach the present height through her efforts also. Since there may be others who are more experienced and had seen life in the outside world, there is nothing wrong in taking their advice. But before implementing them can't she at least tell me about it, she thought. It was this total disregard of her position in the organisation that was hurting Sarala very much. She was sad that the issue of inducting the twins from the slums was kept away from her, and that she came to know of it only through the wife of the chairman.

Sarala had also started questioning her need for continuing with the position of administrative secretary for an organisation which had such little faith in her. More so, when Madam Agatha questioned some of her actions, mostly relating to expenses of a routine nature. She had even cross-checked some of the vouchers Sarala had passed. Indeed, she was aware that Madam Agatha was worried about the declining financial position of the organisation.

Despite her best efforts to cut down the expenses, due to the overall price rise for all the essential commodities, the grocery bill was on a continuous rise. She did have a serious dialogue with Janaki about it many times. That's why Madam had decided, under her advice, not to take any more new girls in until the financial condition improved. Then why this big hurry in inducting those twins, that too from the same family?, Sarala wondered.

It was true that Agatha had started worrying about the future of The Nest itself. The channels of donations from abroad had been drying up slowly for some time, and as one who had been getting nervous easily of late, she had developed a lurking suspicion that some were working against the institution from behind the scene. One possibility was through anonymous emails to the patrons abroad containing unfounded allegations. This was one area Mu. Ka. Raja had warned her about right at the start. Such anonymous messages were the most vicious weapons in the hands of cowards who dared not to come out in the open.

This was corroborated subsequently when Agatha received a letter from a long-standing donor in Germany, enquiring anxiously whether the organisation was trying to promote atheism and blasphemy. It appeared her polite explanation about the objectives of The Nest did not carry much weight with the old lady, since more searching questions followed, possibly on account of anonymous follow-up emails. Is there any smoke without fire, the lady was tempted to dish out the old adage. She was in her early 70s, had once visited The Nest during her tour of the country, was a real opinion-maker, and had a loyal gang of oldies from that place who had set apart a portion of their earnings for charity. Having reached a level nearer to God by now, the lady was probably not willing to accept blasphemy of any nature.

Few such queries of a less serious nature followed from some other countries, thereby making it clear that the overseas donors' list of The Nest had been leaked out. It was a matter of great concern, and a thoroughly shaken Agatha was unable to judge as to who the possible insider was. The colonel was also angry about it, and she cautioned Agatha to be a little more careful with the people around her. Don't trust even your own people, she warned.

It was in this situation that a call from Swamiji at the inopportune time of the colonel's chat session alerted her. Wondering how he got her cell number, she promised to call him back after the session was over.

Profusely apologetic about his untimely interference, Swamiji was unusually generous in praising the uniqueness of the campus. It was simply amazing, complimented Swamiji, and that he could feel the difference as soon as he had stepped out of the car—as if he had the touch of the divine hand on his head; as if the Almighty had blessed him. It was a rare kind of *rashi* (name of the sign in which the moon is placed in one's birth chart) possibly due to the *vāstu* (traditional Hindu system of architecture) of the place. He wanted to know who the owner was and how they could lay hand on such a unique campus.

Suspicious of his intentions, she avoided a direct reply and managed a loud chuckle.

'It is the blessings of the Almighty. When one's intentions are good, God is always with them—be it Jesus, Krishna, or the Prophet,' she quipped.

Having caught the message clearly, Swamiji did not pursue the matter further and offered his apologies for being discourteous during his earlier visit. It was clear that he was trying to get the latest news about Parveen, and Agatha's reluctance to open the topic at all was a clear indication to him that something grave was up. But she was sure that the man was privy to lot of information about the missing girl, which could perhaps be of great use to the investigating team. But it would be better to keep mum on this topic, she thought.

Meanwhile, it was almost decided that in case a girl managed to eke out a living outside, she would be encouraged to leave The Nest and no fresh admissions would be made in her place. While this was still at a discussion stage, Sarala had decided to jump the queue on her own and posted this on the official website of Kilikoodu. This was something that hurt Madam Agatha deeply, since there were already very few in the waiting list anxiously awaiting their turn. They were awfully unhappy that some strangers had been admitted in the past overlooking their claims, but nobody had the courage to question the decisions of Madam Agatha. Moreover, Agatha was unhappy that because of this post they were accepting defeat in the presence of the whole world, and their rivals would be the happiest. Although she did not want to be a rival to anybody, it appeared there were a few who were thinking on those lines.

Then a stray incident of a missing voucher, where the payment had already been made, put Agatha on the alert. Incidentally, long back Didi had also warned Madam Agatha to be cautious of Sarala, who was supposed to be her conscience keeper.

'She has evil eyes,' Didi had warned. 'She would bring bad luck to the birds inside.'

Agatha had taken Didi's initial claim that Sarala had practised sorcery from someone in north Malabar as one of her usual pranks. She had just smiled and left it at that.

Meanwhile, Srinivasan's son, who had since become friendly with Agatha and had agreed to go through their accounts occasionally without any fees, found out some suspicious cases of unsubstantiated entries. He had also alerted Agatha to be more vigilant with the accounts; more so, since The Nest was having a severe funds crunch in the face of rising prices.

This incident, coupled with the issue of the post on the website without her approval, had infuriated Agatha, and she had no hesitation in giving a thorough dressing down to the secretary. Rarely had she seen the former sister flare up like this over trifles. It was clear that something at the back of her mind was hurting her beyond description.

This was the most embarrassing moment Sarala had faced while in The Nest. Suspicion was something she could not swallow. Then, hesitating for a moment, she took out a sheet of paper from her desk and wrote a simple letter of resignation. After taking a quick look at the paper, Madam nodded as if enough was enough, and she was okay with Sarala quitting. Taken aback for a moment and hoping that Madam would reconsider her decision, Sarala waited for some time. But by that time Madam had coolly withdrawn to her room, without even caring to look at her. It was clearly the end of the road for the Sarala, and she was mentally prepared for it for some time. Nevertheless, she was a bit emotional while stuffing her personal belongings in a bag and hurrying to leave, without even caring to say goodbye to the girls with whom she had lived.

Since Karupayyan was not on duty during daytime, there was nobody to fetch an auto rickshaw for her. She had to walk all the way in the hot sun up to the rickshaw stand with her heavy suitcases.

Little did she know that Madam Agatha was watching from the window the departure of her once trusted lieutenant without any remorse at all...

It was dark when Sarala reached home in her village after changing the bus twice. Her mother was waiting anxiously with a sullen face, along with her uncle who had rushed in on hearing the news.

'Are you okay, my girl?' asked the worried Amma.

Sarala could not answer her for a moment. With a bowed head, she was avoiding the sharp glances of her uncle.

'You were quite short-tempered during your childhood and adolescence but I thought that you had mellowed with time...'said the uncle.

'Taking such an important decision without telling anybody, neither your uncle nor me...' the mother said, almost on the verge of tears.

It was this uncle who had always stood by her after the untimely demise of her husband. During the beginning of the school season, he had seen to it that the children were well taken care of with new clothes, uniforms, books, umbrellas and all other essentials. The meagre pension of her widowed mother, a retired primary school teacher, was the only income of the family. The earnings of her husband had already been spent in carrying out some essential repairs to the house. Madam Agatha was quick to understand her plight, and had taken her in at the beginning itself without asking too many questions. The family was so relieved after that, since her mother could take care of the children, and Sarala needed to make only weekend visits. In fact, all her expenses—including essential toiletries, food, transport etc.—could be taken care of at The Nest; Agatha never bothered about such petty things.

How will they be able to take care of the family hereafter, wondered the uncle.

'If all of you start accusing me like this...' Sarala was on the verge of tears. '... After working sincerely for so many years, right from the beginning...'

'Don't think we're trying to find fault with you,' interfered her mother. 'Before taking such a hasty decision you should have thought about the conditions at home...'

'Not that I didn't think about it... But to continue there amidst distrust and suspicion was suffocating for me... How long I could pull on shamelessly?' Sarala's throat was choked with emotion and she found it difficult to continue.

'May be,' said the uncle. 'After all, she is an old nun. Might have been a bit short-tempered. You could have coolly ignored it. I believe this was first such instance. Had she behaved like this earlier?'

'Not directly. But it was all written on her face. Some kind of displeasure in whatever I did... And those unwanted suspicions.'

'Isn't it foolish to read too many meanings from others' faces? After all, we have all worked in government offices amidst such spiteful faces, both from above and below, and in our dealings with all kinds of people. Unless you learn to ignore such things you cannot live in this world.' the uncle, with a long service history in various government departments, advised.

'Not that I don't know all this. I had already suffered enough. When I scribbled that resignation letter in a fit of anger, I was under the impression that Madam would tear it off. That was the kind of relationship I had with her. But when it looked as if she was eagerly waiting for such a piece of paper from me, I lost all my control... I am also an ordinary human being. I might have made mistakes, but as an elderly sister, wasn't it her responsibility to correct me?' Sarala beseeched.

'Responsibility for both...' her mother was quick to correct. 'Listen, anger is not the solution to all the problems. You could've waited for some time for the lady to cool down. After she had settled down, you could've gone to her room quietly for a heart-to-heart talk. After all, she is not a bad lady. She would've understood you.'

Unable to face a barrage of such questions, Sarala went to her room carrying her baggage. The children were looking at her, unable to understand what was happening.

Sadly, Madam Agatha was also deeply disturbed after the unsavoury incident. Although she had watched Sarala walking alone in the hot son carrying two heavy suitcases with cruel pleasure, she was quick to realise later that it was her folly, too. No one in The Nest had the courage to ask her directly but the sulky faces of the girls spoke volumes. Kadambari, who was close to Sarala, was looking at Madam Agatha accusingly. Even Didi, who had warned Madam against the secretary, felt that this step was rather harsh, that poor Sarala should have been put on notice before taking such a hasty action. Strangely, this was the only time when Didi didn't want to confront her with her comments.

But Madam was searching for excuses to justify her action. After all, wasn't it Sarala herself who had volunteered to resign on her own when I had pointed out some of her genuine mistakes? Anyway, I didn't chuck her out, she told herself.

But after some time, when the tempers cooled, she found it necessary to pray. While praying with folded hands, she was muttering 'my fault, my own fault'. After all, wasn't it Jesus who had taught to forget and forgive, and pray for sinners?

It was yet another day of remorse for Madam Agatha.

Parveen's Tragic End

The body was found on the river bed, lying upside down, with the sand-smeared face in the waters and the body on the shore.

A group of ladies, who were regular temple-goers in the morning, had spotted it first. When they let out a loud cry, men taking bath in the adjacent men's area had rushed to the spot. By that time, the dawn had broken and a small crowd had assembled there. The body was that of a young girl, a fair-skinned stranger, which none of the onlookers could identify. The body was partially decomposed after being in the water, presumably for a couple of days. The onlookers were sure that the girl was from some other place, possibly from the nearby temple town, and were anxiously waiting for the police to arrive from the town. One of her eyes had been eaten by fish, and the flesh from some parts of her right cheek was also missing.

It took some time for the police jeep to arrive along with the ambulance. On completion of the initial formalities and taking the statements of the villagers who had spotted the body first, it was carried to the waiting ambulance. Initially, the villagers were too scared to say anything, pretending that they were not the ones who had seen the body first. But the police assured them that they would not be put to any hardship, since it was a suicide case; she had possibly jumped into the stream at some other spot. With the monsoons not far away, there was a fairly good current in the river and the flowing waters would have carried the body this far.

Later, in the government hospital where the post-mortem was to be conducted, the body was identified by the police as that of the missing girl Parveen. The police had the photos of the girl, which had also been published in the local newspapers. Still they had wanted a formal confirmation from those who had lived with her. And so, Madam Agatha was summoned first. While going to the police station, Madam Agatha chose to take Parveen's roommate Apoorva with her as well. Apoorva was closer to the girl and could not stand the sight of her face, which had now gained a bluish tinge. Strangely, the silver ring with a green diamond on the centre that Salim had put so lovingly on her ring finger was missing. Did the miscreants steal it or remove it for some other reason, wondered Apoorva. Although she wanted to avoid such an ordeal, she was persuaded by others that this being a police case, no resident could escape the questioning of the police. After all, the police had to collect all the available evidence, and who else could talk about Parveen than the ones who had lived with her for some time?

Salim was the first to come. Having been apprehended a few days back for questioning, he was in police custody and came with full police protection. Strangely, as one who would not have expected such a sad end to his beloved, Salim was unusually calm and unmoved. After taking a close look at her face, he took her hand and kissed it without any emotion. At the same time, the onlookers knew that he was trying hard to suppress his feelings. After due identification, Salim was taken to the station for questioning. The 'missing girl' case had now acquired larger proportions; it would now be either be a murder or a suicide case.

However, the findings in the forensic report received a couple of days later were quite puzzling. The girl had died of poisoning, the doctor confirmed emphatically, and certainly not by drowning. That meant that she had died before being thrown into the river.

The police was thoroughly confused, and so was the colonel and her detective friend. If it was a murder, who had administered the poison? If it was a suicide by consuming poison, how did the girl living in a protected hostel get it? And how did she get out of the compound? If somebody close to her had managed to draw her out without getting noticed, who was it? A close relative?

Suspicions were too many. Meanwhile, when the police had tried to contact the relatives at her place to ascertain what should be done with the body that had been lying in the mortuary, the response was lukewarm. The police also confirmed that the girl's parents were avoiding a straight answer. The mortuary at the government hospital was not big enough to keep the bodies for an unduly long period, and the doctors were pressuring the police to remove it as early as possible. Since it was a ticklish issue, which could be questioned later, the police were in two minds. Ultimately, they decided to give a newspaper advertisement with the girl's photo and her recorded home address. It was a kind of ultimatum that if there were no authorised claimants, the police would have the right to cremate it as per normal practice.

Meanwhile, political pressure was also mounting on the police and the local authorities to not pursue the matter further, since it involved the administration of two states. Ultimately, having reached a dead end and almost sure that Salim was not involved in the crime as he was in custody, the police decided to cremate the body according to the local customs. None from The Nest attended the funeral at the electric crematorium, since they could not watch their dear friend being burnt like a log of wood.

Later, the colonel shared some of her thoughts on the whole episode. As usual, she had toed a totally different line of argument in the case. Someone in whom she had confidence, or one to whom she could not say 'no' to had managed to take her out of the campus, hoodwinking the drowsy gatekeeper. The person obviously did not want to take the girl to her place and subject her to all the scrutiny there, and would have advised her to end her life on her own. In a weak moment, she would have agreed to it to avoid further complications. However, a more convincing possibility would be to assume that the person or persons would have forcefully administered the deadly poison. They did not want to leave any shred of evidence of a murder behind them, and they did not want to hurt her either.

Anything was possible, Agatha agreed. The whole episode had left a bitter taste in her mouth and dampened her spirit. Running a girl's hostel was not as easy as one might have thought; more so, in this era of highly complex relationships.

Meanwhile, some of the channels in the north had raked up the issue again with their 'breaking news'. Despite the major channels dissociating with such sensational coverage, female TV crew of the language channels continued to be on the rounds around The Nest. Unable to get any further information either from The Nest or the police, they telecast their own cooked up stories with some repeat shots of the campus taken from outside. Agatha was sure that they would get tired after some time, particularly after another sensational piece of news came up, but she was concerned that the rhythm of her daily routine had been affected by the unexpected turn of events. She was even avoiding her usual evening stroll on the lawn. Also, the reputation of the institution was also being tarnished. The sad part was that The Nest was being projected by some as a Christian institution run directly by the Church itself. When Mu. Ka. Raja tried to intervene by explaining to the press that the Church had nothing to do with the institution and the happenings there, they pleaded helplessness, since the drama was being enacted far away and the players being some small-time TV channels.

Then, anxious mails followed from abroad where the donors were inquisitive about the happenings in The Nest. Evidently, scans of media reports would have reached them. Most of them had wanted to know whether there was any foul play in the campus and whether Madam had been questioned. There were a few worried well-wishers who had heard that Agatha had been remanded to police custody as one of the accomplices. This was the height of mischief, and Agatha was unsure of what was going to happen in future.

But, as usual, the colonel advised her to take it easy and continue her prayers and efforts with double the vigour. But Agatha was clearly upset and mumbled 'easier said than done' to herself.

However, as predicted by the colonel, the dust had settled down fast—earlier than expected, since the local police were not keen on continuing with the case. They had found it convenient to close the case as a clear incident of a suicide. Meanwhile, Salim, the only concerned party, had agreed for marriage with a rich girl selected by his parents, and the girl's father had offered to help him with sufficient resources to develop his business. From the cargo business on commission basis, he had shifted to set up his own company with three trucks of his own. More vehicles were to be added into the fleet shortly. In this situation, the inspector was sure that he would have conveniently forgotten about the girl from the North, that, too, from another religion.

Meanwhile, the twins had become very popular with the girls—with their singing and dancing. While Kamatchi sang well, Kamalachi was quite good in dancing, particularly the rhythmic folk dances. On the evenings of weekends, those who had assembled in the main hall wanted the girls to perform before dinner. Although the twins were too pleased to do it (as they used to do in the open ground in front of their hutments), Madam had her own apprehensions. The old matron of the college girls' hostel feared that it might spoil the atmosphere, affect the strict discipline of The Nest even. But it was the colonel who asked her whether such a camaraderie won't be good for the girls to bond, since all of them had come from different backgrounds, and with their own baggage of miseries. Moreover, the Parveen episode had dampened the otherwise calm atmosphere at The Nest. The girls had started feeling that Parveen's voice was still reverberating in the hall. They also commented that while Parveen singing her ghazals soulfully moved their hearts, these twins lifted their spirits. Hence, she agreed to allow it on alternate weekends.

The twins were quick to sense the financial difficulties at The Nest. Having grown up amidst utter poverty, they were used to starving—particularly during the winter months—when their father, under the bout of asthma, could not go out on his old bicycle for selling lottery tickets. Incidentally, some of their neighbours had suggested then that the highly talented girls should not be made to sit idle at home and should perform at street corners so that they could make some money and be of support to the sick father. And who knew, one day they might even be noticed by some stray guy from the TV channels or the film industry even, and then sky would be the limit. Weren't there many stars who had come up from humble origins? Wasn't southern superstar Rajinikanth a mere bus conductor earlier?, slum-dwellers would say to him. But Appa, so conscious of the self-esteem of a former mill worker, despite living in a slum now, had refused stoutly. No, never. My daughters would not perform in street corners or in open *maidans* (ground) like gypsies. They had not been reduced to such a condition yet. They would rather starve to death instead, he had said. When he was a mill worker they were reasonably well off, and the family was not made to look for work. But he had forgotten that unable to see the kids starve, his wife had started working as a domestic help in the nearby apartments... Hence, the girls performed occasionally in front of their huts for the neighbours—just for fun, and not for money. Still, there were a few onlookers who had gifted them some money without their father noticing it.

When he was depressed, he used to take out that old khaki uniform from the almirah and wear it for a few moments. It was almost like a thin skin which could not be peeled off easily from his body. There was a time when that khaki uniform did command good respect in the area.

Later, when the girls wanted to work in an agricultural farm of a Chettiar in the outskirts of the town, the father had to agree reluctantly. At least the daughters wouldn't have to starve, he was advised. Although not used to farming in the past, the hardworking girls took to it quickly and started earning a steady income. The normally stingy Chettiar was wary of paying the normal wages of a farm worker to them. But he fed them well. Feeding the hungry was the best way of pleasing the gods, he had heard somewhere. The girls could also take home the remaining food for their father. It was after a very long time that the father had a taste of his favourite meat dishes. On the other hand, Chettiar's wife was quite generous, and used the give some money to the girls without her husband knowing about it. On the eve of the first Deepawali, she also presented them with gold nose rings on the promise that her husband should not know about it; that they should wear it only on festive occasions.

After their father's death and shifting to The Nest, the girls did not want to go to Chettiar's farm again as ordinary workers. Moreover, Kadambari had agreed to teach them to read and write effortlessly. First they would start with Tamil and a bit of English; latter would be of great value to the girls. Having mixed with the other girls for the past few months, they had changed substantially, and had learnt the basic manners for living in a polished society.

In such a background, when the twins had requested Madam Agatha for a plot of agricultural land that they could grow some vegetables on, she readily agreed to look at it. By working on the farm of the Chettiar for some time, they had also acquired some expertise in farming. Since the land in that area was quite fertile and there were many farms doing flourishing business, why couldn't they start one in the name of The Nest—strictly an organic farm with no synthetic fertilisers and pesticides used. Normal fertilisers like compost, green manure, cow dung, bone meal etc. would ensure clean crops. Moreover, poisonous insecticides would not be sprayed on the crops either. After meeting the requirements in their kitchen, the surplus could be sold through outlets for organic vegetables. Agatha was aware that there was a big demand for organic vegetables and they fetched higher prices in the market, provided the customers were satisfied over their genuineness.

Mu. Ka. Raja also agreed that it was a good idea, and that the earnings from the farm could be considered as the girls' share of contribution to the organisation. He was also happy that his recommendation had borne fruit, and that the twins—apart from earning the confidence of the girls and Madam Agatha alike—had started earning on their own. Then, through his contacts, he managed to get an acre of land lying unused which could easily be converted into a farm on the condition that it would be on lease for a few years—that, too, in the name of The Nest. Surprisingly, the owner was prepared to give it for free as his donation to The Nest; still, he wanted a record somewhere that such a deal had been entered into. He also offered that in case the venture proved to be successful, he was prepared to give the adjacent plot on the same condition as well, since it was lying unused for a long time. In fact, having worked in Chettiar's farm for some time they were missing the smell of the soil, which, according to them, was the smell of mother earth. After taking a close look at the land and tasting the soil on their tongue, the girls were immensely pleased with the offer, and were confident that after the first cropping season, they would be able to take the adjacent land also. The only request they had made was that they needed some money for buying agricultural tools like spades, pickaxes etc. as well as some quality seeds and fertilisers. Agatha readily agreed to lend some money towards the initial working capital.

Thus started the farming exercise of the twins. Having come up the hard way in life, the girls had no problem in working hard in the hot sun. And when they returned in the evening dead tired, Janaki greeted them with hot coffee. Within no time, the girls drew the admiration of all the residents; some of them were remorseful of their initial misgivings about them.

'Life is the biggest teacher of all,' Madam told Kadambari. 'Future was nothing but what one would carve out herself. If each girl learnt from life and shaped her own destiny, the world would have been a beautiful place to live in.'

Kadambari readily agreed. Her own Adarsh Tuition Centre was doing pretty well. She had become popular, since she was not greedy and had not fixed any fees. Instead, the students—many of them being middle-aged ladies from middle-class background—could contribute whatever they could; there was no compulsory fees.

As promised, the twins succeeded in their first harvesting season, and were gifted with the adjacent plot also; the owner was vastly pleased when a bag of organic vegetables like okra, brinjals, peas, tomatoes etc. was presented to his wife and as a gesture of goodwill. He gave the additional land without any legal documentation.

It was then that the twins surprised Agatha beyond comprehension. She was surprised when both the girls prostrated before her with tearful eyes. 'After meeting you, we have decided not to go to the temple. Why worship lifeless idols of stones when there are live idols right in front of us?'

Quite moved, Agatha could not understand what they really meant. But slowly, it sunk in that they were trying to refer to the timely help given to the two unwanted slum-dwellers, despised by one and all. It was then that the younger girl divulged that there were many lecherous eyes staring at her for quite some time, and after the mishap a one-eyed guy with a crooked face, who was earlier one of the cronies of a goon, had approached her with an irresistible offer for acting in a video for a song, to be followed by a telefilm... But she was quick to sense his motive and ignored him. Still, they knew that they would not be able to resist the advances of hooligans beyond a point. If not this fellow, there would be another guy... And that would be the road to ultimate disaster...

How a single gesture from the lady saved the lives of two precious lives.

'Jesus,' cried Agatha. She blessed the girls by keeping her hand on their heads.

Then the girls revealed that by now they had started earning enough to sustain themselves, and that they did not want to burden her further. They had taken a one-room apartment on rent near the farm so they didn't have to commute by bus, and at the same time take care of the activities at the farm.

Agatha was surprised. This was one occasion when she could not assess how The Nest would be poorer by the exit of two beautiful birds. Other girls also joined in the grief.

'Then what about our evening performances of dance and music. Won't we miss those invaluable programmes?' one of them lamented.

The girls themselves did not have much to say. They, too, controlled their tears. After the mishap, this was the first occasion on which they could let their emotions out. Embracing each one of the girls, Kamatchi, the elder one, assured everyone that they would be around whenever needed, and they could be counted on for help, always.

'All good things come to an end, and all of you would have to fly out, one day or the other,' sighed Agatha. 'That's all about the world we live in, and the mothers are destined to wave her little birds off, wishing them all the best.'

Nobody answered. They all stood speechless.

Lisie and the Twins Take Flight

The next one to fly out of The Nest was none other than Lisie. It was on the cards for quite some time, since the ambitious girl had been working hard towards her goal for long. She had told Madam Agatha some time back that she had successfully completed the nursing course and was desperately looking for a job. She had a clear path in mind for taking her career forward. A close friend, who was senior to her in the nursing college and had completed her course meritoriously, had gone to Germany after spending a couple of years in Willington Hospital in Delhi. Being from the same district—Pathanamthitta in Kerala—and having known her family history intimately, she had promised to refer her case to some influential people in Delhi, who could take her on as a trainee. The reference of some such hospital in her CV might help her in getting a job in Europe. Possibly in Germany, Austria, or Switzerland, where there were any number of nurses, mostly from Central Travancore in Kerala. Some of them had been there for nearly a quarter-century, and they would be in a position to put in a word or two in her favour.

The fact that her initial job was in a hospital in Coimbatore did not deter the ambitious girl, and she was sure of getting into a major hospital in a Metropolis later; from there, she would plan her journey to Europe.

Her departure was expected for quite some time and there were no emotional scenes in The Nest, except Lisie's roommate Weepy Seetha being unhappy to go see her roommate go. When she was about to weep, she was comforted by Kadambari who reminded her Madam Agatha's instructions that no one should be left alone in a room, that she could move into Kadambari's room shortly since her own roommate Gouri roommate was waiting for her posting orders from a nationalised bank, and would leave soon. She had received the confirmation letter from the bank, had already completed the preliminary formalities, and was only waiting for the communication about the centre of posting. Since she had indicated that she had no particular preference in this regard—as was the case with many girls—and was prepared to work anywhere in South India, papers might not be delayed too long. The indication from their regional office was that she might land up in a small town in Karnataka, where enough hostel facilities were available.

With so many girls leaving in quick succession, Kadambari was a little concerned about the future of The Nest. But Agatha was unmoved. 'I am delighted, if not excited that the girls found a path of their own at the opportune time,' she said proudly. This was precisely what she had wanted. She had taken a firm decision that no new admissions would be made until the dust had settled down on all fronts. Firstly, the financial position had to stabilise and once she had sufficient back-up funds in her kitty, the next move could be planned. The board had also been apprised of the same; after all those scandals and anonymous emails to the benefactors abroad, the chairman had also advised her to lie low for some time so that her rivals would take it as a tactical withdrawal from the arena.

Among the girls who had left, only Gouri had promised to donate a portion from her salary to The Nest for some time. About Lisie, Madam was aware that there would not be any surplus left from her meagre salary for such donations. She also had to save a little money for her future plans abroad. Surprisingly, the twins were the first to come out with their generous offer. With their store of organic vegetables becoming very popular, particularly among the housewives, they had enough surplus money with them. Strangely, the aunties who had been frequenting the municipal vegetable market in the past, where they used to bargain for each item aggressively, never even looked at the price list exhibited at the twins' store. The prices were written clumsily with a piece of chalk, and were being updated daily. And they were sure that Kamatchi, who sat at the cash counter, would not cheat. They were happy on many counts. Apart from the vegetables being poison-free, the prices were reasonable and the measuring scale thoroughly reliable. Earlier, they used to leave the market grumbling that they had been cheated on any of these counts, or possibly, on all.

And it was one such Iyengar lady in her early 80s and still doing her weekly shopping herself, despite some arthritic problems, who was one of their regular customers. In fact, she used to ask her son to stop the car in front of the shop and let her do the shopping herself, limping all the way. As one who had disliked using a walking stick, she did not want her daughter-in-law to help her in this; she was made to sit in the car. This is my area, by doing this I would continue to have a feel of the market and recollect my glorious Mylapore days at least, she said gleefully. As one who had lived long in Mylapore, Chennai, where her husband was a professor in a college, she was a regular visitor at the market and was aware of the current price of each and every vegetable. Interestingly, the shop-owners used to grumble at the very sight of the limping old lady but they did admire her combative spirit, even at that age.

It was the same auntie who had suggested that if they were fighting against poisoning of the vegetables, why not take a close look at the milk that was being sold in town also. Why not think of starting a small dairy, too, with a couple of animals?

A dairy? What is that, wondered the twins.

Kamatchi did not know what the old lady was talking about. The twins had not tasted milk in their life so far, other than the trickle put in their coffee; they didn't know that the milk in circulation was adulterated and not reliable. So used to black tea and coffee, they just didn't know anything about this milk business and the associated adulteration going on in the market.

'Why milk, even curd, butter, ghee and things like that are adulterated,' alleged the lady. 'They would pollute even mother's milk, if they could!'

What is this adulteration in milk, wondered the twins. They had seen the milk vendor pedalling his old bicycle and ringing the bells in the early hours of morning, using the public tap for diluting the milk, fully aware that the Municipal water could be unsafe, but they were not familiar with what the kind of impurities.

Slowly, things were becoming clearer to the girls. *Mami* (old lady) was talking about rearing cows and buffaloes, and milking them for selling their milk to the people.

Although they had seen cows and buffaloes grazing in the fields near the chawl and Chettiar's farm, they did not know how they could be reared and milked.

When consulted, Madam giggled for some time.

'Well, ambition is always good. I envy you. It's in this age that one should dream,' said Madam.

Kamatchi blushed, thinking that Madam was poking fun at them.

'It was that *mami*, not our idea...' she stuttered.

'So what? Let it be your idea...this is the time to dream the mountain and not the valley!' Agatha added.

But she explained that this one would be a very big project, and one needed a lot of money for it. 'Anyway, let the existing business stabilise for now. You can revisit the idea after two or three months,' she advised.

The girls nodded reluctantly, and agreed to come back after two or three months. But they were to return after two or three weeks, conceding that they could not sleep without brooding on it. In fact, visuals of the animals grazing in the fields and Kamalachi milking them in a small shed had started appearing in their dreams. Kamatchi had even zeroed in on the names for a couple of them after some arguments between them: Lalitha, Padmini and Ragini.

Madam Agatha was stunned. Things had taken a serious turn at last, she realised. Anyway, since it is an expensive proposition, two animals will do for the present. Let Ragini wait!

'We know it,' said Kamatchi, showing her passbook. It appeared they had gone around the cattle market and assessed the going rates for good quality cows and buffaloes.

'But this is not at all sufficient,' commented Madam, eyeing the entries in the passbook.

'We know that, too,' smiled Kamalachi. 'That's why he have approached our Madam. We know that you would be able to find out some way...'

These girls think I have a magic wand, chuckled Agatha. Anyway, she did not want to disappoint them.

'Okay, let me consult Raja sir.'

The girls agreed immediately, since they knew that he was capable of finding a solution.

When Raja returned from his overseas trip he was briefed about the proposed adventure of the girls, and he was very excited.

'Why not? Let it be rearing of milch animals in the beginning to grow as a dairy. After all, isn't it the responsibility of government banks? We hear a lot from the politicians about helping the needy. Now is the time to prove it. A perfect case for photo opportunity, since the girls were the victims of the shameful inferno.'

Then the issue of putting up a shed to house the animals—that, too, in hygienic surroundings—came up. Here again, Raja could convince the landlord who had leased out the farm land to the girls. The landlord was immensely pleased that this land of his that had remained barren for ages had suddenly turned fertile, and was being converted into a farm by the girls through their own efforts. Judging by their past dealings, he promised to help them in putting up a shed himself. After all, the dung and urine used as manure by the twins were going to nourish his land, too.

Thus came Lalitha and Padmini, immediately after the shed was put up.

They had invited the same Iyengar *mami*, who had given the idea first, to the simple opening function; the old lady was made to cut the ribbon and light the traditional lamp. When she was anxious to know why such charming names were given to the cows, it was Agatha who reply with a broad smile. 'Aren't these cows the darlings of the girls?'

'Not only lighting the lamp, I want to be the first customer, too!'

Mighty well pleased with the gesture of the girls, she ordered for delivery of two litres of milk every morning. Their servant will come in the early morning and they should be ready by that time. But the consumer activist in her was to wake up immediately.

'Anyway, let us see whether to continue or not!'

She advised the girls not to experiment too much by mixing exotic components in the milk so as to make their product attractive. 'Milk should be sold as milk, nothing but milk,' declared the lady amidst applause from the audience.

Your next aim could be towards dairy products like butter, ghee, curd etc., suggested the lady. 'But take your own time and never jump into anything aggressively. Over-ambition is the path to greed, the biggest enemy of man which has ruined many good people,' she warned. The twins did not forget to thank the *mami* for her invaluable advice, and touched her feet in reverence.

Madam Agatha was very excited. When Kadambari met her in the evening, she was beaming with happiness.

'Now I feel like a proud mother bird, who had shown their little ones what their wings were for and watched them spread their wings and fly away one day, never to return.'

'Absolutely, ma'am,' Kadambari agreed. 'What could be more satisfying? But one small correction. You should change "never to return" to "return occasionally".'

As destiny would have it, the twins from the slums whose admittance had caused such furore within the organisation turned out to be the ones who came out successful in life, as was predicted by Didi.

'Because they were humble, ambitious and conscious of their own limitations at the same time,' commented Kadambari.

'No wonder... God helps the needy,' nodded Agatha.

They were all sure that the twins were going to succeed immensely in life, and in that process they would make all those behind the Kilikoodu proud.

The Big Crunch

The Nest was just not the same after the misfortune of Parveen and the departure of the twins and Lisie. It was as if a thin shroud of the graveyard's silence has descended upon it. Hushed talk and over cautious tones were prevalent…even the usually boisterous Didi had gone dumb.

Of course, Lisie's departure was not unexpected. But the tragedy of Parveen really shook The Nest. Then that sudden goodbye to the twins. Interestingly, they'd become quite close to the other girls in a short a time, much to the surprise of Madam Agatha and others. They had a rare knack of getting close even with strangers; the kind of energy they spread was amazing. They were also keen on the sustaining the same level of relationship with others through their pep talk. As Didi had commented once, one could learn a lot from the lives of people who had carved out a future on their own efforts, perhaps more than what one could learn from religious texts or the sermons of scholars.

Strangely, Madam Agatha had changed a lot in recent days. She was not seen reminding the girls that this was not a couch to relax on, and only a launch pad for the future. Neither did she repeat that this was just a branch to perch on for some time, a nest to rest for a night. In the morning one has to fly out and

The Nest does not expect her to return. She had realised later that she was a bit harsh in making these assertions. In fact, it had forced the girls to comment amongst themselves that it was sad that Madam had thought of them as unwanted fugitives. But they were to realise later that one should appreciate the kind of challenges the poor Madam was facing to run this unique organisation. This strengthened their resolve to quicken their efforts to fly out on their own at the earliest.

Although encouraging the girls to leave The Nest as quickly as possible, Agatha suffered the pangs of parting later. Within such a short time, the girls had become so close to her that The Nest had transformed itself into a well-knit family. Quite a strange experience when compared to what she had felt during her long stint as the warden of college girls' hostels. Despite trying to console herself that it was the fate of a 'mother bird', the rationalisation didn't succeed in reducing the burden in her mind.

Moreover, the anxiety about the future of the organisation was also on the increase. Started with enthusiasm and missionary zeal, it was becoming clearer that it was not that easy to run such an organisation. Strangely, her trust in fate and destiny was on the increase. It was not that she didn't know that it was an acceptance of one's weakness and lack of will power. But she had realised that, of late, her mind had turned into a quagmire of complex thoughts and beliefs.

'How's everything, Agatha?' the colonel would enquire often, and her response to it would be a casual 'Getting along, Fernandez!' The colonel was quite unhappy with such an evasive reply from her close friend. It was clear that something was bugging her and that she was not as lucid as she used to be. The colonel decided that she didn't want to bother Agatha with more probing questions...

After taking over as the secretary temporarily, Kadambari was to realise that the financial position of The Nest was indeed under stress, making Madam a bit irritable. Since the generation of revenue was Madam's responsibility, she could only look at reducing the expenses to whatever extent possible.

'We may have to tighten our belts a bit, we are in a real financial crunch,' she once told Didi.

'Right buddy! In a way, it might be good for the girls—it will keep their waistlines in check!' quipped Didi, adding, 'And if you look around, you could get easy clues for it.'

When Kadambari blinked, she pointed to the courtyard. It was getting dark and the lights in the garden were in full glow.

'Don't you notice anything striking?' asked Didi.

Kadambari stood clueless.

'Do we need these many tube lights in this small garden? After all, won't the birds returning to The Nest look for a veil of darkness?'

Kadambari nodded in sheer awe of the lady. She is spot on! Karthikeyan had put up lamp posts all around rather lavishly, so that it lights up the entire compound.

'Yeah, he could afford this luxury, but not this poor organisation,' agreed the new secretary.

Didi beamed her typical disarming smile.

It was then that Kadambari remembered about Sarala often murmuring about the rising electricity bills. But she did not do anything concrete to set it right. In addition to the periodic rise in the tariff, the usage had also been on the increase. It was only now that Kadambari noticed that all the lights in the garden were in full glow up to around half past 10 or so. When Sarala had insisted that it should be so since it's a girls' hostel, Madam had nodded in agreement. But Kadambari was sure that this was an avoidable luxury. Although the light in front of Karupayyan's cage could stay turned on throughout the night, others could be put off by around 9 o'clock or so. Moreover, there were street lights close to the compound wall which lit up the northern and southern corners of the garden throughout the night. If two more lights are installed on the vacant poles in between, it would provide enough brightness to the front area. This could be done easily if someone could influence the municipal authorities. And the ever-helpful trustee Anita Subramaniam readily agreed to interfere, and managed the task without much effort.

Although Karupayyan kept murmuring, he did not have the guts to do so in the presence of Madam Agatha. Interestingly, all the girls at the hostel were the first to take a cue from all these moves for cutting the expenditure. They took it upon themselves to reduce the usage of power and water as their share.

Agatha was happy that Kadambari could put the message across strongly to the other girls at the right moment. She also briefed the other trustees about it. Cook Janaki also agreed to bring down the kitchen expenses to whatever extent possible.

When Mu. Ka. Raja came to know about all these moves, he was quick to contact Madam Agatha.

'Do you want me to do anything in this regard?'

Agatha was stunned for a moment, and was thinking of a proper reply. Then Raja added that though he knew many moneyed businessmen—who were known philanthropists, too— it was but natural to expect some kind of *quid pro quo* from the donees, which could possibly go against the ethics of the trust. He had already tied up with some charitable trusts of the area in the beginning itself, and promised to look for more in the nearby towns where he had good contacts.

Didi was also quick to act by following up with her papa about the promises he had made about some prospective Australian donors.

Later, Professor Othello Abdulla complained, 'How come you didn't brief me about your resource crunch? If we're not coming to your aid in times of need, why should we be in the board at all? All along, I was under the impression that the donations from abroad and whatever you could muster from here was sufficient. Anyway, let me see what I can do about it.'

Anita Subramaniam also backed him. These supportive gestures from unexpected quarters did help boost Agatha's sagging spirit.

It was then that she was approached with an attractive offer to do a documentary on The Nest by a gentleman based in Manila, Philippines. He spoke fluently Tamil, since his ancestors were from Madurai. Although Agatha was excited about the project—it being of international relevance and all—she didn't want to take a decision on her own. When the colonel couldn't be contacted on phone, she got in touch with the chairman instead. As is normal, Justice Padmanabhan thought for a while and enquired about the people behind the venture and their antecedents. Obviously, this was an area where the information had to be collected from outside, and when she was about to ask for time, came another sharp question from him.

'Are you aiming for the satisfaction in taking up such a noble cause, or the publicity behind that will come from it?'

Hesitating for a moment, she stuttered, 'Both. Contentment is primary but who would shun a little publicity that goes with it?' The suppressed chuckle from the other side spoke a lot, and Agatha was quick to understand its import.

Later, when she confided in the colonel, she said that she was in total agreement with the chairman, and that publicity ought to follow one day or the other for all such noble efforts.

Weepy Seetha Weeps No More

When Kadambari came to know that VP Seetha had a love affair in the past, she was pleasantly surprised. Strangely, it was Madam Agatha who noticed a visible change on her face.

'Our Weepy can laugh, too,' commented Agatha.

'Yes, our Weepy can laugh, too!' agreed Kadambari.

'But I never knew she could be like this.'

'There was a time when she was known as the "laughing doll"—one who could cut jokes and burst out laughing. We always avoided accompanying her to a cinema theatre; more so, if it was comedy movie. She would just laugh out loud at inopportune moments!'

'When she laughs, the whole atmosphere brightens up. As if all are joining her in gaiety.'

'Perhaps her childlike innocence charms others and illuminates the place.'

'Anyway, a big consolation for me,' sighed the colonel. 'After all, wasn't it me who had christened her a "Weepy"?'

'Not so, Fernandez! She felt the whole world was against her.'

Kadambari had many things to ask when they were alone. But before that, Seetha herself did the talking.

'See, the dawn is so beautiful!' she commented.

'Yeah.'

'Days are unusually bright, too.'

'And the nights are oddly moonlit!' added Kadambari.

Seetha beamed a big smile in return. And Kadambari did not want to remind her that it was the full moon period. By that time the real truth behind the 'unusually bright' days and 'oddly moonlit' nights had come out in the open.

That childhood romance of Seetha! When she heard about it, Kadambari could not control her laughter.

'A romance tale of our own Weepy! Certainly, that guy would have been a virtuous soul. He might have had a magic wand to convert a commoner like Cinderella into a princess,' the colonel told Agatha later.

That sullen look, as if some calamity was bound to happen any moment, had disappeared from her face. Strangely, it was the colonel who had promised to convert 'Weepy' into 'Bubbly' within 41 days. Although nothing miraculous like that happened, she did change to some extent and did not mind listening to jokes…even sharing a couple of them while in good mood—but becoming chirpy or bubbly was a far cry still. She was even prepared to go out for a matinee show of a comedy film, carefully selected by Kadambari. She was afraid that a film that made women cry could be dangerous, since it would have been sufficient to turn Seetha into Weepy again.

Seetha's old love episode appeared to be straight from a Mills & Boon story. It had started at the primary class stage, where a bench mate Ramkumar was her closest pal. This friendship continued until they passed out of the school. During their college days, when they had studied in different colleges in different towns, they exchanged some letters but they were too formal with plenty of courtesy thrown in, not at all sufficient to kindle any kind of fire within them to sustain it further. Like any other episode of this nature where there were no real sparks, the relationship was also bound to be distant; childhood memories were not sufficient to drive it further. As in most of these childhood romances, the boy went his way and the girl on her own. Like all love stories, Ram would have gone to the Middle East or somewhere in the North on the lookout for greener pastures. Similarly, after completing her studies, Seetha would have been waiting anxiously for an eligible suitor to come riding on a white horse, as it so happens in folk tales.

It was then that the tragedy had struck. Seetha's mother committed suicide in unfortunate circumstances and the creditors had started harassing her for recovering their dues. And after that, her father was too weak to handle any kind of situation. It was then that she was forced to flee the place, trying to forget her past and unsure of her future. It was known only much later that he had also committed suicide to join his ill-fated wife.

Then how come did Ram trace out old mate Seetha, living in an unknown town far away? As destiny would have it, having heard of her tragic story, the ever-persistent Ram who incidentally had transformed himself into a successful businessman—owning a couple of stores in Ajman in the Middle East—managed to trace Seetha's whereabouts. Nobody knows how divine love was kindled all of a sudden in his mind, possibly out of sheer sympathy. In this *Kalyuga* where monkeys are not around to assist the proverbial Ram, only destiny—in the form of social media—served the purpose and could unite couple, as it did.

Possibly, somewhat emboldened by the continuous motivational goads by the colonel and supported by Madam, she opened fresh Facebook and Twitter accounts—that, too, in with pseudonym 'Weepy', without revealing where exactly she was located. In fact, she had kept away from social media for a long time for the fear that her creditors would trace her wherever she might be. The fact that one of them did succeed later is another story. Of course, her profile photo was that of Alia Bhatt, the Bollywood movie star, but in one of the group photos on the timeline, she was seen as real Seetha with Lisie and Kadambari, all wearing dark glasses. Possibly an inadvertent post under the impression that such glasses were sufficient to conceal one's identity. However, as a prominent blogger and an active social media person, Ram could easily locate his childhood pal.

Aggressive search followed without the help of any monkeys, which ended in another unexpected call at The Nest. As providence would have it, it was the maid Devaki, again, who answered the phone in the lobby. Unable to forget the unpleasant incident of the past, Devaki had initially refused to connect the call but charmed by the sweet voice of the caller, she agreed to note down his name and the cell phone number.

Thus, like any other Boy meets Girl story ending happily, Ram did meet Seetha in the lobby of The Nest, under the watchful eyes of Madam. It appeared that Mother Mary herself had cautioned her the previous night, against putting any hurdles in the holy communion of Ram and Seetha, which would be nothing but meddling in the affairs of another religion. And even a child knew this communion was destined to happen.

Ignoring the objections of his parents who had concluded a good deal with a wealthy merchant who was desperately on the lookout for a handsome NRI boy for his elder daughter, Ram professed his divine love towards Seetha. In fact, the merchant had offered a fabulous dowry in the form of five grounds (around 12000 sq.feet) of land in Coimbatore, and cash, gold, silver vessels, and a brand new white Maruti Swift Dzire to match. The car had already been registered in the name of the girl and kept unused. This ended in a clash with the typical MN Nambiar-type of villain, rushing out of the Kodambakkam studio floor, without even removing his make-up, to scuttle the proposed marriage to Seetha. But throttling all the plans of his villainous father, Ram got the marriage registered as the first marriage of the day at a remote registrar's office. Interestingly, the registrar, a keen Virendra Sehwag fan, hugely pleased with himself for having achieved his ambition of completing a triple century of marriages before his retirement due at the end of the month, distributed ladoos among the members of the marriage party.

At last, When Weepy flew out of The Nest in a boisterous mood holding Ram's hand, all the girls had assembled at the portico to see her off. Even the colonel had come down to bless the couple. Placing her hand on the bride's head, she beamed that at last 'Weepy' had turned 'Bubbly'.

And taking a last look at The Nest with a deep sigh, Seetha got into the waiting car and disappeared.

It was siesta time and Didi was relaxing in a sofa in the lobby, with her eyes closed. There was a half-opened book on her lap.

Apoorva hesitated for a moment. Is she dozing off? Or lost in one of her own weird dreams? Dreams which only she can conjure. Is it proper to disturb the lady now?, Apoorva wondered. She coughed once, which made the Didi move a bit; but she was still wandering through some wild forests.

Apoorva cleared her throat again, which woke the lady up. She stared at the girl as if she was an alien from another planet. Then quick to come back to senses, she gestured her to come nearer.

'Sorry, *Akka*!' Apoorva flushed.

Didi called the girl and made her sit close to her. She stroked her hair and patted the cheeks lovingly.

'My sweet little kitten!' she beamed. 'The only one of its kind in this Nest!'

It was then that Didi noticed the sullen look on her face.

'What happened Apu, didn't you sleep last night?'

Apoorva shook her head. Didi was the only person in The Nest who called her by that pet name.

'The night before?'

'Nah...'

'Wow.' She fondled her cheek and asked searchingly. 'Isn't this the age to be cheerful, enjoying all those bright things in life? But you seem to be upset about something. About your *Appa* and *Amma*?'

Hesitating for a moment and eyeing a tiny bird trying hard to perch on the window bar, she said, 'Not that, they worry me no longer. They know how to quarrel and patch up later...'

'Then?'

'Tell me frankly, *Akka*, what happened to our dear Parveen? Whenever I close my eyes I can see her glowing face in front of me. In spite of all those horrible problems she used to put on a cheerful face to me. It was only during the last stage, when she found all the roads closed, that she turned grim and found consolation in singing all those sad and soulful songs…'

'Oh, that's what's worrying you,' Didi sat back on the couch. 'Look, Apu, there are certain things one has to forget and forgive in life. You're too young to understand all those intricacies. I always admire Madam Agatha who had the guts to take that girl in without too much questioning. A much-targeted girl from a faraway state. But as usual, Madam's sixth sense would have shown her the way.'

'She is divine. She was like Mother Agatha to my *Appa*.'

'Anyway, no need to worry too much about her. Take it as if she has left The Nest for ever. Hasn't Madam Agatha told you right from the beginning that all of you would have to fly out one day or the other?'

'But this was not the kind of flight she had hinted. How can we abandon her in darkness like that? Don't we have the right to know what happened to her? Doesn't the police have the responsibility to get to the roots of the incident and track down the culprits?'

'Oh, no. The ability to ask questions may be a God-given gift. But one can't expect to get the correct answer always. Life is not like a crime-thriller where the detective would appear in the end and clear all the doubts. Quite the opposite! Life is nothing but an open-ended story. Won't it be better to leave some doubts as they are and make the reader ponder on it later? After all, aren't such clueless riddles the very element that make life interesting?' There was a mischievous twinkle in her eyes. '

'Dunno!' Apoorva blinked, and Didi continued with the same twinkle.

'Once a reader questions a writer—why he made the protagonist of the novel disappear into darkness at the end, leaving the readers puzzled etc.—then the writer has to reply with a guffaw that he naturally expected his readers to be reasonably intelligent so that they would be able to find out a solution of their own.'

'So you also want to leave my Parveen as a character in a novel?' asked Apoorva. She was not impressed by yet another riddle-like answer from the enigmatic lady.

'After all, isn't life like an open-ended book?' asked Didi, and obviously, Apu did not have an answer. It's yet another puzzle of the mysterious 'Lady on the wheelchair, with a Third Eye', as Kadambari used to say, thought Apu.

Madam Agatha Turns Gloomy

Sadly, when Weepy turned 'Bubbly', it was Madam Agatha's turn to become gloomy. Even her close confidante Colonel Fernandez could not identify the reasons, since the Madam was refusing to open up with a convenient excuse that she 'was fine, as she always was'. It was then that the colonel authorised Didi to go after the real reason. She was fairly confident that the clever lady on the wheelchair, who claimed to have a 'Third Eye', might be able to get some answers. The colonel was indeed worried about the failing health of the lady. In fact, after the last check-up Dr Geetha had warned Agatha to avoid 'over anxiety over trifles', since she was a potential heart patient with high blood pressure and cholesterol. The colonel was worried that the youthfulness and verve, which were the hallmark of the lady in the past, had disappeared.

What really happened that made Madam so depressed, Didi asked Kadambari. But Kadambari, too, admitted that she had no clue. However, it was revealed later that a couple of days ago there was a lengthy email from the landlord Karthikeyan, which was later followed by a long-distance call from him that day. After the call, Madam looked downcast and had withdrawn to her office without talking to anybody. It was in this background that Didi wanted to have a frank chat with her, along with Madam's protégé Kadambari.

They were sitting on the benches of the lawn, Madam, Kadambari and Didi. Throwing her glances on stray objects in the lawn, she remarked how disorganised the whole compound had become and how she could not pay attention to all these things for quite some time. 'See that dustbin kept carelessly on the north-eastern corner, which ought to have been in the south western corner? And the dry leaves piled under the mango tree, the heap of garbage among the row of rose plants? The gardener Perumal from an orchard nearby, who used to mend the garden at least once a week, has now become irregular. He is probably not quite happy with the way he is being compensated for sharing his expertise for a while now. After all, by mere experience and hard work he turned from a mere gardener to an expert horticulturist and a specialist landscaper,' she explained. Not convinced by Agatha's repeated assertions that wages could be paid only for the quantum of work done and not for one's experience in the field, he had murmured repeatedly as only a Perumal could do. Even his murmur had a slang of south Canara, and Madam had to caution him at last that she hated murmuring and would rather welcome a face-to-face banter. Amused by these grievances of Madam, Kadambari kept quiet, knowing well that it was not the time to interfere.

But not so with the irrepressible lady on the wheelchair. Never to miss an opportunity for not mincing her words, she remarked, tongue-in-cheek, 'What if the dustbin was kept on the north-eastern corner instead of the south-western? After all, a dustbin is a dustbin and would continue to be so during its life time, and I don't see any apparent dissymmetry in its present position. You now look like an old Mother Superior with thick eyebrows, and thick spectacles, a relic of the past, since that tribe exists no longer, except in movies and TV serials.'

It appeared Madam had not heard Didi properly, and her loud soliloquy followed about the sapping of energy. 'I was this, I was that' etcetera. Kadambari then felt that this was the time for her to intervene.

'It's all in the mind, ma'am,' she reminded. 'It seems you are unduly worried about something and keep on brooding unnecessarily about it. It was you who had told us to forget the past, think about the present, and look towards the future…'

Madam Agatha was silent for a moment. Then she mumbled.

'May be. Anyway, I am not arguing with you. But frankly, I am a bit worried about the future of the institution we all love so much.'

Then the subject of Karthikeyan's mail and call came up.

The generous man had leased out the campus for a fairly long period and did not make further enquiries about it, since he was immensely rich and was not bothered about the paltry returns from the plot. Of course, there were wild allegations that he had leased out the land, mainly in view of the unconfirmed reports that the government was trying to acquire it for their own purposes. Once a charitable institution set up for a noble purpose started functioning there, it was not easy for the government to acquire it and there was public outrage against it. However, it was clarified later that it was a mischievous piece of report spread by the broker lobby who were trying hard for some kind of deals for the plot. Anyway, during his last visit, he was quite happy about the good work done by Madam Agatha and her team, and the way the whole campus had been kept clean and tidy. He was also sure that the lady who had substantial experience in managing a convent hostel would be able to maintain the same standards in the days to come.

'Then what happened now,' asked Didi.

Nothing to panic, Madam assured. But she informed them that a series of mischievous mails had reached him, too, covering all sorts of baseless allegation—from promoting atheism to indulging in illegal activities. It was alleged that the girls from the hostel had been questioned persistently by the local police, and that Madam herself was apprehended by them and was in custody for a day. Also, that she was still on bail, and could be summoned again.

'Oh, this was what was bothering you!' Didi laughed aloud. 'Mind you, ma'am, this world is not in short supply of scoundrels and mischief-mongers, and fictitious mails such as these are one of their popular weapons. Those who do not have the spine to fight face-to-face use such dubious methods. Stabbing from behind is an ancient art, practised from the origin of mankind. After all, won't a broad back tempt one to try his hand with a knife? And about rumours…well, they are meant to be rumours until the Oxford dictionary decides to chuck them out. Obviously, only poor substitutes are available in the market. Anyway, for heaven's sake, please don't be upset by this nonsense. If you start worrying like this, it is a clear victory for them. You getting worried and upset is what they want. Don't give them that!'

'Still… The Nest…'

'Nothing is going to happen to The Nest, come wind, come rains,' assured Didi. 'If you are worried about money, money is something that always frowns at the needy and smiles at the rich. But the world is not that unkind yet, and there are a few noble souls who smile at the needy still. That is how the world had existed this long! And about this gentleman Karthikeyan, I have heard about him, that he is a thorough gentleman. I would like to talk to him on phone or conduct a video chat. There is no reason why he should disbelieve a rank outsider like me, a Jew at that!' Didi chuckled.

Agatha smiled, still unsure of herself though.

'You could count on me, and people like me!' Didi declared. 'After all, what is money for? This institution has been set up for empowering hapless girls, as you had claimed and are well-acknowledged for all over, even by your rivals. But I have always looked at the institution from a totally different angle. In the present times, when the whole world is going back to the days of racist divides, here is a former devout nun taking cudgels and championing the cause of intolerance and pluralism. Unthinkable. I salute you ma'am. You are like Mother Teresa to me.'

'Oh, no,' intervened Agatha. 'No comparison with the great soul.'

'In an era when external forces dictate how one should think, speak and write, the dress they wear, and the food they eat etc., where is the freedom we all boast of? Anyone who dares to defy their diktats are being silenced forever, aren't they? I am saying this because I have the right to do so, as a Jew, more than anybody else in the world. But mind you, I was born a Jew but not groomed as one, since my parents were liberal. Wasn't it George Bernard Shaw who had once said that there was only one religion, though there were a hundred versions of it? My parents believed in that phrase,' Didi said, visibly excited. 'In these days of nationality and sub-nationality, where do the human rights stand? I have heard *netas* (politicians) talk about humanism but do they ever practise it at all? No, they don't!'

Madam Agatha nodded spiritedly. She remembered Albert Einstein's comments on nationality: 'If my theory of relativity was proven successful, Germany would claim me as a German and France would declare me a citizen of the world. Should my theory prove untrue, France would say that I was a German, and Germany would declare that I am a Jew.'

Didi appeared to be in a mood to talk endlessly. She continued:

'We Jews are the most haunted tribe in the whole world. After the destruction of our temple in Jerusalem, we had to flee for life, and had scattered among all the seven continents crossing the five oceans. We were looking for safe havens and greener pastures—all in the name of religion. Even now, in the name of the Palestinian crisis, we are being dubbed as villains by some political forces in India... I was happy that ages ago a few groups of West Asian Jews had taken refuge on the western coast of India, that is now Kerala, where they were welcomed with both hands and assured of protection. In fact, it was one place where even now you can see our old synagogue and other remnants. There is a village where one can find a Krishna temple, a Jewish synagogue, a Muslim mosque and a Christian church—all co-existing within a radius of half a kilometre. Those were the times...when the rulers were so liberal and tolerant.'

Kadambari was looking at her with astonishment. She did not know anything about Judaism and it was the first time she was meeting a Jew. Nostalgic about the past, Didi continued with added vigour.

'In fact, when all our people were ecstatic about migrating to Israel, my family was the one that had thought otherwise. When my parents chose to migrate to Australia instead—where they had some close friends—I wanted to remain here, in the land of my birth. I love this country, the culture, the tolerance, the democracy where everyone has a say, despite some occasional hiccups here and there. But democracy was so strong to survive all such threats back in the day.'

'True', Agatha thought for a while. 'No doubt, this country is great. Where else in the world do so many religions co-exist? With so many castes and sub-castes and a highly complex divides, we have still survived as a nation—a strong nation, too. Haven't we?'

'Absolutely,' agreed Didi. 'That's why I am assuring you that you shouldn't worry about this institution at all. We are with you, at least me and Kadambari. And, of course, that young girl Apoorva, who is bound to continue here until she completes her course. If there is any problem—like paucity of funds, we can look for alternate options, since the world is so wide and large and there is no dearth of noble men, possibly in some remote corners of the world. Leave it to me, Madam. Meanwhile, I'm so happy that grown up birds are flying away, one by one. That is the law of the nature. We should welcome their departure and wish them all the best. That's what The Nest stands for.'

'Then I should think of considering a few deserving cases now, since a couple of girls are due to fly out soon,' Madam said, slightly unsure still.

'Why not?' supported Didi. 'That is precisely what I am emphasising. The show must go on, come what may. The excitement lies in fighting, fighting till we win, as you yourselves have been preaching.'

Kadambari clapped in agreement and got up.

Thoroughly reassured by now, a relaxed Madam Agatha beamed a big smile at them, and it appeared as if she had grown at least 10 years younger.

'Thank you all', she hugged both the girls, and helped Didi turn her wheelchair back to the building.

Sabeena Soars

The next girl to fly out of The Nest was none other than Sabeena. A highly withdrawn girl, reluctant to chat even with her roommate Didi, Sabeena had always avoided talking about her past. Keeping it as a well-guarded secret, she avoided mentioning about it while talking even to Madam Agatha. Accompanied by her step sister Sainaba, she sat with a bowed head at the time of admission while the step sister did all the talking. But taking a quick look at the gloomy face of the girl, Agatha had understood her misery and did not try to probe further. The type of untidy dress she was wearing, when compared to that of her step-sister and the inherent fear and stutter in her speech, said it all and Agatha had admitted her straightaway—much to the surprise of Sarala, the secretary. What had happened to the otherwise tough Madam who used to hurl a volley of questions at the girls—more so, in case of those who were not properly introduced, Sarala had wondered.

Sixth sense! Sarala had told herself later. Madam had this uncanny sense of identifying the right candidate, humbling the skills of a seasoned human resources manager even.

Anyway, Sabeena had kept herself busy with her routine prayers, and reading the Holy Quran and other religious books. The only other book which had interested her was none other than *Arabian Nights*—the fascinating story of King Sharyar and his bride-to-be Scheherazade, who was made to narrate an endless story all through 'One thousand One nights' to keep the king engrossed in thereby escape the sword hanging over her head. It appeared she continued the narration uninterrupted for 'One thousand One nights', so that the enchanted king was kept awake. It was a classic case of how a narrative could sustain the interest and keep the listener glued to his seat. Still, even the never-ending poring over of *Arabian Nights* did not tempt Sabeena to narrate a couple of her own stories to her roommate. A rare breed indeed, who had no friends nor enemies, wondered Didi.

However, it was found later that her main enemy was none other than her own father, a known philanderer. A ruthless moneylender who had never compromised on his dues, he had many mistresses, known and unknown, all in places he had frequented during his sojourns. Besides he had also married two women from respected families. While the elder gave birth to Sabeena and her two younger sisters, the younger wife had two more girls. This infuriated the man very much, since he was desperately hoping for a couple of sons who would have taken care of his business, as he was getting old. When the disgruntled man—suitably empowered by an adequate dose of imported aphrodisiac—married again, this time a younger girl in the hope that at least she would present him with a lucky son, all hell was let loose in the family. Not to bother about the resistance from his women, he did not budge and brought the third wife home. Until then, she was staying in another house he owned. The younger one, this time from an ordinary family, with the added vigour of a virgin, could easily keep the husband under her thumb and call all the shots in the house. This aggravated the problem further.

When the senior women joined together occasionally to fight the common enemy, pandemonium prevailed in the house, much to the annoyance of the neighbours. At last, the secretary of the colony had to intervene and tell him in unambiguous terms that they could not put up with this any longer, and that they had to either put an end to the daily ruckus or move out of the colony. This complicated the issue further, since the secretary and the majority of the members of the colony were Hindus and they were Muslims. Interestingly, the two Muslim members of the committee chose to keep quiet, since they, too, were disturbed about the mayhem in their household and had taken it as a shameful symbol on the community as such.

Sabeena's major problem, however, was the persistent quarrels among the three ladies, who used to pick some issue or the other to settle scores. The old man was least bothered about these squabbles in the house and made it a point to leave early and return late from work. Meanwhile, the youngest wife also delivered a premature girl with visible handicaps, and the old man had no other option but to withdraw from making further adventures on the advice of the Imam of the Mosque, who was also getting fed up with him. He also wanted to stop the man from going for yet another bride at this age.

By this time, the bedlam at home had reached a point of no return, and a grown-up girl like Sabeena could not tolerate it any further. Incidentally, a couple of decent marriage proposals for her were also thwarted due the disrepute the family had already earned in the locality. When the relatives from the groom's side visited the place to enquire about the girl's family, they were told to walk through the bye-lane near their house for about 10 minutes without revealing their identity. While this party chose to return within eight and a half minutes, the next one to follow reversed their Innova car within six minutes. Such was the loud commotion in the family, which could be heard from outside.

Finding that her father was unable to interfere in the matter, Sabeena feared that if one of the women had picked up a weapon in the height of a fury, the whole issue would take a different turn. Spending sleepless nights, her health also deteriorated and she was afraid she would fall ill. To cap it all, when the younger brother of the junior-most wife—a road side Romeo—started visiting the house frequently and began making lewd comments on Sabeena, she could not bear it any further.

It was then that Sainaba, the step sister, encouraged her to leave the family at the earliest.

'Aren't you the elder? Jump out first, and I'll follow you later,' assured Sainaba.

Thus, when Sabeena was forced to take the painful final decision, even her mother did not want to stand in her way. Her father was away in Telengana on work. It was Sainaba who had accompanied Sabeena to The Nest without the knowledge of her mother and step mothers to present her case to Madam Agatha.

How this sudden change all of a sudden, Didi wondered, as did Madam Agatha. The girl was all smiles at the dinner table, and even laughed aloud when one of the girls cracked a stale joke. Since there was nothing new in the joke, other girls were wondering what happened to the saintly Sabeena. Was she hearing it for the first time?

Then one night, while in bed Sabeena narrated a rare love story from *Arabian Nights* where the sword-wielding hero had dared all the enemies in the name of his immortal love. Didi was awestruck. What happened to my virtuous roommate? Has the vicious Satan found an easy prey in the poor soul, she wondered.

But the secret came out in the open soon when her step sister met Madam Agatha with the happy news that, at last, Sabeena was matched with a guy working in an oil company in Qatar, drawing a decent salary. In fact, it was Sabeena's uncle, a younger brother of his father who ran a prosperous tobacco business in Kakinada, who had materialised this alliance. He was just the opposite of her father— a loving person, with an equally affable wife. Their only son was studying in Germany. Although in faraway Kakinada, he would often visit their ancestral home with huge packets of gifts for the kids. He chose such visits on days when his elder brother was out of station.

His visits were literal festival time for the kids, and they were all sad that they didn't have a father like him. It was during one of the visits with his wife that he came to know about Sabeena being in The Nest. This was a rude shock to him, since he had great liking for the girl.

'How come nobody told me about it? I would have taken her to my household! After all, she is my blood, too,' lamented the man to his wife.

But who will tell his brother, who is quite rude and non-compromising? The ladies chose to keep quiet.

Putting her up in The Nest, nothing but an orphanage in the eyes of the public, was a huge disgrace to the entire family—particularly to the uncle, who had a good reputation in business circles. Now that this was not an issue which could be discussed with his brother, he took it up as his responsibility as a dignified member of the family to find a suitable alliance for the girl and take her out of The Nest. Like Gouri's mother, he was also looking for a boy working abroad, preferably in the Gulf, so that the girl could fly out of this country. And it did work out at last, and Sabeena was to fly out of The Nest soon, after all the initial formalities regarding her nikah were finalised. He was particular that the entire family, including her parents, should be kept in the dark about the this until the last moment.

'Yet another Kodambakkam movie script, isn't it?' Agatha asked Kadambari.

'Correct, ma'am. Kodambakkam has a rare knack of sensing the future and putting it on their sets!' agreed Kadambari.

And those usual hugs, kisses, with group photos, and selfies and sobs and goodbyes took place. As one normally not moved on such occasions, Didi found her eyes burning.

'I used to wake up every morning to her reading the Holy Quran, her head covered like a devout Muslim. After all, these holy activities happening in the room, how come I haven't been purified, Madam?' she asked with tears in her eyes.

Agatha had no answer.

One more girl has come of age, Madam Agatha sighed. Although she was sad that yet another bird was to fly out shortly, as Didi had clarified, that's what The Nest was there for; and as the mother bird, she should be happy about it. It was almost like a mother marrying her daughter off at the appropriate age. It was normal for the mothers to cry desolately on such occasions, hugging and kissing her beloved daughter. There was always a lingering concern in their minds as to how this unknown guy, her husband, would treat her darling in the days to come.

Even Rishi Kanva had cried inconsolably when Shakuntala had left the ashram to join her husband Dushyantha, remembered Kadambari. This was destined to happen, one day or the other. A mother bidding goodbye to her daughter, a mother bird watching her tiny ones flying away, flapping their young wings.

The only consolation could be that there would be new birds coming in and taking their appointed place in The Nest. As Didi reminded, the show had to go on. Come winds, come rains, The Nest had to remain on the top.

Yes, I should decide to lift the temporary embargo and look at the list of girls eager to join The Nest, thought Agatha. The list had been kept in the back burner by her for quite some time, and even Sarala had no chance to glance through it when she was the secretary. After all, this had to be her own decision and she did not want others to intervene.

Joe Proposes to the Colonel

'Architects should be dreamers, like Brahma or Maya—the all-time great creators. An artist, and not just an architect! I'm fed up with those stereotyped structures without any stamp of a creator behind it.'

It was in a gathering of the architects that Joe, the architect, had made the comment. Be it a house, a hut or a mall, it should have the brush strokes of an artist...something unique, he had added.

'At last my Joe is becoming an artist. That, too, in this old age!' joked Colonel Fernandez.

'I'm not that old, you know! Besides, love and art can be appreciated at any age,' retorted Joe.

However, it was a friend who had attended that meeting who teased Joe later, commenting that it was about time that they all became artists. 'Let us all be creators; sad that precious time has been lost already,' the friend said.

But it was the colonel who was amazed. In fact, she had taken it as one of those jokes normally shared between a liberal dose of choice cocktails at a dinner gathering. But she was to realise later that Joe was quite serious about it. When he explained that he was trying to expand his activities in the Pune-Mumbai belt, the colonel was pleasantly amused. All along, he was posing as a content man, not eager to venture into any new projects.

What for, darling, he had once asked. Not for money's sake anyway, since he had enough of it already—bank deposits, bonds and other investments, and his earnings were sufficient to sustain a couple of generations. True to her nature, his wife Mary did not ask for any alimony at the time of separation, but he had kept substantial bank deposits for her and their two daughters. He had also promised that all their educational expenses would be met, and that if they wanted to study abroad, he would support them, wherever they might be. After the divorce, the girls were with their mother, with whom they were deeply attached.

But the vicar at the local church was thoroughly unhappy about the break-up at this age, and was not prepared to bless it. After all, Mary and her family were faithful members of the parish. Once one ties the knot in front of the altar, I am not here to untie it, he had said. 'Anyway, think twice and if you still can't solve your issues, better approach the court of the church' was his advice. But the couple decided to approach the civil court instead.

Meanwhile, the father asked.

'Why at all this painful decision, Joe?'

'I was terribly bored father,' was his reply.

'What about you, Mary?'

'I was horribly bored, father,' replied Mary.

Hailing from a village, the old vicar could not find out the real difference between 'terrible' and 'horrible', and shook his head and bade them goodbye. But he requested them to think twice if they ever thought of re-marrying.

Joe had a few clients in the Pimpri-Chinchwad belt, and had already put up some amazing villas there. He had never thought of expanding his activities further in that part of the country though. Despite some friends suggesting that opportunities were immense there, he was reluctant to take the plunge. But a couple of architects from Pune, with whom he had developed a close rapport in the past, had asked why they were not working together. Instead of building complexes, they could look into building 'designer villas' for high net worth individuals like businessmen and non-resident Indians. Incidentally, one of these partners was an artist and a well-known interior decorator, and was dreaming of building designer homes for people with deep pockets. With their long-standing connections in the area, they wouldn't face any difficulties in attracting new clients either.

'It's not for making money but doing something creative that would be seen and admired forever,' Joe explained. They were also planning to take the help of some consultants from abroad for these projects.

But when the colonel agreed that it would indeed be rewarding, Joe revealed that he planned to shift his base to Pune so that he could work more closely with the team. Moreover, such a challenging project involving art and engineering, and based on team work, would require continuous brain-storming among the team. They had already hired a place for their office, which was being done up tastefully. A website would be launched soon after finalising the name of the firm. They were in touch with a numerologist for it, too.

'No problem. But you would be able to fly down occasionally on weekends, won't you?' the colonel asked.

He shook his head immediately and made it clear that he had planned to live there until he had settled down in this new business environment. Of course, he was not sure himself whether he would change his mind later. Then, after hesitating for a moment, he asked if she would join him there.

'What for? I'm not an architect…' the colonel was puzzled.

'Not as a partner of the firm, but of life! We're going to be so good for each other,' he explained.

'Am I not now? Unless someone else has entered your life!'

'Do you consider me a flirt?'

'Not yet, but who knows about the fickleness of a man's mind?'

Then he made his intentions clear. No more of the occasional weekend sojourns and random holiday trips to hill stations. He wanted her to live with him forever. 'And why can't we think of marriage? A civil marriage outside the church?' he asked.

'Marriage?' the colonel was stunned 'Have you gone crazy? No way in this lifetime!'

'I can't wait for the next lifetime, darling,' exclaimed Joe. 'And who knows, we would, perhaps, be born again as animals… different species at that!'

'No arguments on that, Joe,' she pleaded. 'Let's talk about something more sensible.'

Seemingly, the colonel was not at all in the mood to change her mind but she did not want to dishearten Joe either, because he was so excited about the project.

'Let's not talk about it now and spoil your enthusiasm, Joe,' she said. 'Please continue with all your preparatory arrangements. After all, I'm with you always, and there wouldn't be any difficulty in working out suitable arrangements as and when time demands.'

She was not sure whether they could live under one roof without getting 'terribly bored' or 'horribly bored' after some time.

However, Joe did not appear pleased. Apparently, he had expected a firm response from her—a positive one, of course.

'Then what about a baby?' his voice faltered.

'A baby! Are you kidding me? No way!' the colonel laughed aloud. 'Utter nonsense. You live in romantic dreams even at this age?'

'No age limit for romance. And in this country of ours, aren't kids produced more by unromantic pairs?' Joe was visibly hurt. 'What I had in mind was a love child of two people who were so fond of each other…'

Although not romantic by nature, quickly gauging the depth of his feelings, the colonel wanted the matter to cool down for the present so that they could talk it over later in a more relaxed mood. She was sure that it was not a case of casual infatuation. In fact, Joe was deeply in love with her and had really meant what he had said. There was probably a clear void in his life which, he thought, could be filled only by a compatible person like Annie Fernandez.

'Okay, Joe,' she consoled him. 'It appears you are planning much ahead of time, like a real dreamer. Work on your project first, and we can decide on other things later.'

Then she hugged him tightly and kissed him on the lips passionately—quite unlike her. Her gesture put him at ease for the time being.

At The Nest, after the long chat where both Didi and Kadambari assured their enthusiastic support for taking the establishment to the next level, Madam Agatha was much relieved. She had even started scanning the list she had hidden scrupulously from all. After zeroing in on four names and thinking of selecting two out of them before making the next move, she wanted to consult Kadambari first, in whom she had great faith. Agatha wanted Kadambari to extract the information on the pretext of updating of the organisation's records; Kadambari had literally taken over the portfolio of administration once handled by Sarala—quite competently at that, and much to the satisfaction of the partner of Aiyer, Aiyer & Aiyer, no suspicions would be aroused.

It was in the morning the day after she had discussed the matter in detail with Kadambari—who was excited about inducting two new girls and was about to go through the records—that Agatha received a call from the colonel. Kadambari was also in the office after hurriedly being summoned for discussions.

Shaken and speechless for a moment, Agatha could not contain her anxieties any further.

'It would be the proverbial curtain for this institution. At last, I can pull out The Nest from the treetop with a barge pole....'she cried.

Stunned by her response, the colonel tried to explain the situation. In this age of smartphones and tablets, wasn't video chatting fairly simple? Even a small kid could operate such apps. Moreover, she was not going far away, or out of the country. And she assured Agatha that she could easily fly down in case of any emergency. Moreover, did The Nest depend that much on the occasional advices of a well-wisher who was not even a trustee?

'Have I ever considered you as just one of those well-wishers? Yours is the only number I can dial on my landline just from memory. You were the first person I approached to be a trustee after the chairman was inducted, and you had stoutly resisted and said that it was not your cup of tea. You had even said that you hated signing documents! And you are the first person I think of whenever I need to clear my doubts or need reassurance.'

The colonel was amazed by the unexpected emotional outburst from her friend. Her voice quivered many a time while she expressed her thoughts, and it was clear that she was deeply hurt. It was clear that she was trying to control her grief.

'Yes, Agatha, not that I don't understand the value of our friendship but I am faced with a different situation which has emerged suddenly,' the colonel tried to console her. 'I'm sure you would be able to run the show without my occasional visits to the campus. And we can always have a hearty chat on the telephone! And there is going to be no need to discontinue my chat sessions with the girls, which I am told they love. We can always get a projector and do video conference calls on the big screen in the hall.'

Agatha knew that these were mere excuses; she just didn't expect them from a person like Annie Fernandez. Gadgets like tablets, laptops, phone screens etc. couldn't substitute for the warmth and closeness of human relationship. Was there any gadget in the world which could be a substitute for a warm smile or a close hug, and a kiss in the case of lovers? But at that moment, Agatha could not say anything else to her on the telephone. She only wished to visit the campus at least once so they could have a more meaningful discussion on the subject.

Then what made the colonel call her on her cell phone?

Kadambari was also wondering about the same. The colonel could have easily come down and talked it over to do away with the misgivings in Madam Agatha's mind, and to give her the much-needed confidence boost. She probably did not want to face Agatha, thought Kadambari. But she had noticed that Madam Agatha's fighting spirit was now at the lowest ebb, and she was often found complaining of her sapping energy. Since a word of support from the colonel had always worked miracles, that was what she was looking for. But it seemed that the colonel was deliberately avoiding such a situation for fear that it would made her change her earlier decision.

It was a question of old friendship vs. the call of the heart, guessed Kadambari. Her bond with that architect friend of hers appeared to be much stronger.

Despite the telephonic conversation ending with the colonel assuring that she would think it over, Agatha was quite depressed, and Kadambari was also doubtful whether the lady would go back on her earlier decision. Meanwhile, during a recent check-up at Dr Geetha's hospital on her complaint of fatigue and unstable heartbeat, Madam Agatha's cholesterol level was found to be fairly high, coupled with variations in blood pressure. Since Kadambari had accompanied her to the hospital, she was a witness to the friendly advice of the doctor that the time had come for her to take better care of her health. She had even warned that excessive workload and anxiety could escalate her problems further. Kadambari noticed that the patient had nodded to all these briefings like a submissive student. Nevertheless, she was aware that it would be very difficult to discipline her once she was back at The Nest.

The exact same thing happened when Agatha was back at The Nest. Both the colonel and Kadambari had warned her many times that she should not poke her nose in every activity being carried out in the organisation. Agatha was very particular that unless she oversaw everything right from cooking, cleaning and gardening to checking the accounts, things would not be perfect as they should be. That is an old style of management and you should change with the times and try to delegate as much as possible, and supervise them all like a real boss, the colonel had advised. Despite her nodding at that moment, the onlookers were doubtful whether she would change at all.

After the lengthy telephonic conversation, a very depressed Madam Agatha withdrew to her bedroom quite early.

'It's a disaster, nothing but disaster. I need some rest', Kadambari heard her murmuring while walking to her room alone. When Kadambari tried to go with her, she was waved off with a degree of resent. 'I'm okay, don't worry,' she mumbled.

Later, Kadambari found out that she had skipped lunch and had continued to nap for a couple of hours—unusual, since she was not one for afternoon naps; some casual rest by reclining on her favourite armchair which had gathered the dust, sweat and memories of decades, sure. It was the only piece of furniture she had owned while in the convent, and had carried it wherever she went. Hearing her loud snore, the cook tried to peep in through the door which was not fully closed, and had found her sleeping peacefully.

It was the siren of the ambulance screeching into the porch which had alerted Kadambari. When she hurried down the stairs, she saw some hectic activities going on.

Two attendants assisted by Devaki and Janaki were carrying Madam Agatha into the stretcher, and then to the waiting ambulance. Later, Janaki admitted that there was no time to alert all the girls, as she had to summon the ambulance from Dr Geetha's hospital hurriedly. Although conscious, Madam Agatha was visibly tired and sleepy after the long siesta, and was perspiring profusely. She appeared to be in great pain because she was seen pressing her chest with a pillow. While Kadambari rushed in to change so she could accompany the patient, she was told by the attendants to follow in a rickshaw instead, since the patient had to be admitted as early as possible.

On reaching the hospital with Apoorva, they were told that she had been admitted into the Intensive Care Unit (ICU). Dr Geetha, who had known Agatha very well right from her convent days, assured the girls that there was nothing to worry, and that Agatha's condition was stable. They complimented Janaki for rushing her to the hospital in right time, since she had palpitations in the heart and had to be given injections straightaway.

It's all the blessings of Lord Murugan, admitted an emotional Janaki. Since Madam had skipped lunch and was in deep slumber for quite some time, she wanted to peep in and check whether all was well. Only then had she found that Madam Agatha was perspiring heavily, and had kept a pillow pressed on her chest—a sign of obvious discomfort. Dr Geetha's suspicion was that the patient had felt the early signs of unstable angina while at rest the previous night itself, due to over exertion or stress; and she did not want to wake others up, as was her wont.

A couple of hours later, a nurse came outside and told the anxious by-standers that Agatha was stable, and that she was sleeping peacefully.

'At this rate, she could be moved to a private room by tomorrow but she might have to be kept under observation for at least 48 hours. Considering her age and long-standing problems like high level of cholesterol, irregular blood pressure etc., the possibility of discharge from the hospital can be decided only after close monitoring,' said the nurse.

'Fine, let her take rest. It's only here that she would agree to rest anyway!' said Kadambari, trying to inject humour in the atmosphere.

Meanwhile, Dr Geetha, who was passing through the corridor, called Kadambari.

'No need for so many people hanging around. As you know, one can't enter the ICU. Tomorrow, she would be shifted to a private room, and one person would be allowed.'

Thus, Janaki and Apoorva were sent back to The Nest and brief the anxious Didi, who was following up continuously on her cell phone. Ultimately, Kadambari had to switch off the phone, since there was a strict restriction on using cell phones inside the hospital.

Relaxing on a bench near the ICU, Kadambari started brooding on some of the recent happenings at The Nest. The words of Didi and Kadambari had reassured Madam Agatha to a certain extent, and she was planning to restart the activities at The Nest. She had even started scanning the list of the girls who could be taken in after a lull. Then this unexpected torpedo from the colonel hit the scene. Nobody had ever expected such a turn of events. The colonel was the one person who was expected to be at the centre of activities at The Nest for a fairly long period, and was also the main source of strength for Madam Agatha; the only one she could look to for help in case of any contingency.

But Kadambari was sure that this would have been a very unpleasant decision to take for the colonel, too, because she had started cherishing her association with Kilikoodu immensely. The way the girls had taken her chat sessions seriously, and had reacted exuberantly to, had really made her younger and energetic, too.

Now, what next? That was the question facing Kadambari. It was doubtful whether all the pep talk and cajoling of the highly articulate Didi would work now. Madam Agatha looked awfully crestfallen after the call, as if she had lost her walking stick when she needed it the most.

She wanted to have further discussions with her after she returned to The Nest and regained normalcy. Perhaps, the time had come to call it a day.

Yes, all good things come to an end one day, Kadambari consoled herself.

Madam Agatha Surprises Kadambari

'Back to work, Agatha, you're not a patient anymore!' assured Dr Geetha with a broad smile when she visited The Nest.

It was a week after Agatha was discharged from the hospital, and the doctor wanted to comfort her that there was nothing to worry about. Obviously, the blood-thinning medicine had to be taken along with the other drugs prescribed by her religiously. Routine work and continuance of normal life were the best medicines for illness.

Agatha was also relaxed to a certain extent. The sudden attack appeared to have upset her as she had hitherto been reasonably proud of her health—scrupulously maintained through strict diet and rigid schedules.

'It's all a question of aging, Agatha,' said the doctor.

'But I'm not that old, doctor,' Agatha reverted.

'I agree. But please try to keep your mental age lower and lower. That is the best medicine.'

When the doctor had left, Agatha appeared determined about what she was going to do in the future. Perhaps, the long rest at the hospital had given her adequate time to ponder about her future plans. Hence, when she said that she would like to have a long chat with her in the evening in the privacy of her room, Kadambari did not know what exactly was on Madam Agatha's mind.

As expected, when Kadambari entered her room, Agatha was sitting at the writing table, jotting down something in a pad.

'Srinivasan's son, the chartered accountant, has given me the green signal at last. He has assured me that we are on sound footing, and that I can go ahead with my plans!' beamed Agatha on seeing Kadambari. It appeared she was working on future plans, as if nothing had happened.

Relaxing on a sofa, she dragged Kadambari to sit near her. She expressed to her that she had made up her mind, that past was past and there was no point in brooding over it.

'Only the institution matters, and not individuals behind it—be it the colonel or even me. Nobody is indispensable in this world, and it was a huge blunder on my part to have thought that The Nest could not function without one colonel, or Agatha, or anyone for that matter!. After all, human beings are sometimes reduced to mere alphabets, as that Jewish girl used to say… Come rain, come winds, the Kilikoodu will remain, since it is perched on a solid branch. When our intentions are good, it has to remain solid—despite all adversities.'

'And may it be so, Madam,' Kadambari agreed reluctantly.

'Come on, let's relax for a while,' Agatha was in a jovial mood. 'I shouldn't be asking a girl, groomed in a Brahmin household, but still…how about a glass of wine?'

Kadambari was shocked. She had not expected such a question from anybody, least of all from Madam Agatha.

'I don't drink,' she said tersely.

'Neither do I,' Agatha smiled, and added, 'but this is an important occasion, an important time, and an important drink, too! Holy wine for special occasions!'

She took out an unopened bottle of red wine hidden inside the almirah.

'Gift from a visitor last Christmas—a cake and a bottle of high-quality French wine, not knowing that I don't drink... but who knew it would come in handy on such an auspicious occasion?' Madam giggled like a young girl.

'Auspicious occasion?' Kadambari raised her eyebrow.

'Yeah!' smiled Agatha. 'A gift meant for the holy birth comes handy for the re-birth of The Nest. But I don't know whether this is the proper wine glass. I have heard some sisters saying that a particular type of glass should be used for each type of liquor. What sort of etiquette to a former sister!'

Kadambari was amused. Madam was in good spirits.

'I had tasted it a couple of times while I was in the convent during Christmas and Easter, but had never enjoyed it. I wonder how people drink it. You, perhaps, don't know that many of the priests drink wine, and some, even whiskey!'

Before Kadambari could stop her, she had poured red wine in two glasses...less quantity in Kadambari's glass.

'No one would come at this hour, but it's better we close the door,' cautioned Madam.

After closing the door, Kadambari did not know what to do. Her first reaction was to withdraw from the room on some excuse or the other but she felt it would be terribly discourteous, and that Madam Agatha would feel hurt. So she sat on a chair nearby and took the glass to her lips. A tiny sip, and she felt compelled to spit it out, for the bitterness really put her off.

'Relax, relax. Nobody is born a drinker, only circumstances lead them to drinking. And this is probably an occasion when one can let their hair down, to give company to this old Madam Agatha. In fact, I was planning to talk to you in solitude, for a heart-to-heart chat.'

Kadambari sat back and wondered whether it was all right for Madam to consume alcohol after her hospitalisation. Quick to understand her anxiety, Agatha explained with a broad smile.

'Nothing to worry about, dear girl. A couple of glasses of wine is perfectly okay. It would only smoothen the blood circulation!'

It appeared Agatha was enjoying her wine and seemed quite composed; in fact, like never before.

'I have decided that we should re-start our work with double the vigour. You would have gone through the list I had given you, I believe. Did you?'

Kadambari had done it, and had carried that list with her.

'Of the four girls shortlisted, I think we can select two of them to start with, and perhaps others later. One Kumudam and a Karpakam, both from poor backgrounds, if I remember correctly. Highly deserving cases who could fly out later on their own, I believe. Wouldn't they?' asked Agatha.

'I think so, Madam,' said Kadambari.

'There was another case where the girl threatened she had no other option but to commit suicide. It might, perhaps, be true but I don't believe in such pre-announced suicides, as most of the suicides are nothing but wild decisions taken at the spur of the moment.'

Kadambari nodded. Meanwhile, Agatha had lifted the glass and signalled Kadambari to catch up with her. 'After all, it's only wine…with low alcohol content. And it is so boring to drink alone,' she complained. Reluctantly, Kadambari gulped some more and leaned back on the chair, closing her eyes. As a novice, her head was swivelling slightly.

'So let's start the process and display a message on our website. Let the whole world know that we have not pulled down the shutters, and are not the ones who falter in the face of a few adversities. If necessary, we would manage a small news item in the local newspapers with the help of Raja sir. And again, why not give a formal reception to the new entrants? After all, it's a rebirth for The Nest.'

Madam Agatha seemed to be quite excited about the proposed revival.

'No, ma'am. Let's not go to that extent. Let us lie low for some time. Of course, we can post it on the website but let's keep it to only that for now,' Kadambari was quick to react.

Agatha saw some reason in her reply, and really admired the fact that the girl had acquired the maturity of a seasoned administrator.

'Now that you you've been looking after the duties of Sarala, why not make it a permanent arrangement? My dream was to make this Nest bigger, much bigger. If we could win over Mr Kartikeyan during his next visit, the possibilities would be immense. As you know, he is enormously rich. A known philanthropist, grieving the untimely death of his only daughter Kartika, who had died of a mysterious disease which could not be diagnosed properly by even some of the major hospitals in the United States. It was a curious genetic problem, possibly a one-in-a-million case, they had concluded. Anyway, this unexpected departure of his darling daughter a few years back literally made him depressed, and it took months for him to return to normalcy. Now that he does not want to bequeath his wealth to his only brother and family, he has been rather liberal with his donations to charitable institutions. After all, wasn't that brother responsible for his leaving the country and seek permanent settlement abroad? I've heard that he has already written a will but nobody knows the content.'

'What more do you expect from him? Hasn't he given us this space free of rent?'

'If we tickled his ego, he might loosen his pockets further and build another block in memory of his late daughter Kartika. That block could be designed as a hostel for accommodating more girls. For this, the initiative should be from your side, since you youngsters alone can run the institution in future. Of course, for tackling Kartikeyan you could take the help of that Jewish girl. Pretending to be nutty, she is actually a sweet-talker and has winning manners, too. Don't you remember how she had once video chatted and charmed him into reckoning the true facts behind those anonymous mails?'

Kadambari was clearly embarrassed, unable to react immediately. She was not quite sure how she would conduct herself with that kind of responsibilities.

Madam appeared to be enjoying her drink, and had exceeded the quantity she had poured earlier. But Kadambari did not know how to interrupt and stop her from drinking more.

'Look, I have already taken you as my daughter, a dear daughter of an unwed mother. It's a wonderful benediction by none other than Jesus and I'm thankful for it. This has been a rare occasion where a mother could choose her daughter!'

Agatha was clearly excited, and was in the mood to open up to the young girl.

'Come on, I don't know what to call you… Kadambari is too complex a name, and not easy on one's tongue. Anyway, you have not revealed everything about you. You had promised to do it at a later date. Don't you think that this is that occasion for you to open up, when your poor mother is in such bad health?'

Stunned for a moment, Kadambari hesitated and shook her head. Then Agatha herself made her lift her glass and offered the toast.

'In memory of your Devagiri days that you desperately want to forget!'

That was a smart move. Kadambari finished the glass in slow gulps without uttering a single word, wiped her lips, munched a few more cashews to remove the bitterness of liquor from her mouth and delved deep into her memories. Agatha sat attentive and unmoved, with the glass of wine in her hand.

Those Devagiri days trickled into Kadambari's mind, and not in sequential order but as scattered visuals and events. How difficult was it for the four-year-old orphan to get accepted in an orthodox Brahmin family of repute… The clumsy footprints left by the muddy toes of the child on the first day had remained in the mind of Amma for many more days, despite trying to erase it incessantly. Then the gradual change in the attitude of both the parents occurred, and how the girl became their darling daughter... Those nights of thunder and rains when the child had found solace in the tight embrace of her mother. How she had accompanied them for many festivals, clinging to the hand of Appa. Those were the days...

Only when she had grown up as an intelligent and attractive youngster that things had changed all of a sudden. A very bright young girl, too good in studies with a radiant face, charming everyone around. Further, when Shankararaman started bragging about the intelligence of the girl and that they were planning to get her admitted to the medical college, the jealousy of others had started working; particularly in the minds of the Sastrigal and his two daughters. The mischievous Sastrigal could not accept the thought of that girl overtaking his daughters, who were supposed to be the brightest stars of the whole village. Then one day, he commented how Shankararaman could take pride in the achievements of this girl, who was of unknown origin. Certainly, she did not have the looks of a Brahmin girl like his daughters. Look at her complexion, doesn't it indicate the traits of a low-born, he had mocked.

It was only then that wild thoughts of religion, caste, *gotra* etc. had entered the parents' mind. They realised they didn't know for sure if she was even Hindu at all! Where was the proof, since she was picked up from the temple compound—a girl who did not have genuine birth credentials of her own.

'That is a long story,' Kadambari continued. 'Despite my best efforts to forget the past, strange thoughts started streaming into my mind. Who was I? A Hindu, a Christian, or a Muslim? Who were my parents? Why didn't they look for me in the temple compound or even resort to the public address system, where any number of 'lost and found' announcements were being echoed? There was every reason to believe that they had abandoned me on the hope that someone good would pick me up... It was clear that they wanted to discard the unwanted baby. Possibly an illegitimate child; a cursed birth... And those canards spread by the Sastrigal and others were so venomous that the attitude of Appa also started changing slowly. Was I from their clan? Whose daughter was this girl? What was our relationship with her? Thereafter, some distance started developing between me and Appa. He had started looking at me with different eyes.'

Then suddenly, she remembered that teacher Vedanayakam again, who had once played a major role in her life. Then, as if shaken, Agatha remembered again.

'Oh, that kiss!' Agatha sat motionless, closing her eyes for a moment. 'A stolen kiss!'

'Do you know how precious is a stolen kiss of a lover?'

Back to the days in the convent, when she was none other than Sister Agatha... Didn't the story sound familiar to her? Did Vedanayakam remind Father Andrew, quite charming with winning manners, teaching in a Christian college in town? Did he have curly hair falling on his forehead, and melancholic eyes of that romantic hero Gemini Ganesan?

And then that kiss...

Kadambari was probably too young to understand the import of that solitary event. But here was a nun, mature enough to understand all the aspects of this forbidden relationship. It's a fact that she had been planning on quitting the order for quite some time but was unable to make up her mind; the first kiss had possibly aroused the woman in her. Certain tender feelings that had been suppressed for long came rushing into her mind. Then she had no misgivings in taking the crucial decision, as is the case of any other lovelorn woman. But, strangely, the much-respected Father Andrew, who was initially inclined to quit the order and marry her, later withdrew—probably on the advice of his seniors in the clergy. But having made the decision, the resolute woman could not retract. And so, Madam Agatha was born, in a new avatar.

When Agatha narrated it without remorse, Kadambari could not believe that she had such a colourful past. Looking bewildered, she tried to comfort her by patting her back, forgetting for a moment that she had turned her mother.

'Did you know dear,' she said lovingly, 'when I decided to leave the convent, a senior sister whom I had respected very much asked me whether I was really serious about my decision. But I avoided giving a direct answer to her. It was embarrassing to tell many things straight to her face... That rebel feeling deep in my blood. A wasted life...'

It was the offering of her mother to the church when her grandfather had fallen critically ill and was doubtful of recovery. When the doctors washed off their hands and all the offerings to various churches were in vain, it was grandma who prayed that she would offer the eldest grandchild to the nunnery if the old man recovers. After all, there were two younger girls to be married off and the eldest one was not quite good looking... Miraculously, he was to recover later, much to the surprise of the doctors and relatives alike, to live longer and healthier until his normal death in the old age.

'Yes, I was a sacrificial lamb on the altar of belief,' lamented Madam Agatha. 'Nobody had asked what I wanted.'

None knew that that the childhood dream of Agatha was to become a nurse and work in a missionary hospital so she could be of some service to the poor. In fact, Florence Nightingale and Mother Teresa were her all-time favourite role models at that time.

Having exhausted her version of the story and eager to know more about Kadambari, Agatha was looking expectantly at her.

'Still, you are keeping something to yourself, aren't you? Now, tell me, what made you flee from your beloved parents? After all, you owed them a lot.'

Kadambari nodded. Devouring the remaining liquid in the glass, she tried her best to put on a brave face. Agatha was waiting anxiously for her reply.

'Well?' she said.

Kadambari pondered for a moment...

It was the end of the *Chitterai* month (in the Tamil calendar, Chitterai begins with the Sun's entry into Aries in mid-April, and is the first month of the year), when the *Agni Nakshatram* (the hottest day of the year, marked by the celestial movement of the sun through the star *Kritika*). It was the festival time at the Lord Muruga temple on the hilltop. After an unusually hot summer noon, when her body was burning and sweating profusely, Kadambari wanted to take a cool bath. She was the one who had always hated her own body odour, and liked to take baths as frequently as possible. But one couldn't afford that luxury in that place, since water was generally in short supply, more so in the summer.

Amma was in the kitchen and Appa on his usual easy chair, reading a magazine. It was a makeshift bathroom covered with wooden planks, not arranged properly and shaky as well. There were a couple of gaps on the northern side, and Kadambari had asked for getting a carpenter for aligning them properly and fixing it permanently with screws many a time. But lazy as he was, Appa kept on delaying it... And on that evening, when she had removed all her clothes and was about to pour the first mug of water on her head, there it was: two eyes between the shaky planks which had a gap between... For a moment, she did not know what was happening and who it was. The eyes were so fixed on the plank that she could only guess who the person was and then she heard herself screaming madly without knowing what was happening. Blood was rushing into her head and eyes were burning... Then those eyes disappeared suddenly. Hurriedly covering her body with a towel, she rushed out. Amma had come running from the kitchen, enquiring what had happened. Appa was not seen anywhere at all... It was only after a few moments that something exploded in her head all of a sudden.

'Who was it?' Agatha asked anxiously. Then pressing her forehead, she thought for a moment.

'Was it....? Was it....?'

Kadambari was sitting wordless with her head bowed.

Then as if shaken by a wild thought, Agatha asked, 'He?'

Kadambari hesitated for a moment.

'He?' Agatha repeated the question.

And Kadambari nodded.

'Jesus!' Madam Agatha was shaken beyond description.

She wanted to pray. She drew a cross in air and then again on her chest. As one who had not kept a picture of Jesus on the wall of her room and had not prayed in the traditional manner after leaving the convent, she kneeled for the first time and prayed to Jesus like a true devotee. She regretted that it was a great sin on her part to have asked the girl to narrate that sordid episode. She prayed for forgiving all the sinners, which she believed, only the Almighty could do.

There was a long silence. While Kadambari sat motionless, Madam Agatha got up and hugged the girl lovingly.

'Anyway, past is past. Please forgive me for bringing back all those cursed memories to your mind. Let God forgive all the sinners! It's time to forget and forgive, as the Lord had said.... Now that you are at the right place at the right time, you have a great task ahead. Let's all work on it together. Hereafter, you will be the real boss running the show here....'

'No ma'am, but...?'

'Don't worry, I'll be behind you always, keeping a close watch. After all, it's my baby. I would continue to be active, but certainly not overactive as I've been in the past because the doctor has advised me otherwise. You youngsters are better equipped to run organisations like this.'

With these words, she took out a bunch of keys from the almirah, kept it close to her heart for a moment—obviously in prayer—kissed it and handed it over to a hesitant Kadambari.

Kadambari was moved. She did not know what to do. Such a bunch of keys in the hands of a beggarwoman's daughter... A girl discarded by her mother... She could not say no to her. And Agatha could easily understand her predicament.

'Don't worry, dear. Take it easy!' she comforted her. 'Please give it some time to sink in. We are all with you! All beginnings are like this. A few years back, when that Karthikeyan extended his hand after handing over this bunch of keys to me, I was speechless for a moment, too. Too many worries echoing in my mind... Would I be able to handle all these responsibilities? I am handing over all those worries to you now. Mind you, there would be God's will behind all such things... And you're young enough to take it.'

Waiting for a moment and appearing thoroughly confused, Kadambari bowed her head in reverence and touched her feet. Madam, in turn, hugged her and kissed her, with tears rolling down her cheeks.

'But I have a small request to make. Don't say no to me. As I said earlier, this is the day to forget and forgive. What has happened cannot be changed but you have to go to Devagiri one day, meet your parents and talk it over. It would be a day of atonement for all.'

Kadambari was looking at her with disbelief.

'After admitting all my sins to you, I've done my confession after a very long time. I'm so relieved!'

'A confession. That, too, to this worthless girl,' murmured Kadambari to herself.

'A confession need not necessarily be to a priest. It can be to any noble soul close to you.'

Kadambari did not know what to say. In fact, she wanted to call her Amma once again but was hesitant to do so. By that time, Agatha seemed to be in a hurry to retire.

'Do well, my child. Jesus would always be with you, or perhaps Lord Murugan... Now, better rush to the dining hall before Janaki closes shop. Let me relax for some time. I don't need any dinner, my stomach is pretty full.'

Without waiting for an answer, she walked with tottering steps towards her room. Kadambari noticed that she was tired, but relaxed as well. Kadambari accompanied her till she sat on her cot.

'Before you go, one last thing,' Agatha faltered with an unsure voice. 'Sorry for asking this… I had also asked the colonel a couple of times but she avoided a reply.' Pausing for a moment, she continued, 'Now, tell me, has Agatha failed? Was it a wasted life? At times, I felt like asking the mirror, my most truthful companion, "Mirror, mirror, on the wall, have I failed?".'

Kadambari was surprised. Why this question now?

'Tell me frankly, have we moved an inch forward from where we had started?'

'Why this doubt now, it has been proven umpteen times and acknowledged by one and all... You can't measure it in inches. Don't we have longer tapes?'

But Madam Agatha was muttering to herself.

'Was it wrong to leave the order, the path of the Lord?'

'Isn't this also one of the paths of the Lord?'

'But I have miles to go before I sleep.'

'Of course!'

'And promises to keep, as the poet wrote...'

'Poets are prophets, too...'

'The woods are now darker and deeper, aren't they?'

Kadambari was stunned.

'And a day of atonement for me, too...' she mumbled half in sleep.

'Good night, dear!'

And Agatha slipped into deep slumber while the woods got darker and deeper.

A Morning of Lightning, Thunder, and Rain

It was a flash of lightning which split the skies with a golden sword, followed by a deafening thunder which shook the entire building, that woke up Kadambari. A strong wind was blowing across, smashing the window panes, with splinters of glass scattering around. Her head was still reeling under the previous evening's wine, and it took some time for her to comprehend what had happened. Then the rain started, followed by intermittent lightning and thunder. Suddenly, the power went off, plunging the whole area into pitch darkness...

Sometime later, Kadambari heard a wild noise down below. Was somebody crying? She could not understand for a moment but after listening intently, it was clear that someone was shouting at the top of their voice. Hurriedly, Kadambari located a candle inside the table drawer, lit it, and scampered through the steps without waking up her roommate Apoorva. When tripping between the steps and about to fall, she held on to the railings firmly and managed to reach the ground floor.

There was a commotion in front of Madam Agatha's room. Janaki was beating her chest and crying aloud. She was heard blabbering something in between. Karupayyan was behind, leaning on the wall, unable to cry aloud. Then Kadambari realised what she had feared had happened.

Gesturing to Janaki to stop crying, Kadambari paced into the room quietly. Agatha was fast asleep, as if unaware of the fuss around. Her face was peaceful, with a wry smile on her lips. A feeling of contentment? The serenity of one who had lived a full life and did whatever she could in the service of the community. As a true believer in Jesus, she had tried to accomplish what the Master had wanted.

'But it's not time for the mother bird to fly out,' moaned Kadambari.

Kadambari could not do anything other than touching her feet and prostrate in front of her.

'Amma, *pranamam*!' she whispered.

By that time, the thunder and lightning had stopped. But it was raining heavily. Unseasonal rains.

And the rains continued...

Acknowledgements

I am extremely thankful to my editor, Ms Vibha Chakravarty Kumar, who took pains to go through the manuscript of my first English-language novel and turned it into the book it is now. Her editing skills, and sharp and discerning literary acumen has been beyond helpful in tackling the sensitive issues that I have tried to address in this novel.

My sincere gratitude also goes to Mr Nirmalkanti Bhattacharjee and Niyogi Books. Without their support, this book would not have been possible.

Last but not the least, I am indebted to my wife Raji and my readers for standing by me all these years. Their support and love mean the world to me.

About the Author

A Sethumadhavan (Sethu), born in a small village in Kerala, has been writing stories and novels in Malayalam for the past five decades. He belongs to a highly innovative generation of fiction writers in Malayalam, who pioneered a radical transformation of sensibility during that period. Widely travelled abroad and having worked in different parts of India, many of his writings have a global flavour and a pan-Indian canvas. A winner of many major awards in Malayalam, he has 18 novels and 20 collections of stories to his credit. His novel *Adayalangal* won him the Vayalar Award in 2005 and the Sahitya Akademi Award in 2007. Many of his works have been translated into English and other Indian languages. *The Saga of Muziris* was published in English translation in 2016, and *Aliyah: The Last Jew in the Village* in 2018. *The Cuckoo's Nest* is his first novel in English. He is known for his magical rendition, weaving in 'a sense of the impossible' in a haunting manner, remarkable for the way it attracts a subtext of profound psychological, anthropological and, at times, mystical significance. A banker by profession, Sethu was also the chairman of the National Book Trust, Delhi, for three years.

Reviews of *The Saga of Muziris* by the same author

'…a gripping mix of history, myth, legend, fiction and magic reality.… Beautifully written, the book is a masterpiece.'

—*The Book Review*

'…this novel is a skilful construction of myth and memory … Sethu has an eye for detail…'

—*Sreevalsan Thiyyadi, Outlook*

'It is…a voyage through history, mixed with myths, legends and pure fiction.'

—*Jayalakshmi, The Huffington Post (blog)*

'…a novel within a novel, juxtaposing the present against the immediate past, the immediate past against the ancient past, and colliding them through a thread of loss and continuity.'

—*Madhavankutty Pillai, openthemagazine.com*